STRANGE

STRANGE

James Buxton

WARNER BOOKS

A *Warner* Book

First published in Great Britain by Warner Books in 1994

Copyright © James Buxton, 1994

The moral right of the author has been asserted

A CIP catalogue record for this book
is available from the British Library

ISBN 0 7515 0753 9

Typeset by Solidus (Bristol) Limited
Printed in England by Clays Ltd, St Ives plc

Warner Books
A Division of
Little, Brown and Company (UK) Limited
Brettenham House
Lancaster Place
London WC2E 7EN

Part One

CHAPTER ONE

Hard light. Hard walls. Hard beds. Hard faces. Hard luck?

Jim Carroll picked up his slop bucket and walked out into the corridor. Up and down the landing, men were standing with their plastic buckets outside the cell doors, eyes blurred from sleep, hair unbrushed, yawning, looking grey. The smell was foul in the cold air.

Hard nosed. Jim added that one to the list.

The thing about prison ... the thing about prison was ... As usual the grinding boredom of it all stopped him from finding out what the thing was. Boredom, probably. Or something. The thing about prison was you always knew what was going to happen next.

Right then. Off you go, he thought.

'Right, then. Off you go!' the guard shouted.

The men turned and shuffled towards the head at the end of the corridor.

The smell of urine grew stronger as he got closer to the head; a thick, choking, rank smell. It echoed off brick walls that were shiny with condensation and thick layers of green gloss paint. You could see the steam and did not want to breathe in.

It was cold outside today and a warder called Mansell, a wizened lemon of a man with a small, old-fashioned moustache, was supervising the slopping out. Mansell had no sense of smell and a bad back, so he refused to open the window in case the draught brought on a twinge. That was that. It was a petty irritation, but the sort of thing that you noticed, that niggled.

But that, Jim thought, was typical. In a place of locked doors, three-foot walls, old cast-iron bars and new steel mesh grilles, barbed wire, sirens, and spotlights, you could get annoyed about a six-inch gap in a window. And if you could get annoyed you could get furious. And if you could get furious you could get crazy. And if you got crazy ... There was an apocryphal story of a man who was released from prison and discovered that he was unable to open doors or windows for himself. Always had to get someone else to do it for him, and tended to spend a lot of time in the great outdoors for convenience sake more than anything else.

He burned to death when his digs caught fire. He couldn't open his bedroom door.

Jim looked at the small window and blessed it for being closed. He was not annoyed at all. Not him.

His cell was on the second storey of the prison, or Level Three. He was in A Wing. All four wings of the prison opened on to a central hall. From outside his cell he could see down to the other levels in his wing and across into the main hall. The prison did not have floors outside the cells as such – just metal walkways. The main hall was lit by windows set into the lantern where the four pitched roofs met.

Across the lantern ran metal struts, once painted white but now patched and blistered by rust. This morning the struts were crowded with sparrows. The sunlight was cold and bright. It hurt your eyes to look at it, and made you want to cry, it was so clean.

The man behind him nudged his ribs gently and nodded in the direction of the central hall. The governor, a small man in a pale grey suit, was making one of his rare appearances, escorted by Jack Lyall, the head warden.

'Three to one it's yellow.'

'I'm skint.'

'All right, half an ounce.'

Some of the men would bet on anything: how many birds would land on a telegraph wire in an hour; how many seconds before or after the Radio 4 pips the lights went out in the evenings; how long it would be before Snotty Smith, one of the screws, picked his nose.

Jim could take gambling or leave it. He calculated quickly. Another half ounce of tobacco would be nice, but then again, if he lost it would mean borrowing from Joe. Still, as a red-band Joe earned pocket money so it was not that much of a problem, and on top of that he'd never seen yellow before.

It was worth the risk.

'Done,' he said.

Half-way across the floor, the governor took out a handkerchief and wiped his lips with it. Blue this morning. Jim saw Lyall raise his eyes to heaven. He knew what was going on. There was a muttering from the landings as bets were called in.

Jim smiled. Half an ounce of tobacco and he'd only been awake ten minutes.

The head was a small oblong room, lined with white tiles. There was a porcelain hole in the floor at the far end where you poured your slops, and a urinal along one wall.

He pushed past a man having a long and noisy piss,

emptied the bucket and began to walk back.

Mansell barred his exit with his truncheon. 'Look what you did, Carroll. You, get out.'

The other prisoner shook, buttoned his flies, and walked out, eyes fixed forwards.

Jim said nothing.

'You splashed me. Look. On my boot.'

Jim knew better than to look down or look up. He looked straight ahead. He knew he could do nothing to make this situation go away, but by being very careful, by threading a path between the Scylla of anger and the Charybdis of dumb insolence, he might at least be able to keep it under some sort of control.

Mansell pushed the truncheon tip under his chin and smacked it upwards. Jim's tongue jumped. He stepped backwards.

'I don't like splashes on my boots, Carroll. I don't like them at all.'

He punctuated every word with a jab of the truncheon. At the end of the room he stopped and said in a low voice, 'Stay in your cell over breakfast if you know what's good for you. Someone wants to talk to you.'

Then he whacked Carroll hard in the stomach, but not as hard as he could have done, and shouted, 'Next!' over his shoulder.

Jim stumbled back to his cell, pretending to be more hurt than he was. He wondered what was going on.

The prison was quiet but the fly kept on getting away. It was the quietest Jim had ever known it but that damn fly just kept on escaping. Jim had got it to walk along the table edge, pausing, stopping, starting again, but every time he lowered the chop sticks and snapped them shut, it whirred out of reach, hovering in front of his closed eyes. Try as he might, they just snapped in thin air and the fly zigzagged away, sometimes growing, sometimes shrinking, sometimes metamorphosing into something ridiculous like a dish of beef and green pepper in black bean sauce or an Austin Allegro. That was the trick, to keep on concentrating. It was amazing how time flew and flies flew when you were having fun.

It was a craze – catching imaginary flies with imaginary chop sticks; apparently it was a mental exercise that Taoist monks did. Mick South, a safe cracker of the old school, claimed that he could get five out of ten on a good night, and a few of the more excitable younger prisoners claimed that they were shooting scores of Scud flies with cosmic Patriot missiles. But they always got away from Jim.

He was concentrating so hard that he did not hear Jack Lyall come in. It was the sound of leather-soled shoes scraping on the floor that brought Jim back to reality. He stood up feeling slightly nervous even though he knew he had nothing to be worried about; Lyall would not have bothered to go through all this rigmarole if he had simply wanted to punish him.

Lyall nodded to the landing orderly who closed the door behind him. It thumped comfortably into its thick frame, then bounced an inch or two open. Lyall pushed it to with his index finger, then looked at Jim and said: 'Well, aren't you going to offer me a seat?'

Nonplussed, Jim pulled back the plastic chair from the table, and waved a hand at it. He waited for Lyall to sit down, then perched on the edge of the bed.

There was an awkward pause. Jim reached into his pocket for his tobacco, then on impulse offered it to Lyall who rolled a minute cigarette, about the thickness of a matchstick. He waited for Jim to do the same, then offered him a light from an old petrol lighter. Jim watched him closely. Lyall's face was as dull as crumpled tissue paper and the rings under his eyes were as heavy as tyres.

'Am I in trouble?' Jim asked.

A ghost of a smile passed over Lyall's face.

'Not yet, Mr Carroll. Sorry. I didn't mean that. I mean ... what do I mean? I mean that I'm about to ask you to do something for me.'

Jim glanced nervously at the door.

'Don't worry. It's a secret. Just you, me, and the gatepost. I mean that. The only people who know about this little meeting won't tell.'

'Why go to all this bother? Why not just call me in to the office?'

'Because that's official and what I want to ask you isn't.'

'I don't want to know,' Jim said. It was pure reflex, as automatic as jerking your hand when a wasp lands on it.

'Whoa! You don't even know what I want yet.'

'Please leave my cell.' Voice very flat.

'You should hear me out.'

'Get the fuck out!' Jim shouted, feeling panicked. Fear balled in his throat and squeezed his voice. 'I am not a squealer. I am not a grass. I do not talk to screws.'

'You used to be one.'

'I was a policeman, not a gaoler. There is a difference you know.' He swallowed bitterness and reminded himself that it didn't matter. Nothing mattered. 'It doesn't matter anyway,' he continued. 'Now I'm a convict. I'm wearing a different sort of uniform now.' He said it like a litany.

'It doesn't suit you,' Lyall said.

'What do you mean by that?'

'It doesn't go with your eyes.'

There was a pause. Lyall's joke sounded flat and more aggressive than he had intended. He passed a hand in front of his face, pulling the skin into a different expression. Jim looked at him, shocked. Lyall wore the expression of a man with nothing left to lose – there was a brightness and defiance around his eyes, and his mouth was tight at the corners. Jim had seen it in interview rooms a few times and it had always made him feel odd in his stomach, and slightly guilty. This time he did not feel guilty, but he still felt that he was watching something he did not want to see.

'I'm going to talk,' Lyall said. 'And then I'm going to leave. At the end of my little speech I'll make you an offer. The choice will be yours – take it up if you want, or drop it if you don't. If you want to take it up, get an appointment to see me and say that you've heard that there's a possibility of a vacancy in the library sorting books. I'll think about it and then give you the job. It's in my remit. That means that you have taken up my offer. But, and I want to get this into your head, what I am going to ask you to do does not involve squealing, grassing or anything else. I wouldn't ask you to do that because I wouldn't trust you. Now just listen.'

Lyall spoke without moving, his face blank, his voice very even as if he had gone over the material so many times there was nothing left in it that surprised him any more. All that changed, Jim noticed, were two tiny blobs of white spittle in the corner of his mouth that grew larger as he talked. He concentrated on them. It gave him detachment. Detachment was a cultivated habit.

'I expect you've heard people talk about the suicides in Long Barrow prison?' Lyall asked. 'Any idea how many there have been?'

There had been six in the last year, Jim thought. Two in the remand cells, one in the secure wing (which was tricky and required great determination and guile, owing to the level of supervision), three in the main body of the prison. He did not say anything.

'Six,' Lyall said. 'That's not unusual for a prison this size, and this old, and this understaffed. I think there's a confidential Home Office report that correlates suicide against certain fixed criteria. Six is about average. A target figure.' He paused. 'Which is why we chose it.'

Jim looked non-committal and wished Lyall was somewhere else. Lyall was staring at him with the intensity of the ancient mariner.

Hold off! unhand me, grey-beard loon!

'We chose six,' Lyall said, 'even though the real number was two. Two is below average. Two is a very good figure. Two is a pat on the back.'

He struck another match and waved the flame in front of his cigarette, thought better of it, took the cigarette out of his mouth and lit it that way. He blew out the match, blew on the tip of the cigarette.

He's not finding this easy, Jim thought, which at least gave him something to think about.

'This is harder than I thought,' Lyall said. 'The reason we did that is that four of the men were killed.'

Jim could not quite suppress a tight little smile. Every time there was a suicide it was blamed on the guards. Coroners' reports, autopsies ... no one trusted them. By the time a cadaver had been attacked on the coroner's slab, no one was going to be able to say for sure how the person had died.

In truth, in the end it was an academic question anyway. Suicide or murder; prison killed them. Smokers, non-smokers, haemophiliacs, homosexuals, heroin addicts, sniffers of strange distillations of bleach and paraffin – prison killed them all even though some people blamed the deaths on AIDS, cancer, solvents or even God. Lyall's voice bored into his thoughts.

'The single major cause of self-inflicted death in prison is asphyxiation. Twist your shirt into rope, tie it into a loop around the bars of your cell, stick your head in the loop and let your legs go. It takes time and quite a lot of effort but it doesn't hurt. Last year we had two go like that, and four that didn't. We were able to say that those four did kill themselves like that because no one else could have done it – video tape from the security cameras showed no one went in or out of the cells, no evidence of anyone tampering with the tape, full cell integrity, that kind of thing, but the men were dead. And they didn't kill themselves. No signs of asphyxiation, no signs of self-mutilation, no chemical abuse—'

Jim raised an eyebrow.

'In other words they didn't take an overdose. Neither were there signs of epidermic or subcutaneous trauma. I mean they weren't beaten up. So—'

He was watching Jim's face now, staring at the bridge of his nose to stop his eyes moving. Jim kept his face absolutely still.

'When things like that happen you start looking for common factors,' Lyall continued, 'and like the nice people we are, that's exactly what we did. We came up with a lot of blanks.' He took a breath and his mouth formed to say something else. Something beginning with B.

'But?' Jim suggested.

Lyall shook his head. He looked angry. Glanced at his watch.

'But nothing,' Lyall answered. 'I should go now. What I want you to do for me, if you have a mind for it, is to find out what killed them. You're intelligent, you're respected, and—'

'I used to be a policeman,' Jim said.

'I don't care about that. But you're here, inside, and I'm

not. You know how to look for things and I don't. And you had a good reputation.'

'And you think I'm innocent?'

'Frankly I don't care. What I do know is that you're the only policeman that's ever been inside who hasn't been sectioned. One of these days I'd like to find out how you managed that. I'd better go now. One last thing. I meant to say it earlier. These deaths. Like I said, we couldn't find a pattern, but there was something all the men had in common.'

'What was that?'

'They all thought they were innocent too. All four of them.'

'Thanks for that,' Jim said. 'There's just one thing I'd like to know.'

'What is it?'

'No epidermic trauma or whatever you call it. No chemical abuse. No self-mutilation. No signs of asphyxiation.'

'That's right.'

'So what was the cause of death?'

Lyall pursed his lips then went and stood in the doorway. 'Their necks were all broken,' he said. He left without looking back, closing the door softly behind him.

Jim went to the tiny window and looked out of it. Four or five miles away the moors rose in steep, dun undulations. The ground changed colour stealthily as clouds moved across the sun.

But the great grey bulk of the prison sat in the middle of his mind.

He pressed his cheek against the perspex. To his left he could see the blunt end of D Wing sticking from the main body of the prison at a right angle. Beyond that was the first wall, then a gap known as the canyon, then the perimeter wall. Over the wall, under a blue sky scratched with thin clouds, the town lay like a gritty pool contained by the brown rim of the moor.

The prison was built in the shape of a stubby cross, the four wings sticking out from a large, domed central hall. Jim Carroll was in A Wing. B Wing was given over to administration. D Wing was mainly high security and C Wing was occupied by remand prisoners and sectioned prisoners who had to be kept separate from the rest of the men for their own safety. The sectioned prisoners were police informers who had got banged up anyway and certain categories of sex offenders – child abusers, rapists, and anyone else who made men inside the prison feel worried about their families outside. Sectioned prisoners were considered fair game if you caught one, and sometimes the guards, who, they would argue, were only human after all, let you do just that. Jim had resisted being sectioned and so far had managed to avoid getting killed, but then he was a suspected murderer, and to some that gave him an aura of respect.

Above the main hall stood the water tower, resting on vast pillars which pierced the dome like massive tree trunks. There was a bell in there which used to be rung on Sundays for the service, but the service was optional now and the last time the bell was rung bits had started falling off the roof.

Far below in the yard between A and D Wings he could see the fatigue party poking in a desultory way at the piles of rubbish that accumulated there. Ever since the roof had started to leak in the gym the authorities had been finding things for the prisoners to do for extra exercise. There was a rumour that they were going to put in a vegetable garden so the men could have fresh greens. There was a rumour that Elvis Presley had been seen on B Wing.

Jim could do three things in his cell. He could look out of the window, sit on the bed, or sit on the plastic chair. He decided to save the chair for later, for when he got really bored. He sat on the bed.

Should he take up Lyall's offer? He could think of many reasons why he should not.

First there was the danger. He had, through a combination of violent behaviour and sheer force of personality, carved out a niche for himself inside. Lyall was right. Most bent coppers were beaten up so regularly by the other convicts that they sectioned themselves. Jim had decided he did not want to go that route because it sounded like a prison within a prison.

The first time a group of men had come for him in the showers he had been lucky. A mop had been leaning against the wall close to him. He had jabbed it into two of the attackers' bellies, hard enough for them to be hospitalized, and broken the handle against another man's head. After that there was the odd attack, but they were infrequent and Jim tended to beat them off because he knew he had to. Over the course of a couple of years he won respect and now he was left alone.

If he started snooping, all that respect would go. He wasn't the same man who had been convicted four years earlier. He was less fit, less angry, less everything. If the other prisoners found out, he would get the treatment that was always doled out to informants and this time he would not be able to fight them off. He was too apathetic.

But wasn't that the problem? It all came down to boredom. If he turned down Lyall's offer, it would be because boredom had eaten into him, eroding that very part of him he needed to prevent the boredom.

He turned the conundrum over in his head carefully.

There was a choice: to risk death from apathy or to risk death from trying to beat it off.

He opened the old tobacco tin on the small table in the cell and took out a worn old penny. He rubbed it between his finger and thumb, enjoying its smoothness, then flicked it. Heads he would take up Lyall's offer, tails he would not.

Tails. Wasn't that typical. He stretched himself out on his bed and decided in that instant that he was not going to be influenced by the spin of a coin. He was going to take up Lyall's offer. He was going to take up Lyall's offer, but he was not going to get excited about it. Lying on his bed, trying not to think of anything, he felt a tiny twitch of excitement flutter the muscles of his belly. Then he fell asleep.

CHAPTER TWO

Jack Lyall dipped a plain Hobnob into his mug of tea and opened the file on his desk.

His office looked like a prison cell but he wouldn't have it any other way. Other screws might try to soften reality by laying down carpet tiles and installing potted plants in their offices but Jack Lyall was not that sort of man. What was real was real and should be faced. So the walls of his office were brick, the texture smoothed and made slick by coats and coats of green gloss paint. The floor was painted with red, rubber-compound paint. There were filing cabinets along one wall, a calendar with a photograph of the Lake District *circa* 1950 on the other. A fluorescent light hung on thin chains from the high ceiling and its harsh glare shone on his scalp through his thinning layer of hair. A cigarette burned in an ashtray made from the foil tray of a meat pie.

He flipped through the file to remind himself of a few facts, then linked his hands behind his head, relaxed his neck and closed his eyes.

Inspector James Edward Carroll. Age forty-three. Suspected of murdering two prostitutes, finally convicted only of accepting bribes. The murder charges would not stick but the police had not come up with another suspect. Yet.

Single. A stable personality with a range of interests that included hill-walking, opera, food and reading. After the trial the papers said he lived a double life, that he was a Jekyll and Hyde figure. Well, some put it like that. Others said he was Inspector Morse and Jack the Ripper.

He had denied both murder charges and the bribery charge and claimed he was the victim of a cover-up and corruption. Well, he would, wouldn't he?

He had appealed and his appeal had been quashed on the grounds of no new evidence. He had spent a total of three weeks in solitary confinement for violent behaviour which had not bothered him a bit. He had one friend in prison – his cell-mate Joe Cohen – and that was all Jack Lyall knew about him and it was all he wanted to know. If he succeeded, fine. If he failed, he failed.

There were things he could have told Carroll about the deaths but something had stopped him. It was better that he find them out for himself, and if he couldn't find out what they were, he certainly wouldn't be able to discover how the men had died.

Jack Lyall shivered and tried to make his knackered captain's chair swing round. He was on his own, unable to trust anyone. Prison could corrupt the guards as much as the prisoners. Perhaps there was a perfectly reasonable explanation. He hoped there was. Otherwise it meant there was a very clever murderer loose inside the prison, a murderer able somehow to stretch his hand through brick walls and steel doors and snap a man's neck while he slept.

Snap. He felt the back of his neck, the two ridges of muscle that ran up the side of the vertebrae, the dinosaur knobbles which began between the shoulders. How do you begin to break that?

He knew one other thing, sitting at his desk, sipping his

tea, scratching his scalp which was rather dry. He knew that if the governor found out what he was doing, he'd be fed to the sharks. Snap.

CHAPTER THREE

'**R**oses is a new one.'

Joe Cohen's voice was sarcastic and it woke Jim up. The dream faded – the oddest sensation, rather like walking into a room just as everyone stops talking. Tears had pooled in his eyes as he lay asleep and he brushed them away.

Joe turned heavily in the bunk above his and the basket of metal that held up the mattress bulged dangerously. Jim looked up at the window. It was a square of dirty orange against the black of the wall. The street lights were still on in the town, staining the night sky.

'Bad dream?' Joe asked.

'Yeah.'

'Punishing yourself.'

Jim groaned and rolled over. 'Spare us the psychology. It's five o'clock in the morning.'

'I know it's five o'clock in the morning. You've just woken me up. It's like sharing a cell with a sound effects tape. Just remember, the beauty of Her Majesty's penal system is that you get someone else to punish you. You don't have to do it for yourself.'

Joe would never accept Jim's innocence – he said it was

irrelevant – and Jim had given up caring what Joe thought. His arms and shoulders ached as if he had been hugging himself, and he had a cricked neck. His pillow smelled and feather stems pricked his cheek through the ticking and the grey cotton cover. The rough blanket pricked his neck and rubbed the stubble under his chin. It was all so frigging uncomfortable. Above him the thin wire grille creaked again. It was Joe's week in the upper bunk – if the bed frame lasted that long.

Joe weighed sixteen stone and had worked various boxing rings up and down the country until the evening he discovered that his manager had been screwing his wife and skimming the cream off his winnings. Joe had lost his temper and a wild haymaker had driven some of the man's nose up into his brain, killing him. Anyone who had watched Joe fight knew that it must have been accidental – he had not landed a blow like that for six years – but the judge did not go for that line of defence. Life for Joe, and a space problem for anyone who had to share a cell with him.

Joe started to snore.

Jim folded his hands behind his head and stared out of the narrow cell window. He could not get Lyall's offer out of his mind. It was almost as if he were waking up from a long sleep. What was it? A call to action? He felt bits of his mind begin to stir, bits that he had forgotten about. Some of them were where he stored his experience, the experience of twenty years or so investigating crimes. Don't look for clues; look for evidence. Don't look for a big mystery. Don't try and be clever. Don't attempt to concoct any sort of theory until every single shred of evidence is gathered in.

But other bits began to stir as well. After the appeal had been turned down he had deliberately numbed himself to all feelings of hope. Now he could feel it moving in him like a treacherous little flame, warming him with its trick warmth. He could not help it. He was innocent, damn it.

If he helped Lyall, perhaps Lyall might help him. He still had friends out there, people who believed in him, of course he did. There was Brian White, his old sergeant. Sure, he had been rather slow to come forward at the trial, but – and this was the crucial thing – the tide of opinion inside the force had somehow changed. Solidarity worked both ways. It kept you in or it kept you out. Once they had decided that he was guilty he was finished, and anyone who then stepped up and came out in support of him risked exclusion. In the police, where you relied on your colleagues and they relied on you, that could literally be a matter of life and death – a call for back-up not relayed as fast as it could be, people not prepared to risk a damn thing to help you. Jim knew how the pressures worked. He remembered that Brian had a wife, a young child – a girl with flaming red hair – and no doubt he wanted the best for them. Certainly he would not have wanted to be filing parking tickets for the rest of his life, or be bleeding to death in some filthy alley because the back-up team felt like finishing their tea before they came in support.

But now it was just possible that enough time had passed for him to look at the facts with a fresh eye. Perhaps Lyall would visit Brian; talk to him, pass on a message. Lyall looked like a decent sort of bloke. Then some new evidence might turn up. Then—

STOP IT!.

He looked at the sky. It was just turning grey. He tried to make his mind that colour.

Joe was out of the cell early because as a wearer of a red arm band he was privileged to skivvy around the prison.

He was always trying to get Jim to apply but it went right against the grain, somehow, and now Jim had Jack Lyall's offer to think about as well.

'You just can't bear the thought of clearing up after the poor old sods you put away,' Joe told him, not without edge. 'You're just a snob, or something.' There was more than a grain of truth in what Joe said.

Jim shuffled into the day.

And when darkness falleth, yea shalt thou piss into a bucket and hope that it runneth not over. Breakfast.

Thou shalt stand in a long line and thy food shall be cold and it shall be dropped from a great height on to thy tray so that the egg shall mix with the porridge and the porridge shall lay down on the toast.

Joe was serving the porridge and deliberately gave Jim a mountain of the stuff. Nothing else in the known universe had quite the same consistency as prison porridge. It was as thick as clay, as sticky as glue, and had lumps in it the size of marbles.

'You're a pal,' Jim said. 'Sorry about waking you up.'

Joe gave the pile of porridge an experimental tap with the ladle. 'My revenge,' he said. 'Clone it. It lives.'

'Move the fuck along there,' a guard said.

And thou shalt utter no sentence, but that thy words shall be profane and obscene. Fuck shalt be thy motto, and shit thy punctuation, and every man who dwelleth in Her Majesty's prison shall henceforward and forever be known as Bastard, now and forever more, a-fucking-men.

Jojo Neill, a burglar, slid into the bench beside him.

'Hear the news?' he said.

'One of the Royals isn't getting divorced?'

'Funny man. No, about this place. Hey, Mickey, you hear the news?' He leant across to the man next to Jim.

'What news?'

'They're privatizing us.'

'What do you mean they're privatizing us?'

'They want to sell the prison to a private firm.'

'They want to sell the prison to a private firm?'

'This is a beautiful conversation,' Jim said. 'Where did you hear it?'

Jojo stabbed his egg excitedly. 'I heard it from a bloke who heard it from his wife who heard it on the radio.'

Jim and Mickey nodded at each other. 'A rumour,' they said in unison, crooked their little fingers, gripped the other's with it.

'Kelly,' Jim said.

'Sheets,' Mickey said.

'What's going on?' Jojo asked. 'No one listens to me. This is true.'

'Like Elvis was on B Wing?'

'He looked like Elvis, that was all I said. Anyway, they're privatizing the place. Knocking down this one, and building a brand new prison instead.'

'Crap,' Mickey said. 'Why knock this one down? I think it's perfick.'

'They could turn it into a museum,' Jim said. 'Call it Dingey World.'

'Yeah, if it moves, theme it,' Mickey said.

'This new prison,' Jojo said, 'will have a video in each cell—'

'Camera or recorder?' Mickey asked.

'Toilet and shower suites—'

'Shag pile fitted carpets,' Mickey said.

'You're taking the piss,' Jojo said.

'He's taking the Mickey,' Jim said.

The bell rang for the end of breakfast.

Breakfast was over by eight. By eight-thirty the men had to

be back in their cells which would be locked until lunch at
eleven-thirty. In the afternoon, they might have half an
hour's exercise if they were lucky, or they might be locked
up until tea at six. Recreation, when they could pay visits
to each other, play cards, or chess; trade dope or tobacco
or sex, or just watch TV in the great central hall, was
limited to about two sessions a week these days. The
authorities said it was due to staff shortages – but everyone
knew they were being punished for an incident the
previous summer when the library had been trashed by
some delinquents and three lifers had broken through the
roof and shown their bums to the world for an hour or two.
It was the silly season in the Press so it was front-page
news. A junior minister had been forced to break his
Tuscan holiday and quack platitudes in front of the prison
gates for the television. An opposition spokesman who had
not been on holiday had toured the prison and said that
'questions would be asked and answers demanded'. The
screws were still furious. They could give him his precious
bleeding answers, but no one ever asked them, oh no, so
they were extra foul to the prisoners instead.

Jim sat on the edge of his bed. 'I could have a smoke but
then I wouldn't have enough for this evening. I could play
patience but I'd cheat and that would depress me. I could
read but I don't feel like it.'

He half-heartedly went through some half-remembered
t'ai chi exercises, over-balanced and bruised his temple on
the metal frame of the top bunk. Then he sat down again
and tried to make himself cry. He failed.

In the end he turned on the radio.

'... standing by the great bulk of Long Barrow Prison,
here in this pleasant suburb of the town with the moor
behind me and the low roof-tops of terraced houses, so

characteristic of the industrial midlands, marching down to the town centre, five miles away.

'Until a few months ago, this would have been a scene almost unchanged from Victorian times, when the prison was built and the town expanded to meet the growing needs of the mills and factories which provided so much employment. It's all changing, of course. The mills have gone, the factories and warehouses closed down. Their blank and broken windows which once glowed with light, now stare emptily over an industrial desert of weed-choked canals and deserted um, places. The prison alone remains, a great yet bleak reminder of times gone by, but even now its future is debatable.

'For behind me the ground has already been broken for another Long Barrow prison, one of the new generation prisons, concrete, not brick, and built literally to withstand the worst anyone can throw at it. They argue that increased security will in fact lead to more humane conditions for the prisoners: they can cut down on supervision and increase day-to-day freedom. More remarkably perhaps, the actual financing of the new Long Barrow prison is a unique joint venture, with the Home Office, the Conservative-controlled local council, and a consortium of local businesses all chipping in to this new enterprise. I have next to me Councillor Hitchens who thinks that . . .'

Jojo was right then. Someone out there thought that prisons were an enterprise.

This place was modern once, Jim thought. He stretched his arms out but could not quite touch the sides of his cell with his fingertips. Twelve foot by eight. When the Barrow was built, this would have been a one-man cell. He'd read a book on Victorian prisons once. A great many of them were built on a wave of reforming zeal and strict scientific principles. The devil made work for idle hands so the prisoners walked treadmills, picked oakum, moved piles of stones from one corner of the yard to another – and then back again – all day long.

Prison was an opportunity for reflective repentance in those days so prisoners were not allowed to talk. They existed in solitary confinement for their entire term, sleeping alone and eating in silence. Even the treadmills had cubicles to stop them communicating with their neighbours. They lived in silence, slept in silence, died in silence. Silence was not just an absence of noise. Silence was a thing.

Not surprisingly a lot of the prisoners went mad.

The radio cut out suddenly. Silence rushed at him from the four walls of the cell. He flinched, tapped the radio and was relieved when it fizzed back to life; '—bringing the expertise of the private sector—'

He looked out of the window. By leaning against the wall he could see a patch of land that had been flattened on the other side of the perimeter wall. *Was that where the new prison was going up? What would they be doing with the old one?* he wondered.

'Rumours that the men inside the old prison are mistreated are entirely unfounded. They get jolly good food, plenty of exercise—'

Jim stared at the radio in disbelief. Perhaps he was out there now, talking lies. The reporter's voice cut in.

'Nonetheless the suicide rate inside—'

'Grossly exaggerated, I assure you. I have it on the best authority that it's hardly any more than the average housing estate.'

'Nevertheless—'

'But whatever the reality, it all just goes to show how

important the new prison is going to be.'

Down the wing, from far away, he heard a man begin to laugh. He started high, swooped down low, rose again, then started to whoop like a siren. He heard people shouting angrily from their locked cells. Then there was the echoing crash of the cell door swinging open and the man stopped.

The door closed and the man started laughing again. Sometimes you longed for silence.

CHAPTER FOUR

'S tand to attention, hands behind back, prisoner.'
Jim stood straightened and clasped his hands
behind his back. Tried to look keen, as if the rigmarole
made him the happiest man alive.

'Head up, prisoner.'

'Oh yes. Sorry.' Jerked his chin up. Stared at the ceiling.
Lowered his eyes.

A small square room painted gloss green. The air stank
of cigarettes with the creosote tang of the disinfectant floor-
cleaner; the walls held the light from the twin fluorescent
tubes in their sheen. Lyall's office on the first floor of the
admin. block had a grille behind the glass, not bars, Jim
noted.

Lyall had not looked up yet. He was writing something
on an official form in blue ballpoint. He had a strong,
looping hand and took his time.

'I'd like to volunteer for library duty, sir.'

'Don't speak until spoken to!'

'That's all right, Officer,' Lyall said to the guard. 'I'll be
all right.'

Renfrew stamped a foot, executed a clumsy about-turn
and clumped out of the office. He left the door open and Jim
heard him sit down.

'Carroll, James Edward,' Lyall said. It had taken Jim two weeks to get this far. He looked down at Jack Lyall's scalp. His hair was dragged across a bald patch like Bobby Charlton's. The man had scurf – a terrible case of it; the tops of his ears seemed to have scales on them. Jim resisted the temptation to pat his own head.

In the stillness Jim heard the humming of the fluorescent light, wet sounds as Lyall swallowed, a gurgling somewhere in his gut and a distant clacking, almost like a printing press.

Lyall opened a folder with a great show of paper rustling. He slid four black and white photographs out of the cardboard folder.

'Your file shows that you have a nasty temper, Mr Carroll,' he said.

His fingers spread the pictures out on the desk.

'Not really,' Jim answered, rather taken aback.

'Sir,' Renfrew's voice came from the other room. Jim moved sideways to block the view of the desk from the ante room completely.

'Sir,' Jim repeated. 'Well, yes, actually. I did three spells in solitary for assaulting other ...' He paused. 'I did one spell in solitary for assaulting four other prisoners—'

'Hospitalizing two of them. You alleged at the time that they had been trying to introduce a broom handle into your person.'

'A mistake, sir. They were just mopping the floor as Mr Scott testified at the hearing. I misinterpreted their actions.'

Lyall raised an eyebrow. Before he could continue Jim went on. 'And I did two other spells for assaulting prison officers. I was having some difficulty in coming to terms with my, er, situation, sir.'

He hadn't always been apathetic, he remembered with

dull surprise. In the first few months he had been manic.

'Right. And you consider that you have adjusted now?'

'Yessir. Certainly, sir.'

Lyall tapped the desk. He had arranged the photographs the right way up for Jim. Jim looked down at them and knew that Lyall was looking at him, trying to read his face. Four studies in colour. Four dead men in living colour. He wouldn't have long, a minute, maybe two.

All four men were naked and lying on top of their bedding. Their skin had that peculiar swollen dullness of death. It was ashy and yellow but that might have been an effect of the wall colour and the flash. Their eyes did not look up, or out, or anything. They were just there: indentations in the skull with soft things in them. Slight signs of lividity in the dorsal regions – in English that meant the blood had started to drain downwards and pool in the back and the buttock, but perhaps that was shadow from the flash. Their faces were distorted but whether by fear, or pain, or pleasure it was hard to say. Their mouths were wide open and the insides looked very dark. There was too much similarity in their position for it to be coincidence, so what could the link be?

Each man was flat on his back with his arms down by his side. Each man had his palms facing the ceiling.

The complete relaxation of the body was in strict contrast to the contortions of the face. Their names were written across the bottom of each of the photographs. Powell, Burroughs, Masters and Campbell.

Jim wondered about the secrecy. Four dead men. All thought that they were innocent. What did Lyall expect? That he'd go the same way as them but keep a diary? Had these men left nothing behind?

If news leaked out – via an enquiry for example – that the suicide level was too high, or better still, there had been unexplained deaths within the prison, the governor might end up running a borstal in Essex, if he were lucky. Lyall could not tell his guards because he could not be sure that they were not involved. Nevertheless he wanted to find out what was going on inside his prison.

Jim liked him for that, or thought he did. You could never be sure.

He realized Lyall had said something. 'I beg your pardon sir, but I didn't catch that.'

'Are you aware of the responsibilities that you will be asked to discharge?'

'I expect I'll find out, sir. I expect it all comes down to people trusting each other.'

Lyall raised an eyebrow and almost smiled. Jim squinted at the pictures. If only he could talk openly to Lyall about this.

Four dead men in different cells at different times, but all in the same position.

The more he looked at the pictures, the less he liked them, and he hadn't liked them very much in the first place.

'I said: have you any questions?' Lyall was looking impatient. He glanced over Jim's shoulder and slid the pictures away.

'The more I know about it, the better,' Jim said, hoping that the conversation did not seem too nonsensical to the guard.

'Try and find out a bit for yourself,' Lyall said.

Jim forced the four names into his mind. Powell, Burroughs, Campbell and Masters. He nodded.

'We'll consider your application,' said Lyall. 'You can go now.'

Jim reached into his pocket and took out a small piece of paper folded twice. He slid it across the desk and walked out.

Lyall watched him go, waited until Renfrew had pushed him into the corridor, then unfolded the paper.

> In return for my pursuing certain investigations within Long Barrow prison I would like you to contact my old colleague Brian White and urgently ask him to visit me in prison. He will be reluctant and will take some persuading but I'm sure if you convince him of my innocence, he will be prepared to come and see me. He used to live in Egerton on the moor. He will be easily traceable.

Lyall shook his head. Surprise and disappointment washed through him: surprise that Jim Carroll was still banging on about his innocence, disappointment that he was not man enough to accept his guilt. He looked at the address written at the bottom of the page. It was not far away, a small village up on the moors, quite nice if you liked that sort of thing. Well, maybe he would go up there and pass the message on – when he had the chance.

In the corridor outside the guard said: 'I heard you giving the old man cheek. If you hadn't been screwing up your chances of getting a privilege I'd have been down on you like a ton of bricks.'

Two days later, to everyone's surprise, Jim Carroll was told that he was to start work in the library in a month's time.

CHAPTER FIVE

Tea – dark brown stew and grey potatoes – had come and gone. It had come on dull metal trays and gone down seven hundred throats with numb disinterest. It was recreation time until eight when the shifts changed and the men had to go back to their cells. All the doors were wide open – hooked back, so that when the men went visiting the insides of the cells were visible. That was the theory anyway. In practice you just crowded the door with people and got on with whatever you wanted – deals, poker games, beatings – inside.

Jim leaned on the railing and looked down. In the middle of the hall was a perspex command box. A guard sat inside it, watching a bank of twelve video screens. The pictures flicked over monotonously – there were more cameras than screens. If the controller saw something suspicious he could hold one of the screens and, theoretically, talk to the nearest guard on a walkie talkie. But as he and everyone else in the prison knew, the walkie talkies did not work properly inside the prison – something about the mineral content of the brick – so the whole exercise was useless. The command post had a siren on its roof now, which had never been used, and some of the prisoners thought it had hidden strobe lights that would disorientate potential rioters.

Sparrows – gaol birds – were fluttering in the huge open space, darting through a hole in one of the windows, perching on the metal girders that ran across the lantern. Like everywhere else, prisons have their legends. The story at Long Barrow was that when the birds left, the prison would fall down and that was why the screws did not put bird lime down on the girders. Some prisoners said the governor had orders to keep them fed and Jim half believed it. After all, they cut the primary feathers of the ravens in the Tower of London to stop them flying away.

It was the same story – if the ravens left, England would fall. Jim wondered how many prisoners in the Tower of London had prayed for the ravens to leave.

He looked across the hall to D Wing where Powell's old cell had been. Powell had been the last man to die, according to Lyall. There was a chance that his old cell-mate was still in the same place.

Jim pushed through the crowds milling around a trestle table.

'Jim, come over here.'

Joe beckoned him over.

'What's going on?'

'Draughts knockout competition. You put in a quarter of an ounce of snout to enter. Winner takes everything.'

'Everything?'

'Well, there's a rake-off for the organisers.'

'Who are?'

'Randall.'

'You amaze me,' Jim said sarcastically. 'Actually you do amaze me. I thought he was on the punishment wing for a month.'

'He is, but Gorgeous George is organizing it for him.'

'He should watch it. When the cat's away and all that.'

'No chance. George is as loyal as a dog.'

Jojo was moving through the crowd, picking up the entry fees and noting names down in the book.

'Gentlemen, can I interest you in a small wager?'

'How many people have entered, Jojo?'

'Fifteen so far. Big prize for someone.'

'The more people who enter the less chance of winning,' Joe said.

Jojo patted him on the cheek. 'It's a game of skill; luck doesn't come into it. And what's more, the more people who enter, the bigger the pot.'

'And the rake-off,' Joe said.

'Fair's fair.' Jojo looked hurt.

Jim looked through a gap in the milling figures and saw Gorgeous George, Randall's lieutenant, say something to a man who shrugged and turned away. George's arm shot out and grabbed the man's wrist. Jim could see the muscles tighten like ropes in George's arms, as he squeezed and twisted. The man began to buckle at the knees. George let go of his wrist. The man dipped into the breast pocket of his tunic and pulled out a twist of tobacco.

'You said George was loyal as a dog? A Rottweiler more like.'

'Man's best friend,' Joe said. 'Going to go in for the competition?'

'No chance. I'm not contributing to Randall's little empire. The man's evil,' Jim said.

'Come on,' Jojo whined, 'you're making me feel bad.'

'He's powerful,' Joe said, ignoring him.

'Forget it, Joe.' Jim moved away. 'Don't worry Jojo. We all do what we can to survive.'

'Who's worried?' asked Jojo, raising his eyebrows and looking from Joe to Jim. 'I'm not worried.' He caught sight of George looking around for him and moved quickly away from them.

'He's not worried,' Joe said. 'He just does a good impression of it. Where are you off to?'

'Got to go and see a man about a book. See you later.'

'Nothing like stating the obvious,' said Joe.

Jim climbed the stairs to the second level of D Wing. The door to Powell's old cell was open. There was one man inside, sitting on the edge of his bed. He was chewing solemnly. As Jim watched he cupped his hand under his mouth and tongued a wad of grey slime into it. He looked at it, then pressed it into a small square mould made from a hollowed out block of wood. He then took another piece of wood, exactly the same size as the hole in the mould and pressed it in, carefully. He maintained pressure steadily for about ten seconds, then up-ended the mould and tapped it on to a tray. A tiny block of compressed paper fell out.

On the bed by him was a paperback book. He tore a page out of it carefully, stuffed it in his mouth and began to chew again.

'Evening,' Jim said.

The man looked round. He was middle-aged with a deeply lined face and dull eyes. His teeth were round like pebbles and grey from the printers' ink.

'That's interesting.' Jim nodded at the pile of paper blocks.

The man stared at him, chewing all the time.

'Making something?'

The man stared at him a second longer, then reached under the bed. He pulled out a board. On it was a half-finished model of a church.

'The house of the Lord,' the man said. He looked at it

sadly, then put it back under the bed. 'God shall live in it and it shall reside with me.'

'Very nice.'

'The house of the Lord,' he repeated. 'I burned down my house with my wife inside it. Now I shall build the house of the Lord and it shall be a place unto Him.'

'Let's change the subject, shall we?'

'I'm not insane,' the man said. 'Just evil. The spirit of evil resides within my body. That makes me a very interesting person.'

He began to chew again.

Jim smiled encouragingly at him, feeling slightly queasy as he did so. 'I'm sure it does. I've come to ask a question about your old cell-mate, Powell.'

'What do you want to know about him for?'

'He borrowed a book from the library. I'm on book duty now and I saw that he hadn't given it back.'

It was a bad lie but it would have to do. Jim wanted to get the other man talking.

'This one?' the man said. He held up the torn paperback. A Sven Hassel Eastern Front book.

'No.'

'What book then? I eat books, but often remember what I've eaten. This church is made from words. God spake and it was so. And the word was God.'

'A course book. Open University. One of the other men wants it.'

'I never knew he was doing a course. He never told me that he was doing a course,' the man said.

'Oh really. I wonder what he wanted the book for then.'

'The question is: what do you want the book for?'

'Me, I want it to go back into the library.'

'Other people have come looking for his books. Other men came looking.'

The man was rocking from side to side, gently at first but getting faster and faster. Jim tensed. He felt a rush of adrenalin. The man was like a volcano waiting to erupt. Suddenly he stopped, turned and spat a wad of paper at Jim who just managed to duck. It hit the wall, stuck, then slowly slithered down.

'Evil seeker,' the man said. 'Evil will come to the evil seekers. He was an evil seeker who made the devil his God. And those that follow him will be smitten.'

'What?'

'Evil is that evil does. And evil is he that does evil. Evil and devil are divided only by D. D is present in one, absent in the other. The D is death. The devil is evil made manifest in eternal death. Are you with me?'

'No. I'm afraid not.'

'Evil is he that evil does. And evil is—'

'All right.' Jim put his hand up to stop the man. The man sat still as if held by the hand and stared at it. Jim frowned. 'Are you telling me that Powell was evil?'

'I am telling you nothing that you do not know. This is a den of evil, a cesspit of evil. Only the pure can prevail.' He began to chew again.

'Please don't spit at me again,' Jim said. 'I really didn't know anything about this. Can you tell me again exactly what Powell did?'

The man looked at him. Sweat had broken out on his forehead and his face had lost its colour. When he spoke it was in a hoarse whisper. 'He made a pact with the devil,' he said. 'And the devil took him. Now leave.'

Jim woke up in the night with a start. He looked for the patch of sky on the wall but a huge shape was blocking it. He struck out in panic, but his arms were suddenly grabbed and pinned down by his side.

'Easy, easy,' Joe said. 'Take it easy, mate.'

'What's going on?'

'Can I let you go or are you going to try and hit me again?'

Jim let his arms go limp. 'I woke up and it was dark. I couldn't see a thing. It was as if someone was trying to smother me. You know. Or just drop a bag or something over my head.'

'You were shouting.'

'What?'

'That you were innocent. Then you started screaming. I came down to wake you up. Are you all right now?' Joe asked.

Jim's head hurt all around the inside. He thought perhaps that someone had just stuck a steam hose in his ear, blasted his brain out and left the inside nice and clean. New. Waiting for someone.

'I'm fine,' he said. The bunk rocked as Joe climbed up.

'Sorry,' Jim said.

'Don't even think about it. We've all had bad times.'

'What was I shouting?'

'I didn't say shout. I said scream.'

'My throat's sore.'

'You sort of screamed, then cut off terribly suddenly. Like this.' Joe went 'EEEEE', then made a little click in his throat.

'EEEE? That doesn't sound very frightening.'

'It did from up here. It was blank. Like a kettle going off.'

Steam cleaned. 'Anyway, thanks,' Jim said.

'*A votre service*,' said Joe, who had once done a French O level.

The bunk creaked as Joe settled down again. Jim put his hands behind his head and watched the sky get lighter. If he was having nightmares, he supposed he was having bad times, but in all honesty he was quite enjoying his new role inside the prison. Perhaps that was the problem. Perhaps he was just a miserable old bastard and should stay that way.

CHAPTER SIX

Jim followed the guard along the clanging balconies across the main hall and into the entrance of B Wing. The guard unlocked a door and almost pushed him in.

There was no library when the prison was built. It was situated in the hall where the men picked oakum, unravelling the thick naval ropes until their fingers bled. The wall still carried messages from those days, painted on to the stone in large, clear letters, so that the men could read them easily if they lifted their heads.

Above is Heaven, below is Hell.
Faith in the Lord preserveth well.

A charming sentiment, Jim thought, but changed his mind when he read the next lines.

The Lord shall smite thee with a consumption, and
with a fever, and with an inflammation, and with an
extreme burning, and with the sword, and with
blasting, and with mildew; and they shall pursue
thee until thou perish.

Deuteronomy 28:22

Old Testament prophets were not exactly imbued with the spirit of sweetness, light and forgiveness, Jim thought. The God of the prison was clearly an Old Testament God:

bloodthirsty, self-righteous and terrifying.

People must have been tough in those days. After being
struck with fever, consumption, inflammation, extreme
burning, sword, blasting and mildew Jim did not think he
would need pursuing until he perished. The mildew on its
own would do for him, he thought. Mildew grew on roses
as a sort of clinging grey mould. It made the leaves wither
and drop off. It spread with horrid speed through a garden.
He saw a tiny cottage, its door framed by a trailing dog-
rose, buds just opening in the spring sunshine. He reached
out and touched one of the buds. Inside the tense package
of stem and outer leaves it was liquid with rot.

He started. It was almost like an hallucination – the
cottage, the rose, the rot. Perhaps they really were drug-
ging the tea, he thought. His head felt clear now, but his
ears were blocked. He shook his head and felt them clear.

*Now this man purchased a field with the rewards of
iniquity; and falling headlong, he burst asunder in
the midst and all his bowels gushed forth.*

Acts 1:18

Great place to work, Jim thought. He looked around the
room.

He had discovered books in his twenties. When he was
a kid, reading had been considered evidence of a feeble
mind, impotence, effeminacy ... all that kind of thing. You
did your work, your school work, to get your certificates,
but you didn't do more than that. In the evenings you put
your dad's grease on your hair – if you had finished your
homework – and hung around the fish and chip shop or
the bus shelter in the municipal gardens. There was always
a gap in the railings and the park keepers would pin dire
warnings on the wall about Illegal Entry After Official Park
Closing Time and What Happened to Persons who Committed Nuisances, Obscene Acts or Littered the Floor Area

with Cigarette Butts and Other Sundry Items.

Bus shelters and chip shops. A pinched adolescence spent reeking of nicotine and different kinds of oil. Hair oil. Engine oil. Chip oil. OK, so the chippy wasn't that cool, but there was nowhere else to hang out – no brightly lit coffee bars like the places where Cliff Richard or Tommy Steele strummed their guitars, and certainly none of those places that looked like stranded flying saucers, all glass and chrome, where American teenagers went in the movies. Driving Dad's Ford Popular down to the chippy wasn't quite the same as rolling up at a drive-in in a Chevrolet shark-fin special, but it was better than nothing.

Then they got older. They stopped meeting in parks and bus shelters. Some of them got jobs and the ones with jobs met in pubs and dance clubs, under-age and still handing in their wage packets to their mums, spending their pocket money on booze and fags and terrible clothes.

Jim was still at school when the first of his friends got married. At the ceremony Jim looked at him and didn't know him. He wasn't a friend any more. He was an alien creature with a thin neck sticking out of a cheap suit, his face still green from the stag night forty-eight hours before. He was working down at the factory with his dad and a lot of other people's dads and uncles and brothers. There were rumours even then, and by the time Jim left school with his certificates, ready for the clerical job his mother had meant him to get, the factory had closed and his father was drinking and his mother was beginning, just beginning, to cough too much.

He saw their life like a prison. He saw the world slamming its doors shut around him. He wanted to be free, like the hero in a cliffhanger. With one mighty bound . . .

He wanted something more. He wanted variety, he wanted respect, promotion, security, the chance to look at

dirty books and to drive a dark blue Wolsey with a bell on
the roof too fast. Had he really wanted that? He joined the
police.

> *Drought and heat consume the snow waters: so doth*
> *the grave those which have sinned.*
>
> Job 24:19

Repent or burn.

Be good or hurt for ever.

After everything, could it really come down to that? Did
it take a prison to teach him that?

'Ah, Mr Carroll?'

Jim spun round as if he had been caught doing something
illegal, automatically snatching a book. The man who had
spoken to him was dressed in a suit. The first thing Jim
noticed was high, arching eyebrows that looked strangely
heavy for such a pale face, and small red-rimmed eyes.

'I see you're catching up with your reading. Now let's
see . . .'

He took the book from Jim's hand. A policeman with a
cheeky gap-toothed grin, a tarty woman leaning on his
shoulder. *Confessions of a Bobby on the Beat.* Christ!

'Oh, I see. Goodness gracious me!'

Jim raised his eyes to heaven.

> *Though art weighed in the balance and found wanting.*
>
> Daniel 5:27

'It was never that much fun,' Jim answered through a
tight smile that threatened to crack his face.

'No. No. Quite. What?' The man looked at Jim nervously.

'I used to be a policeman.'

'Oh. I see. Rather – er – ironic your being here?'

Now he looked hopefully at Jim.

'You could say that. I must say it hadn't quite struck me
that way.'

'Well then. Now, I'm told that you are keen to help. There's a lot that needs doing. This place is chaos, simply chaos.'

He gestured around the room, at the piles of books on the floor, on the desks, lying any old way on the shelves.

'How come it's so bad?' Jim asked.

'I dare say you heard about the way some young toughs got in here last summer. They ruined the place. Pulled the books off the shelves, made some of them into bonfires, used others to – well, let's say they introduced them into their toilet routine. There was nothing for it but to throw everything away, especially after they had been doused by the fire services, and start all over again. We – that is, the volunteer association – have been collecting books ever since, but as you can see most of them are still in boxes, those that are on the shelves are in no order whatsoever, and in the stores down in the cellars there is any amount just rotting away, I'm afraid. It's all too much for me, the – er – lifting and carrying, that is. So the first thing to do is some elementary sorting.'

Jim soon found out why the library was in such chaos. Tindall, an elderly volunteer prison visitor, was incapable of doing anything for more than thirty seconds without dropping it and moving on to something else. Jim, still ingrained with the rigid discipline of police procedure, would, in amazement, watch him pick a book off the shelves, peer at the spine, lift his glasses for a closer look, examine the fly leaf, flick through it, find that it reminded him of something, put it down and wander off to another part of the library, see another book and start the whole procedure again.

Jim spent the morning taking the books off the shelves, content to classify them as fiction and non-fiction for the time being. He somehow communicated to Tindall that he should try and sort the non-fiction into categories before arranging them alphabetically. But when they had finally sorted the non-fiction to one end of the room, Mr Tindall suddenly decided to take Jim down into the cellar to see what books might be down there.

At the back of the library was a small panelled door. Tindall unlocked it with a key on a pink plastic tag and led Jim into a short corridor. At the end of the corridor a metal spiral staircase led downwards. Jim could feel different air on his face. Colder air. Darker air, somehow. Secret air.

Tindall nodded and Jim led the way down. It got darker and damper with every step. He breathed in the deep must of old cellars.

'Any chance of a light?'

'There's a switch at the bottom. Are you there yet? I don't want to come tumbling down on top of you.'

'That's very thoughtful of you.'

'What? Ah yes. I see. Very good.'

Their voices were punctuated by the clanging of their feet on the metal rungs.

Jim's feet touched stone. 'You'll find the switch high up on your left.'

His fingers scraped across the wall. Loose paint caked behind his nails.

'Or low on your right. I'm afraid I don't come down here very much. The damp, you see. My lungs.'

My brains, Jim thought.

He found the switch high up on the right and flicked it. A tunnel unrolled in front of him, lit by light bulbs at ten-foot intervals. The bulbs had old-fashioned metal shades and hung on twisted flex. Mould bloomed between the brick courses, and the floor was covered with flakes of distemper.

'It's shocking down here. Really shocking. The state they've allowed it to get into. We're under B Wing incidentally. These were old punishment cells, I believe.' Tindall joined him and pointed to what looked like small alcoves set into the walls. The doors were hooked back, flush against the wall, showing a bench which was too short to stretch out on, and an iron hoop set into the floor. Carroll felt the cold wrap long flat arms around him. He shivered. His back tensed.

'Where are we going?' he asked. 'I don't see—'

'Here we are.'

Tindall unlocked a wooden door, opened it and flicked on the light. Carroll expected to see a small cupboard. Instead he found himself in the mouth of a corridor about the same width as the one they had been standing in. It was vaulted, and lit again by light bulbs hanging from cord. Alcoves were spaced at regular intervals, piled high with cardboard boxes, wooden boxes, sheaves of paper, bundles of notes spilling on to every surface, falling on to the floor. Boxes had been dumped all the way down the middle of the corridor. The damp had softened the cardboard and they bulged like soft sculpture.

'What is it?' he asked.

'This,' Mr Tindall said, 'is where the books have been kept. It's the others in the visitors' association. They will keep on sending them in. I tell them that we've got ample but still they arrive.' He picked one up from the floor. '*Bee Keeping for Beginners*,' he read. 'Mostly unsold books from jumble sales, I fear.'

Jim looked down the tunnel. 'What are all the others?'

'The others?' Tindall asked. 'The others? Files, I suppose. Confidential possibly. Oh dear, does that mean that I have to be down here supervising you? I suppose I should be really, but the damp down here, you know … My lungs …

I do hope I can trust you. If I ask for your word of honour?'
Jim nodded. 'Don't you worry, Mr Tindall.'
Tindall left, holding a handkerchief up to his nose.

Jim walked a few paces down the corridor, and took out a
box at random.

   Item: Seventy Tunics (pattern d) Grey. @ 3s.6d.
   Item: Two hundred squares towelling (low grade) @ 6d
   Item: Two hundred squares towelling (" " small) @
   2s.2d

Pre-decimal prices. If you could prove that no towels had
been bought since decimalization, that would be no
surprise at all. He looked at the date: 1962. Cheap towels
even for then.
   He took another step in. There was a heavier box with an
official Home Office crest on the front. He tried to brush the
dust off but it was damp and just left dark streaks. The top
slid off with a soft thump, as if it were breaking a partial
vacuum.
   More papers, heavily foxed.

   Name: Thomas Anthony Carpenter
   Birth date: 25th February 1908
   Sentence: 15 years (parole denied)
   Previous convictions: None
   Crime: Attempted murder, daughter, wife. Gross bes-
   tiality
   General comments: Prisoner was apprehended having
   intercourse with goose in kitchen when daughter and
   wife returned from shopping. On being discovered
   attacked both with ladle and carving knife. Showed
   remorse at trial and claimed he acted out of shame.

What's sauce for the goose, Jim thought and turned to the
next sheet.

Name: Mark Andrew Smithies
Birth date: 3rd July 1900
Sentence: 10 years
Previous convictions: 1923 – Embezzlement; 1927 –
Fraud; 1930 – Embezzlement
Crime: Theft
General comments: Hard regime recommended.

Will someone be looking at my file in sixty-odd years time?
Jim wondered. He closed the box and picked up another at
random. It was light and rattled. He opened it. A knife, with
an old luggage label tied to the handle.

There's a story there, but I don't know it.

The further he went in, the older the records were. He
picked his way over piles of mildewed rubbish to the end of
the corridor and knelt on the ground.

As far as he could gather the records went back to
beginnings of the prison. Here was a folder full of yellowing
press clippings. Letters from the builder. Letters to subcon-
tractors. Strange that they weren't all kept by the Home
Office. Perhaps there had not been a Home Office then.
Receipts, more receipts. He poked around half-heartedly,
looking for an architect's drawing of the prison. The sheer
weight of paper, and the smell of damp and mould began
to oppress him.

Back to work. The door at the end of the tunnel looked
very far away. He turned, accidentally knocking a loose
pile of papers on to the floor by his feet. They fell in a dry
avalanche. He tried to push them back but only succeeded
in dislodging more.

Something underneath seemed to arch a soft back. Darkness shifted under his hand.

With a yelp he pulled his hands out and leapt back, knocking his head on the light bulb, sending shadows tearing crazily against the wall. A shadow moved suddenly from behind a pillar. Hid again, jumped again. Hid, jumped. Hid, jumped. He put a hand out and steadied the bulb. Nothing. Never was anything. Just shadows.

Still, I'd better sort out those rats.

In the far corner a collection of planks and timbers had been propped against the wall. He picked one up. It was about five feet long, quite thin. Finished wood with holes drilled at each end – like a part of a dismantled frame.

With the plank he prodded the pile of papers on the floor. Nothing moved, only a folder slid off the pile and fell to the floor. He prodded again, feeling the muscles knotting in his calves, waiting for the giant mutant paper-eating sabre-toothed rodent to leap out at him, telling himself all the time to grow up. Yet there was . . . something.

He grew more confident and began to knock the papers off to see what was under them. It was cloth of some sort. Someone's folded up jacket? A blanket?

He poked it thoroughly, partly unfolding it in the process. He guessed it was a rug or blanket and it seemed to be covered with silvery slug trails or spider's webs, criss-crossing each other in close skeins, in places closely bound together, in others single, thin, wandering lines. When he looked more closely he saw that they were threads. Whatever it was, blanket or rug, it had been closely and obsessively embroidered.

He knelt and peered at it but it was too dark in the cellar to see what the pattern was. He put it under his arm and went back upstairs.

*

It was light in the library, and dry and warm. The smell of the books, one of his favourite smells, comforted him. He shook the blanket in the air and let it fall flat to the floor. Then he stood back.

It was a picture of a village, stitched on to a black blanket in white thread. The first thing he thought of was a child's blackboard drawing, white on black. But this was not the work of a child. This took a remembered reality and drew it out along a thousand tiny stitches of despair.

A church stood in the middle of the village, surrounded by a graveyard. A road ran up the middle of the picture by the side of the graveyard, meeting another at the top.

On either side of the road stood a line of houses, quite small for the most part, one or two storeys high, some built in short rows. To the right of the junction was a pub – you could tell it was a pub because of the sign hanging in front of it. To the left a small square of what looked like alms houses.

Further on, to the left, was a smithy with a chimney, and then the village petered out with a small cottage opposite the smithy and a larger, rambling farmhouse behind that.

The very last house was the largest. It was set high up on a rocky bluff above the village, a large building with one of those Georgian fronts that seem to be all windows and can be quite forbidding. Tiny flowers were clustered in the flower beds. There was what looked like a pavilion set by a rocky outcrop.

The detail was overwhelming. Window frames had been embroidered with tiny stitches, there was a duck on the village pond. The gravestones had grass growing up against them, and there was a half-dug grave, the earth piled up in a shimmering mound by the side of it.

'Good heavens! I wondered what you were doing.'

Tindall came and stood by Jim, leaning across him to get a better look. 'Phew. Needs a jolly good airing, I'd say. You found this down there?'

'Right at the back,' Jim answered. 'Under a pile of papers.'

'Well, well. It is rather interesting. Interesting. Something charmingly naïve about it.'

Jim stared at Tindall with an expression that had once made strong men tremble in their shoes. Tindall smiled timidly.

'What do you mean to do with it, then?' he continued.

'I don't know,' said Jim.

'It might look rather nice hung on a wall somewhere.'

Jim was not sure about that. Tindall bent his head, then picked delicately at a stitch with his little finger. 'Good heavens! Would you believe it? The thread appears to be made of human hair. Long white hair. Not all of it. Look, this is hemp, but just here, around the church.'

His finger hovered over the graveyard. Suddenly he stood up very suddenly, staggered a bit, then sat down heavily in a chair.

'Are you all right?'

'Yes, yes. I thought ... I just thought. Sorry, I felt a little faint. Yes. I really don't feel very well. I really think ... I really think that I might be feeling rather ill. There. It seems to be passing now. Perhaps if you would be so good as to look in that carrier bag, you could bring me the little packet of powders that you find in there.'

The little packet of powders turned out to be Lemsip. Tindall watched Jim furtively out of the corner of his eye as he held them up.

'And perhaps you could bring over the packet of biscuits? And the tea bags. I think we might have a brew up.'

'A brew up?' Jim said.

'Isn't that what you men call it?' Tindall asked. Jim smiled.

'Yes,' he said. 'Yes. A brew up. I'll brew you some powder and make myself some tea. But where's the kettle?'

'In the desk,' Tindall whispered. 'It's my little secret.'

Jim favoured him with a conspiratorial wink. Tindall blushed.

It turned out that Tindall knew something about fabrics. His parents had been arts and crafts revivalists. He rubbed an edge of the blanket between his finger and thumb and pronounced it very fine: 'Well not fine exactly. It's coarse material but very well woven. I wonder. I wonder . . .'

Jim finished his tea. As he walked back to the shelves his feet scuffed a piece of yellow paper. He was about to screw it into a ball when something made him look more closely. It had been neatly folded. He opened it. A diagram, drawn strongly in freehand.

'This will interest you,' he said. Tindall looked up. He had been staring at a corner of the blanket.

'What?'

'This. Look, it's a diagram. Some kind of machine.'

'Good heavens! So it is. A loom. How extraordinary. I wonder if it's the loom that wove this blanket.'

'Wait a minute,' Jim said. 'Down in the cellar, right at the back where I found the blanket there was a stack of bits and pieces of wood. Could you take a loom like that to pieces?'

'It's possible, I suppose. I'll have to do some research into the subject. The Victorians were great believers in the redemptive powers of work, you know. The devil makes work for idle hands and all that kind of thing. Mind you, sometimes I think we might take a bit more notice of that these days. Could you bring them up? I think I should speak to someone about this. It could be extremely interesting.'

All the time Tindall was talking he was fingering the blanket between his thumb and forefinger, and peering at it. Suddenly he stiffened. 'Now that's peculiar. It's rather macabre. The tombstone. I've just noticed. That tombstone has a name on it.'

'Someone was being morbid,' Jim said.

'Yes. Someone was. This biggest grave; the open one. It's almost like a signature. Look. S T R A N G E. Strange. What do you make of that?'

Jim bent down to look. The blanket smelled of old, damp rags and sweat. The lines of thread danced before his eyes. But it was not only the large grave. Other graves had names on them as well, stitched in writing so small it was almost impossible to read them. Jim squinted; the words danced. His eyes were drawn to the grave in the middle, stitched with florid elaboration. Strange: the S curling around in a serpent's tail, like a trailing root, almost like a hook.

'Well, Time's winged chariot and all that,' Tindall said. 'We should get on with sorting out these books.'

CHAPTER SEVEN

The chaplain was a large, youngish man with a big crinkle-eyed smile and a broken nose. He had partitioned an area off at the back of the chapel with hessian panels; inside stood a cheap desk, a swivel chair, and two institutional easy chairs upholstered in flame red tweed and set at right angles around a low table. There were pamphlets on the table. The odd word stood out. Friendship. AIDS. Forgiveness.

'Come in, come in,' he said.

He folded an enormous hand around Jim's. Jim caught a warm, rather oppressive blast of personality. *A rugger player for God*, Jim thought. *Spare me. And don't try to be my friend.*

'Take a pew, take a pew,' he said. 'The name's Jerry by the way, Jim. Coffee?'

Jim nodded. 'Stick the kettle on then, there's a good chap. Just off to have a slash.'

He strode out of the cubicle.

The chapel stuck out of the main body of the prison between A and B wings. It was an awkward shape: too high for its length. It gave the impression of having been hastily finished off. It was simple inside, just a main nave pierced by narrow windows, glazed in semi-opaque, slightly yellow glass. Above the altar the glass was blue and red. A large figure of Christ, almost life-size and bleeding from his feet, hands, side and forehead hung in front of the window.

The chaplain strode out of the vestry shaking water from his hands.

'Been in here before? Bet you haven't. Not so bad is it?'

The kettle boiled.

'Help yourself, that's it. Ladle the brown stuff in. Plenty of sugar if you want it. Don't take it? Fair enough. Biscuit?'

Jim considered then took a biscuit. The chaplain watched him bite into it and nodded approvingly. The biscuit was stale and disappointing.

'Now then. What can we do for you?' Jim wondered if 'we' was meant to suggest that Captain God was on the team. 'Home problems? Or just a bad case of the Long Barrow blues?'

'Not exactly,' Jim said.

'Something to do with . . .'

The chaplain's hand hovered around his flies.

'Not that either, I'm afraid,' Jim said. And thought: *I'm afraid or I should be if this is the last spiritual bulwark against the forces of evil.*

'Right. Fine. Brilliant . . .' He opened his great big hands. 'How can I help?'

Jim tried to inject a note of deceitful ingenuity into his voice. He fiddled with a button. 'It's like this. Someone I know, in here, seems to have got involved in something like black magic. I wanted to find out a bit more about it.'

The chaplain's jaw wavered then decided not to drop. He clamped it shut and looked firm. 'You came to a priest to ask about black magic? Surely you know what sort of answer you're likely to get from me.'

'What?' Jim asked. 'I'm sorry, I don't.'

'You play around with things like that at your peril,' the chaplain said.

'Oh, I didn't mean ...' He let his voice trail off.

'And why? Because it's lethal. Black magic, the occult arts—'

Jim looked intent. There'd been a Ouija-board craze when he was a teenager. Apart from a few arguments over who was pushing the planchette to spell rude words, it had been considered pretty tame as entertainment went. No one's head turned round 360 degrees, no one sicked pea soup, no one walked like a crab across the front room floor and hissed when the vicar came to call.

'But what?' Jim persisted. 'Ouija-boards? Water divining? Running naked through the woods on Midsummer Night? That's all occult, isn't it?' He stopped himself running on.

The chaplain looked masterful. 'Yes. It is. I can't put it strongly enough. However harmless it may seem, it all can be dangerous. I have to say that. When people ask me about this, they always choose these trivial examples. Fortune-telling, palmistry, Chinese horoscopes, The Exorcist. But what about the abuse of children? Vile practices and betrayals in neat little homes? What about the terrible damage people are prepared to do to themselves? Look, there was a time—'

He stopped. He looked up at the huge crucifix. Jim turned. The daylight was going and darkness was gathering on the walls of the chapel. Rain spattered against the lanced windows. The chaplain gathered himself. Jim waited for him to speak, unwilling to make it seem that he, a prisoner, was pumping the priest.

'There was a time when I might not have been as convinced as I am now. But now I have to say: deal in any occult practices at your peril.'

'But are you saying that they are actually dangerous? Or just spiritually dangerous?'

The chaplain smiled thinly. 'Do you believe that you can separate the two? Physical danger is spiritual danger, fear can corrode the soul.' He leaned forward in his chair, held Jim with a worried stare. 'Look, I can tell you something. It will frighten you. Some men were involved in this prison. Four men talked, I believe, to the devil. They were tempted in some way, they were lured into his clutches and in his grip they found despair. Do you know what they did?'

Jim shook his head.

'They killed themselves. All four of them. But before they died one of them came to me. He asked me, as you have just done, about occult powers. I realize now that I was not as forceful as I should have been. He died.'

Jim opened his mouth to say something, then closed it again. The hairs on the back of his neck had just bristled, and all the skin across the breadth of his back had crawled. He shook the feeling away. It was nonsense. The chaplain had said nothing new, just put a different slant on things. Although if one of the men had been worried . . .

'Are you talking about Burroughs, Campbell, Masters and Powell?' he asked.

'Yes. I am. Indeed I am. I suppose you all know about it?'

'It was hushed up. I – I found out. So you say it was despair that caused them to take their lives. Is that all it could have been?'

'In the grip of the beast, it might seem like the only way out.'

'Hold on, hold on,' Jim said. 'You're talking to someone who doesn't believe in this sort of thing. Let's look at it objectively anyway. Suicide is a sin, isn't it?'

'Yes, though compassion suggests—'

'No, it's a sin. If someone was in the grip of the devil, or something, killing himself would just push him further in, driving him towards the devil.'

'We are not talking about rational people here. The devil erodes reason. Reason is light.' And the chapel was getting darker.

Jim paused and tried to think clearly. The four of them had died, and they had killed themselves in a way he did not yet know. They were in identical positions. That suggested ritual, or an accomplice, he suddenly realized. But what could they hope to gain by it?

'When he came to you, the man who was worried, what did he say? That he was in the grip of the devil?'

'Not exactly. He said that he had made contact with a spirit.'

'Like Doris Stokes?'

'Do not make fun of this, Mr Carroll,' the chaplain said. 'I beg of you. That man, Campbell, is dead now.'

Jim filed the name and switched tack.

'How did they make contact?'

The chaplain looked at him aghast. 'Do you really believe I would tell anyone that? What do you want? Why do you want to know this?' His voice rose. He stood up. 'I don't believe you when you say you're worried. I believe that you're just trying to find all this out for your own ends. This has gone too far. I—'

'All right. I'll stop,' Jim said. 'One last thing: was there anyone else involved – a fifth person who might have got into their cells and killed them?'

The chaplain gave a sickly smile.

'I think you know what my answer will be. Must be, Mr Carroll.'

Jim shook his head.

'The devil can walk these corridors, Mr Carroll, as can

God. Do not let him into your cell.'

He looked up again. Jim could not tell if he was looking at the crucifix or beyond it to the windows. While they had been talking the darkness had thickened. It was urban dark, choked with soot, clotted by the glare of lights caught in its misty dampness. The darkness was out there. It was just the night but it seemed to be pressing inwards with slow, remorseless pressure.

Recreation time, but Jim did not want to play table-tennis, draughts, poker. He didn't want to do anything. He just wanted to think.

He pressed the heel of his palms into his eyes until the redness turned black and the veins danced orange against his eyeballs.

Four men had died. Killed themselves, he was sure of that. Now why? He didn't think it was despair. He thought back to the photographs. They seemed so calm, so prepared somehow.

And yet four men had died. Four men who had been into some kind of occult worship.

Worship. What happened in religion?

There was ritual. Death often came into it. God gave his only son as a sacrifice. Sacrifice often came into it. Why did people offer sacrifices? You gave something valuable to God to get something back. You killed a cow to make the rains come; you gave up your wealth to go to heaven. Sacrifice. Life. What was more valuable than life?

The word seemed to come from nowhere.

Freedom.

Yes. Suppose – just suppose they had given up their lives for freedom. For other people's? No. Their own? So what were we talking about here? Death and freedom? Death, the ultimate escape? Could that have been why they looked so calm? Jim remembered back to school – how they were taught that the Christian Crusaders went laughing into battle, secure in the knowledge that if they died the Pope had booked them on to the Paradise express; how the Persian assassins, high on hashish and the promise of an afterlife of houris and sherbet, would willingly kill themselves if the Old Man of the Mountains so much as snapped his fingers.

They all went smiling to their God. But how had the four men died? Who had snapped their necks?

Someone whooped in the hallway; someone else shouted. The sounds of a fight flared up, then just as suddenly died down.

This is ridiculous, Jim thought. *I'm getting obsessed because one crazy old lag says that his cell-mate was into black magic and a chaplain's got a guilty conscience.*

Surely to claim that every occult game was dangerous was ridiculous. Fortune-telling: what could be the harm in that? A thought stirred at the back of his mind. Fortunes. Wasn't there someone in the prison who told fortunes? Joe would know at any rate.

Joe was playing table-tennis. The ball went back and forth across the net, plinking as it hit the table, plunking as it was struck by the bats. Half a dozen men were watching. Joe blocked a smash then sent a winner back. He was light on his feet, rising to the return then putting his shoulder into the shot.

He left the table while twists of tobacco changed hands. Two more men began to knock up. Joe looked pleased with himself; his face was slightly flushed and carried a sheen of sweat.

'Table-tennis,' he said. 'The sport of lags. If I knew then what I know now. Could have been a champion.'

'Someone in here does fortunes,' Jim said. 'Who is it?'

'A fortune-teller?' Joe asked. 'Have you gone mad?'

'Quite possibly. I thought I remembered something.'

Joe took Jim by the arm and turned him so his face was away from the main hall. Eyes followed them.

'Look Jim. I've heard rumours, no, not even rumours, just a word, just someone bringing your name up in conversation and looking at me in a funny way, as if you're up to something.'

'That's nonsense.'

'There you go, of course it is. But in a way it's irrelevant because if someone – anyone – thinks you're up to something – anything – it amounts to your being up to something more or less. It's what people think and say that counts in a place like this, not what people do.'

'All I did was ask you if you knew of anyone who told fortunes.'

'But that's not like you, Jim. People think you're a cross between a psycho and Brain of Britain, you know. You've got an image, and a bit of respect. Don't blow it.'

'Who?'

'No idea, mate.'

'Joe. What the hell is going on? Tell me what you know!'

'I don't know anything, Jim. I'm just a punch drunk old killer, me. Here, I'll tell you what, there's a new bloke in today. Know what he did? He was a nice bloke, job and everything, staying in lodgings up in Lancaster. Anyway, one day, it's raining and he needs to go to the shops. He doesn't want to get wet. His landlady's out, so he sneaks into her bedroom and nicks her car keys. Well, her car's her pride and joy so he knows he's got to be careful. Anyway, he takes the car down to the shops, very, very carefully. Parks it carefully, loads it up carefully, drives it back carefully, then half a mile from the house some joker goes clean through a red light and totals it. Car's a write off. What can he do? Tell her? Move out? He panics. That evening he hears her coming in. Judgement day. He's about to own up when he reckons he can't. So he creeps downstairs and you know what he does?'

'What's this all about, Joe?'

'He kills her. He hits her on the head with an ornamental poker that sits next to her flame-effect gas fire. What do you make of that?'

'Joe, I love your little stories. They fascinate me, truly they do.'

Joe wrinkled his face. 'It's got something to do with putting your foot wrong and everything fucking itself up from that moment. You see, if he hadn't gone for the drive he wouldn't have killed her. He didn't think for a second that he would crash the car, and when he crashed the car, or when some prat rammed it, he didn't think for a minute that he was going to bash her blue-rinsed head in with an ornamental poker. But situations have a way of slipping out of control. You with me?'

He had a hand around Jim's wrist and was squeezing the nerve. Jim wanted to hit him, but suspected that Joe wanted him to start a fight.

Jim patted Joe's knuckles and said: 'It won't work. I don't need distractions. I just want to know this: is there anyone in here who tells fortunes or anything like that? I can find out from other people, and I will, which according to you will do my reputation even more harm. So just tell me.'

'People are strange, Jim. You don't want to disturb them.'

'Joe. Tell me.'

'Old Mother Skinner. Safe-cracker on D Wing. He's not very good though.'

'How do you know?'

'He didn't see his time coming, did he?'
'Haha. D Wing. Thank you very much.'

Jim found Skinner playing snakes and ladders with another
man. Skinner had a smooth, pink, baby face and a low
fringe; the other player was bald with rolls of fat sitting on
the collar of his tunic. Jim watched the counters move
across the board, down the snakes, up the ladders until
Skinner won.

'I think our friend wants something, Mother,' the bald
man said.

'Wonder what that is?' Skinner said. He turned his eyes
on Jim. They were like two wet pools, very dark and
covered in a film of tears.

'I heard you did fortunes,' Jim said.

'He heard I did fortunes,' Skinner said to his friend. 'Did
you hear anything else?'

'No. I just wanted to ask you some questions.'

'You haven't crossed his palm with silver yet.'

'Shut up. Look, I think he's serious.'

'I do believe he is.'

'Do we talk to him here or somewhere more private?'

Skinner rubbed his fingers together and closed his eyes.
'Somewhere more private, I think. Don't you?'

Skinner led the way to the top floor. The bald man followed.
Eyes turned as they walked past open cell doors. Heads
bent. Lips moved. Jim began to see what Joe meant.

In Skinner's cell there were magazine pictures of animals
and exotic landscapes on the walls: Ayers Rock, icebergs,
elephants. Under the window was a small window box.
Geraniums trailed their bleached and knuckled stems over
its edge.

Skinner sat on the bottom bunk and indicated that Jim

sit next to him; the bald man leant in the doorway, taking up a lot of space.

'Now then,' Skinner said. 'What do you want from me?'

'I thought that'd be obvious. I want my fortune told,' said Jim.

'Your fortune? My my.' He licked his lips. His eyes darkened. Somehow his lips had got wet. Jim wished he was back on his bed cleaning his finger nails. He just wanted to do something straightforward.

'You were recommended.'

'Oh, and who recommended me?'

'Burroughs.'

'Burroughs? The name isn't familiar.'

'Perhaps he heard it from a friend.'

'And who were his friends?'

'He used to knock around with Powell and Masters. Campbell was a friend as well.'

'Campbell was a friend, was he? Did you hear that, Spike? Campbell was a friend of our friend here.'

'Campbell was never a friend of the filth,' Spike said.

'And none of them are friends with anyone now. Four dead men, Mr Carroll, or shall I call you Jim? Four dead men, Jim. Why should you be interested in them I wonder?'

Jim felt the situation begin to slip and thought of what Joe had said. People knew things he didn't know they knew. He was rusty. There was an art to conducting an investigation and he had lost it. Skinner was ahead of him. 'I'm not interested in them,' he said. 'Like I said, I just wanted my fortune told.'

Keep your lies simple, then stick to them.

'All right then.' Skinner smiled.

He reached across to the table and took a large pack of cards from it. He rolled off the rubber band.

'Card tricks?' Jim asked.

'The Tarot,' Skinner said.

They were bigger than playing cards, with different proportions. They were thicker too. Jim caught a glimpse of their pictures: a fool, a woman in what looked like a white nightdress . . .

'Can I have a look?' he asked.

Skinner waved a finger. 'Naughty, naughty, no touchy,' he said. 'You'll spoil it for yourself. You've just got to let them fall.'

'How does the pack work?' Jim asked.

'How does it work, he asks. We all want to know how it works.'

'No, I mean what do the cards represent?'

'Everyone's different,' Skinner said. 'It's not what they mean, it's how they fall.'

While he was talking he executed a couple of quick shuffles. As he said 'fall' he dealt four cards and laid them in a row.

'Thirty-two cards form to make up the Lesser Arcana,' Skinner said. 'Twenty-two the Greater. Those are from the Lesser Arcana: two in batons and king of swords and the ace of denari. The first card to fall was the fool, from the Greater Arcana. The fool is everyman, that is you and me, and the path he walks is folly. Batons are money, swords bad luck. Denari can be business, journey or message, determined by the card before – ill fortune. Be careful, Mr Carroll. A dangerous journey or a dangerous message awaits you.'

He dealt four more.

'Three of the Greater Arcana. The hermit, the wheel of fortune and the tower. And a three in cups. That is family life. The hermit is withdrawal from the world, and the quest for untainted knowledge. The tower is a symbol of defence or loneliness. Nothing very clear, Mr Carroll.'

He picked up the cards. Jim noticed that his hand was shaking slightly as he reached over to them.

'Getting to you, is it?' he asked.

Skinner looked down at his hand and frowned. He made as if to deal, fumbled the card, dropped it. It fell to the floor.

'Bad luck,' he muttered. He reached down and began to slide the card into the pack.

'No,' Jim said. 'I want to see it.'

'It's bad luck. I don't like it.'

It's all part of the act, Jim thought. 'Come on Skinner, show me.'

Skinner laid the card on the bed, and flicked it over with his finger, as if it might bite. A thin man with goat's feet and a small beard.

'The devil,' Skinner said. He licked his lips and swallowed. Sounds got louder. Jim could hear his heart thud.

His hand was shaking so badly when he dealt the next card that it clattered against the pack. He turned it over quickly.

A red skeleton danced on green grass.

'Death,' Skinner said. He gave a quick nervous smile. 'You been stirring up trouble, Mr Carroll?'

He put the pack down, picked the next card.

His hand flew up. The card stuck to his fingers. He shook his hand, flapping it to get the card off. The card sucked on to his palm. Jim caught a glimpse of a young man with long hair and doublet, hanging from a tree. His neck was cricked. Then Skinner's body seized.

His head jerked round to Jim, as stiff and sudden as if it had been on a ratchet. He blinked. When he opened his eyes again it seemed that the eyeballs had retreated minutely so that a tiny gap opened up around the lids. His eyes wept blackness in thin streams. It fell on his cheeks in a curtain.

Jim pushed himself back on the bed, rigid with shock. The face stared, the darkness flowed like tears. The hard skull was a cage and the soft man of darkness was trapped inside.

This is not an act, Jim thought.

Terrible things seemed to be happening inside Skinner's tunic. It flapped. It clung. It was sopping wet. It snapped like a sail. The hands flew apart. The cards span out and shot across the room. Skinner's face began to writhe. His mouth opened. Jim looked inside and saw red, but it was red earth, the man's mouth was full of earth and it was dropping from his mouth like shit, smelling of earth, heavy, dead and damp, falling on to his lap in heavy lumps.

Skinner's arms were hinged in funny places. They flew up, bending backwards at the elbows, the hands slamming into the metal grille of the upper bunk. Skinned knuckles. Blood. His face grew. There was air behind it. A sound came whistling up from his throat from far away, getting closer, a sound muffled by earth, but heavy and thick, a human voice made without air, an echo from the other side. The room danced. The bed began to shake. Jim was thrown to the ground, his head crashing against the other wall. The smell of earth was gone now, replaced by something else. Death. Sweet. Cloying. Bitter. Corrupt.

Skinner was shaking his head, hard, as if he had regained some kind of control. 'No.' His voice was muffled and shrill. 'No. NO!'

His mouth roared more earth. Jim heard himself scream and his skin crawl. He fell to his hands and knees as the stone floor twitched like a carpet. His hands felt it. It was as soft as skin but cold as stone.

'No.' Jim looked up. Skinner had slapped his hands in front of his mouth as if he wanted to keep whatever was inside from getting out. He began to bounce on the bed.

Jim started to inch towards him. In the doorway he could see Skinner's friend as if through a veil of water, his face blurred with horror.

He reached the bed just as Skinner stopped bouncing. There was a pause, a horrid and heavy moment, then – Skinner's face turned black and swollen as a mulberry and the neck began to stretch.

'NO!' Jim launched himself at the man. He grabbed the head. Hugged it. Tried to control it. He could feel it move in his arms. He hugged it harder, as it began to whip back and forth like a punchball on a stick, battering him against the wall behind the bed, trying to shake him loose.

'Stop it!' he shouted. 'Whoever you are!'

It stopped. The face looked at him, eyes popping in surprise. The mouth opened. 'Togh—' The word came from nowhere. As bitter and thin as outer space. 'Taw—'

The mouth bubbled. Jim felt the body heave and suddenly mud and shit and blood and chopped up food was flooding from the mouth and nose in a terrible relaxing flood.

The body went limp, the stiffness left it, the face deflated and the air was white with the tarot cards but Jim saw that they weren't cards but petals, petals, falling in a thick carpet, petals, bursting into the air from somewhere else. They muffled the place in thick swathes. A booming that Jim had heard without being aware of faded to nothing, and then all was silence, a silence as thick and oppressive as the smell of too many roses.

And dimly in the distance, far away but very sharp, Jim heard a wooden, rhythmic clatter.

CHAPTER EIGHT

Jim told one of the guards that he thought Mr Lyall should come to the library and see something. It was a risk: some of the guards would push information like that at the prison barons in the hope that they would be repaid by the network of contacts on the outside. There might be a good deal on a second-hand car in it for them, a night out in a club with the wife, credit in a massage parlour, or just credit.

Jim hoped that no one cared enough about him to think that he was worth reporting on.

Jim was shocked by the change that had come over Lyall. The rings under his eyes were as blue as his uniform; his skin was the colour of recycled paper and as dull. They sat at a table as far away from Mr Tindall as possible. Tindall was pretending to catalogue some books but he kept on tilting his head and cupping his hands over his ears to hear better.

'You knew there was something going on here and you didn't tell me. Why didn't you tell me?' Jim hissed.

'What?' Lyall asked coldly.

'Oh come on. Black magic, occultism—'

'What?'

'Stop being so coy, Mr Lyall. The whole bloody place is riddled with it, reeking with it. I was in Skinner's cell last night. I saw—' He heard his voice rise. The memory of Skinner's terrible swollen face, that neck, that . . . fury.

'Was that before his epileptic fit?'

'His *what?*'

'He had a massive epileptic fit. Horrible by all accounts.'

'That was no epileptic fit. I know. I was there. He covered me with vomit and shit and—'

'That can happen.'

'And *earth*. It was coming up his throat and out of his mouth. He was trying to talk but his mouth was full of earth. It was no trick either.'

'He had a window box. It fell off.'

'Into his mouth? He was eating a growbag?'

'I've seen the cell. There was a window box, wasn't there?' Lyall seemed almost amused.

'There were flowers in the air, petals, rose petals to be precise.'

'Chase me Charlie I'm a fairy. Flowers in a window box. Whatever next?'

'But not that one. It just had a few geraniums in it that had gone over.'

'Is that geraniums or gerania, I wonder?' Lyall pursed his lips.

'I don't know what it was. I can't explain. It was like – he changed. His body went rigid. He started spitting earth. Then he was battering the bottom of the top bunk with his knuckles. The cards just sort of flew up. They turned to rose petals, for Christ's sake.' Jim glanced across at Tindall whose eyebrows were like two strained arcs.

'Right.'

'I know it doesn't make sense but that's what I saw.'

There was silence in the room. Jim suddenly felt deflated and empty. He had anticipated this as a big show-down with him squeezing the truth out of Lyall who had been using him to do his dirty work. Suddenly it didn't seem like that. He sounded shrill but then he felt shrill. He had seen something in that cell, and he had never seen anything like it before.

'Well,' Lyall said. 'If the earth didn't come from the window boxes and if the petals didn't come from the flowers in the window boxes, where did they come from?'

'He was spitting earth.'

'Hmmm.'

'He was bringing it up.'

'And what were you doing when all this was going on?'

'I was trying to stop it, him, from shaking himself to pieces.'

'So it was an epileptic fit.'

'I am – was – a police officer. I know what I see. I don't make it up.'

Lyall snorted.

'I never did that – never. Look, for the first time since I was convicted, I feel like someone. I've got something to do. Would I blow that? Would I try it on? I'm not stupid. I know it wasn't in my interests to tell you things that you wouldn't believe. But that is what I say.'

Lyall exhaled heavily. Jim watched his face. 'All right,' Lyall said. 'What's your explanation?'

'I don't have one. But—'

'I'll tell you what, Mr Carroll. I've got two explanations. One, you were hypnotized in some way. I remember seeing a conjuror pull a pigeon out of a lady's mouth once. She swore that just before he took it out, she actually felt it in there, feathers, claws on her tongue, heart beating. The fact that she felt it, the fact that everyone else in the room

saw it, doesn't mean a thing. You were set up. Fortune-
teller, cards, bet he acted a bit weird – it's all to prepare
you. Then it went wrong – he had a fit.'

'Was he an epileptic?'

Lyall shrugged. 'Not registered, no, as a matter of fact.
Either way—'

'Wait. Listen. You know that Campbell went to see the
chaplain?'

Lyall's face hardly changed but Jim thought he caught a
flicker of interest. 'Right, you didn't know that. He went
because something had scared him. I'm sure he said
something to the chaplain – something he wouldn't tell
me.'

Lyall took a packet of Silk Cut from his pocket and offered
it to Jim. Jim took one, broke the filter off it and bent his
head over the lighter.

'All right, Mr Carroll. Yes. There was something I didn't
tell you. I thought you'd find it for yourself sooner or later.
Basically, if you did you'd be on course. If you didn't, you
weren't that likely to find out what was behind all the
killings.'

He lit a cigarette for himself and took a deep drag, then
doubled up in a fit of coughing. Jim waited. When Lyall sat
up his lips were deep blue.

'All those men, well three of them, were planning to
escape. Powell, Burroughs and Masters had some sort of
scheme cooked up. Absolutely sure-fire thing.'

'What was it?'

'I don't know. We were told about it by Campbell. He
was a grass. You see what I'm getting at? If you'd
uncovered anything else about it, chances were that you'd
have found out who else knew.'

'Why didn't you tell me about it, though? I could have
used that as a starting point.'

'Didn't know if I could trust you. If you had found out about the escape plan, maybe you would have been tempted to use it for yourself. From my point of view, it was as much a question of what you told me, as what you found out.'

'And how can you be so sure that I haven't found out?'

Lyall stubbed his cigarette out. 'I'll give you one last chance, Carroll. Now, is there anything else?'

'Have you kept your side of the bargain? Did you go and see Brian White? I need to see him.'

'I was not aware that there was a bargain as such, Mr Carroll. But, in answer to your question: No I have not, but yes, I will see him. All right?'

'It has to be, doesn't it.'

Lyall stood up. 'By the way, how's the library? Enjoying it?'

'Oh yes,' Jim answered. 'It's a riot.'

Out in the corridor, Lyall screwed his face up. Black bloody magic. That was great. All he needed.

Of course it wasn't that surprising. The men were bored, out of their minds with boredom. At best they had just two forty-minute exercise sessions a week, and one shower in the same period. He simply did not have the men to supervise them for more. The governor was so keen to show that he could run the place on a budget that it was falling to pieces. If you were an engineer in charge of a huge boiler, or if you ran a nuclear power station, you didn't wait until things started to go wrong before you took action. It was too late then. Trouble fed on trouble.

He walked into the central hall. The sound of radios stopped down by heavy doors. The liquid chattering of sparrows in the lantern. The hum, the buzz of the place.

And underneath it all, running behind, underneath the

little noises, a still, heavy blanket of silence. He tipped his head on one side and tapped an ear with the heel of his palm. Something roared faintly. Must be water from the shower.

He walked up the metal stairs to a landing on the first level.

A sound behind him. Hollow. Metallic. Round. Lyall turned quickly.

The sound stopped. Nothing. He shook his head and walked on along the balcony. If the roof in the gym hadn't collapsed he could have put men in there, but the floor was soaking wet and covered in debris. He could have them clear it up, but that meant tools and tools meant more supervision. Supervision meant guards and he didn't have enough of them.

That noise again.

He whipped round. The sound stopped but he had seen movement. Above him. He looked up. The landings were made of cast iron, stamped into heavy grilles. You could see through them. Shapes that moved made shadows. There was something up there.

He turned and walked to the staircase. There, the noise again. He looked up. A shadow was following him. Something was rolling along the floor. He stopped. It stopped. He walked. It moved.

He ran for the stairs. The prisoners were in their cells, apart from the red-bands, and they would not play a trick like this.

All the guards were off the wings.

The sound grew louder. He looked up, swore and took the stairs two at a time, not sure if the sound was in his head or up on the landing. Ten steps. At the top he turned. He was under the roof here, the prison murmuring below. The metal walkways had 'Bleasdons Iron Works' stamped on an ornamental lozenge in one corner. He had seen something move along it, something pale and shadowy that bobbed and flowed. It had limbs, he was sure of that. A naked man? It had not moved like one and any man moving that fast would have made more noise on the metal, even in bare feet.

An old soft drinks can was rocking slightly on the top stair. Barr's Irn-Bru. Lyall walked slowly, placing his feet down carefully. There was nowhere to hide. He could see each door. He walked softly down the corridor, testing each one. All locked.

The sound from the top of the stairs made his heart race.

The can was gone. He could hear it tumbling down the metal stairs, the only sound in an empty prison.

He heard laughter, a sound that started on deep, dark notes and rose to a saw-edge jag of hysteria.

He turned to try and find a direction, turned again and the sound turned. It was with him. There was no sound in the prison. The laughter was in his head.

CHAPTER NINE

M r Tindall was looking at two lengths of one-inch by two-inch batten when Jim walked down to the other end of the library.

'Ah, Mr Carroll. I say, I do hope everything is all right.'

'We'll get by, Mr Tindall. Thanks for asking.'

Mr Tindall said: 'Good good,' as if he did not really care and then looked grave. 'Now then, I expect you're wondering what I'm doing with these two pieces of wood.'

'You've got me baffled there, Mr Tindall.'

Tindall pursed his lips in gentle satisfaction. 'It is perhaps not entirely regular, but I thought that our little library might benefit from some decoration.'

'Abstract art. Two bits of Wood on a Wall. Am I right, Mr Tindall?'

Tindall looked confused, then laughed. 'Good heavens! Good heavens no! You know, I really think we might make something of this place. It seems odd to say so, but I'm actually enjoying this. I ... hope that doesn't seem insensitive to you.'

'Just as long as you don't expect me to dance a jig,' Jim said. Tindall peered at him. 'Joke,' he added.

'Oh. Yes. I'm sorry. Gallows humour I suppose. You

know I did have an assistant before you. Smooth as butter but somehow – you know – rotten. He frightened me and I'm afraid I asked for him to be removed. Was that terrible?'

Jim shrugged. 'You get to meet a lot of funny people in here.'

'Yes,' Tindall said decisively. 'Yes. And that rather leads me on to something rather exciting. You remember our find of the other day, Mr Carroll?'

'I can hardly forget it.'

'Well, I've decided to hang it on the wall. Now, I'll need your help. What we will have to do is this.'

Tindall explained how they would have to fold the rug over the battens and tack it along the back at the top and bottom. He had brought in carpet tacks and a hammer as well as a good length of wire and they could hang it from one of the window catches above them.

Jim pushed the sagging boxes of books he had not yet unpacked into the corners of the room to clear a space. Tindall then swept the area fussily with a broom. Together they laid the blanket out.

Memory had served it well. It was less dramatic than Jim remembered, and his mind had interpreted the scene, filling it out, rearranging the pattern of threads into something more than the reality.

Before, he had seen something charged and intense; now it looked like a picture scrawled on the back of a schoolbook: embroidered graffiti, nothing more. The road was wider at the top than at the bottom; the church spire leaned on one side; the left-hand side of the scene was done in particular detail, as if the embroiderer only really cared about it, while the right-hand half of the village, above where the road forked, was shadowy and ghost-like. He had paid particular attention to the big house that stood slightly outside the village above a rocky bluff, and a tiny, two-windowed cottage that sat in a hollow under the cliff.

Jim looked at the tiny cottage. It had roses growing up the sides of the door. Screens of memory shifted in his mind like old stage flats. *I've seen that before*, he thought, and his heart quickened in treacherous excitement. But he could not find the memory and decided it was just *déjà vu*. A scrambled synapse. A thousandth of a micro-second delay in the soft mesh of the brain so that you saw an image before you recognized it for what it was. When you did recognize it, gave a name to it, and put it in context you did so with the oddest feeling that you had seen it before, which in fact you had, half a millionth of a second earlier.

His eyes drifted over to the graveyard. There was too much detail there, far too much. The tombstones were sharp and crowded so that it looked like a mouth too full of teeth, leaning over, sticking out, tumbled. Jim had not remembered it quite like that; it looked as if it were breeding graves. And the big grave, the empty grave with the word 'Strange' embroidered on to the stone with something like defiance, looked more familiar than it should.

They folded the top and bottom edges of the rug over the battens and drove the tacks through the doubled-over edge. Jim moved a chair over to the wall and held the rug above his head while Tindall took the long hooked pole that was used for opening and shutting the windows and fiddled the wire over the window catch.

'There. That's done it. Very nice. Very nice indeed.'

Jim shrugged. The more he looked at the rug, the less he liked it. It might be no more than a trick of perspective but he thought that the whole thing looked top heavy and wanted to topple over towards him. He turned his back on it and began work on the books.

CHAPTER TEN

John Ratcliff, Rat to his friends, was not feeling lucky. He'd scrimped and saved for a little twist of happiness, trading cash for tobacco, tobacco for cash, winning a bit on the poker, making a bit more from the laundry. He'd got hold of a nearly-new syringe, shot himself up the night before and – nothing. God knows what the powder was, but one thing was for sure, it wasn't heroin. Now he had been issued with an ancient pair of dungarees and told to go join the work party clearing up the Old Yard.

Why it was called the Old Yard he had no idea. Everything in the prison was old, and this didn't seem any older than anything else. It was a bare triangle of flag-stoned court bounded by the inner perimeter wall on one side and A and D Wings on the other two. He looked up at the blank walls, pierced by windows. Beneath each window-ledge was a dark stain, pointed like a goatee beard, as if there was some slow seepage from the cells. It was a depressing place. The prison reared up behind it and the walls were too high. Ivy had rooted itself along the perimeter wall and lichen had stained the stones black.

A needling wind pricked his skin through the patched boiler suit, carrying with it Midlands damp, the faint smell of coal dust and the dull malt tang of the gluten factory on the industrial estate. Goose-pimples ran along his forearms.

The men were being kept at their work today. They had been paired off and told to lift the York stone flags and stack them against A Wing. Easier said than done without spikes or crow bars. As it was, one man had to kneel on one side and try and slip his fingers under the free edge, then the other would join in, then the first man would get a hand under and then they would heave it up the vertical and stagger off, as bow-legged as chimpanzees, to the wall. The men were unfit; the work was hard. But this was paid work and it was a chance to get out of the cells. The plan, if it could be called that, was to sell the stone – which was worth a bomb apparently – and use the money to repair the gym roof. It would not happen; things like that never did. The other idea was to turn the yard into a vegetable garden, and that would not work either. The yard was in shadow and the earth needed a couple of years feeding to be any good, Ratcliff thought.

'Pick up that hoe and get to work.'

He had been told to weed the thin strip of soil along the first perimeter wall. He shrugged and began to prod away at the earth. He had worked as a gardener once and quickly got the feel of sliding the hoe blade along the earth, cutting the stems of the weeds with its sharp blade. In the middle of the wall, in a place where no ivy grew, someone had planted rose bushes. He'd leave them until last.

There was some commotion among the men who were lifting the slabs. Rat leant the hoe against the wall and wandered over to them.

'That's a hole,' someone was saying.

'A what?'

'An 'ole.'

'It can't be.'

'Why not?'

'There's no mint.'

'Perhaps it's a tunnel.'

'Quick. Make a vaulting horse.'

'Everyone walk around the yard shaking earth out of their trouser legs.'

'What's going on?' The guard who had been smoking round the corner walked smartly over.

'You can't look, Mr Smithers.'

'It's hole, sir.'

'It's our little secret.'

'Permission to escape, sah!'

Rat pushed his way to the front behind Smithers. A hole, maybe a foot by six inches, cut into the earth and covered over with a slab. You could see a tangle of dead grass roots furring the hard edge of earth. He thought of the small square holes that goal posts sat in. Not that anyone would play football in here. Would they?

'Get on with your work. Now.'

'It's dangerous sir, we should fill it in. Someone might break their neck.'

'I'll decide what we do. Hey! Who's that?'

Rat glanced up. Something thin and black, man height, moved with sudden jerkiness into shadows that seemed to knot themselves around the foot of one of the wall's buttresses. He blinked. He had an impression of two long legs, fluttering rags, pink skin, and a head that flopped around loosely like a balloon in the wind.

He thought it turned and looked at him, then stretched out a long, thin arm. He blinked. Nothing.

'Who's what, sir?' one of the other men asked.

No one else saw it, thought Rat. Smithers shook his head. 'Thought I saw someone, that's all. All right. Down tools.

Dinner time. You lucky men can have a wash.'

Rat's hands were stinging. Even with the gloves there was a line of little white blisters along the pads of his fingers. He worked his way along the flower-bed, cutting at the weeds, but avoiding the rose bushes. He was feeling rather strange and beginning to wonder if there hadn't been something in the syringe after all.

He took a breather. The earth looked bare and dark and tidy. He looked up. A spurt of starlings scattered across the sky, wheeled above the prison, looking for somewhere to settle. Every time they found a place they took off almost immediately, fluttering like leaves, and grouped before settling again. The yard brimmed with their shrill chatter. Suddenly they flew upwards, wheeled, and in strange, intent silence poured over the perimeter wall. Rat thought they looked panicked. The sun had broken through the clouds and was impaled on a lightning conductor standing on the tip of the water tower. The earth began to steam.

Windows everywhere, little square eyes, stared out above the walls to the town beyond. By the position of the sun, Rat reckoned that the two arms that enclosed the yard must be facing North East and North West. They would never see the sun. In the angle of the wall, where they met, another smaller window was set, hardly visible in the shadows.

He leant against the northern wall, trying to soak up the sun's faint heat. His skin was so pale that he felt the radiation prickle his face.

Shadows. What had he seen? Something made him look up to the angle between the wings. What was that window doing looking down at the yard? The detention cell. A shape bobbed behind it. Who the hell was that looking out of it?

'Right little dreamer, aren't we? Looking at walls, calculating angles. Tututut,' Smithers said. 'Now get over there and start digging up those bushes. This isn't an ornamental garden. We're meant to be clearing this place.'

'Yes sir, at once, sir.' To be honest he felt like being sick. It had to be a combination of the stuff he'd had the night before and the exercise. Perhaps he was about to have a heart attack. He felt wet on his cheek. The weather changed quickly here. Heavy rain clouds were boiling up from above the moors, crawling across the sky, drowning the sun.

He stood for a while looking at the roses. There were nine or ten of them, all blotched and diseased. They hadn't been tended for years, and long, trailing branches hooped and crawled along the ground. The leaves were liver-spotted with blight; the buds, tightly furled, red and rotting, nodded like tiny boiled heads. Most of them were thin-limbed and sick-looking but in the middle of the flower-bed one stood out, towering above the others, trailing its stems through theirs, smothering and strangling them, more like a bramble than a rose bush.

When he sliced at the first stem it gave easily. A bud broke into petals and for a second he smelled the flower. Perhaps it wasn't going to be too hard after all. He sliced again. Wet stems snapped, some bleeding milky sap and there was something rather awful in the way they broke, as if they were alive but rotten, kept alive in order to rot. He raked them away with the hoe, clearing the ground until there was only the one rose left.

It had a thick stem, fat as a child's wrist, and was covered in wickedly hooked yellow thorns.

All right bush, he thought, *your turn*. He reversed the hoe and aimed the sharp cutting edge at the base of bush.

The scream was inside his head and it was like a cat had

got in there and was being roasted alive. The sound writhed, twisted, filled his head with cold, paralysing anger.

The bush shivered. The pain went. He blinked away the tears.

It was odd, but the tears were lenses that made him see more clearly – the bricks around him were no longer black but the dull red of new stocks. Fleeting impressions were like acid scars on his mind. The bright yellow mortar between the bricks; the flag stones hard-edged, whole and unworn. There was a dull roaring in his ears, a creak, a snap and thud. He whipped round.

Christ. What the hell was that? He looked at the hoe, then at the bush. There was quite a deep gash in the stem. He prodded it nervously with the hoe. Nothing. No scream. Had to be the drug. That was why the sky was darkening. That was why the birds had flown. He hit the bush again. And again. It was tough. Now that he had weakened it, the stem was harder to break. It just kept on giving and the tough fibres stopped it breaking properly.

Perhaps he could snap it with his hands.

He knelt by the bush and grasped the stem. His gloves were thick, but not thick enough. The thorns seemed to leap through the fabric, pierce the flesh, scratch the bone beneath. He screamed, tried to pull his hands away, but the thorns held him, twisting, tightening, working their way through. He saw them break like yellow shark-fins through his hands, their points shaggy with his flesh, and slowly, slowly, he felt the pull on his arms.

The bush was sinking into the earth and he was being taken with it. A hole was opening, lips of mud puckered in the soil. Smoothed, belched open.

Come with me, prisoner, come to me . . .

*

It was Smithers, the guard, who noticed him. Rat's arms were twisted at an odd angle and it looked as if he were forcing them into the earth. Smithers wandered over, saw the expression on his face and slapped him across the cheeks. Then he called some men over. It was hard to get him away, and they only broke his grip on the rose bush when two men got their arms under his shoulders and pulled him until the damn thing ripped itself out of the ground. The bush lay on its side, trailing its roots; they seemed to go about six foot down.

Rat kept on complaining about his hands which he held away from himself like dead flippers. When they got in from the yard he soaked them in cold water until the numbness killed the stinging and brought on its own dull ache. He was too ill to have his tea and asked to be locked in his cell. The officer on his landing obliged, saying that he would be back to check in an hour.

It did not quite work out that way. As it happened, the guard was called away to calm down the sectioned prisoners on C Wing who were claiming that one of the regulars had been down their corridor all evening rattling their eye hole covers. They were a vocal lot, the sectioned prisoners. Earnshaw, an elderly solicitor who had got into trouble with a video camera, a large dog and his grand-children, was their spokesman and insisted on their rights to protection.

But had they actually seen anyone? the guard asked. Well yes, sort of. One of them had seen him through the peephole. He was tall and thin and walked strangely. They also thought that he might have been planning to leave dead rats in front of their doors because there was a terrible smell – and there was a plague of rats, wasn't there?

So the guard took rather longer to get back to Ratcliff

than he had planned. And the sectioned prisoners were right in a way.

There was at least one dead rat in the prison, or at least there soon would be.

Rat lay on his bunk and shivered. He didn't see how he could be so hot and so cold at the same time. His veins were full of acid and he had lost all specific feeling in his limbs from his finger-tips to his elbows. But he could feel something. It was as if his arms were slowly being hollowed out and a slow fire, the sort that creeps underground in peat fields, was smouldering in the long cavities of marrow.

He looked at the door, then at the cell window. Something rattled at his eye piece. Thank God – it must be the guard come back. He tried to raise a hand to attract his attention, but it would not move. He got to his feet, arms swinging like soft, empty tubes.

rattle rattle

a rattle for a rat

'Come in, for God's sake,' he said, and wandered over to the door.

rattle rattle

Screws never bothered to warn you when they were coming in. Perhaps it was someone with a message for him. He put his eye to the hole and peered out.

It flies in, a ragged stream of black, through the spy hole and into Rat's eye, piercing the membrane over the retina, homing like a smart bomb on the black of the pupil.

Rat staggers back. He hasn't long to live. Though blinded in that eye, he somehow sees through it as if he is looking down a straw, sees through a peephole into a land of black and white, of weird spectral shapes, where voices are calling him. He sees a face he recognizes, a face from the past. He's in this place – Rat's never seen it before – there's a little village with a green and a great rolling moor stretching away to the horizon. It's warm there. There's a pub. A little shop. It must be heaven.

He feels his brain turn to jelly, and is thankful because it eases his passage up that strange straw. Yes, suddenly he's free, spurting through the air like a cloudburst, his toes already curling with pleasure on the warm turf. He turns. The cell is a small door in the sky. There's a body in there, with something terribly angry inside it – something so angry.

It's like watching a dog in a sack, digging away, scratching away. The torso's twitching. Pink worms keep on being thrown out of the open mouth. They're hanging down now like a gaudy beard of pinks and browns and blues. Under the old blue prison tunic the belly splits, then the fabric splits, and the guts that aren't hanging out of the mouth are kicked into the air like heavy streamers. Blood is washing over the floor. A shin bone erupts from a split in the knee. Something is in there, trying to do what? Make room. He has a momentary impression of something lying inside him, as if it's trying out a sleeping bag, then the body sort of collapses. It's an anticlimax really – like watching a paper bag disintegrate underwater. But it was him once and he feels a momentary pang of nostalgia.

Back in the cell what's left of the body gives a twitch. Then another. A shape hovers above it for a moment. We sense that it wants to cry, to howl, to feel solid. It compresses to a tiny ball then like a dark, dirty sun explodes, scattering through the box shape of the cell, to spray upon the walls, coating them evenly with the lightest, most depressing shade of grey.

*

That night, lights out at Long Barrow prison is a good two hours later than usual, but in these days of cuts in the prison service, guards refusing to do overtime, low staffing levels, and even lower morale, the men in the cells have got used to practically anything. Along Ratcliff's corridor there has been a lot of activity. His neighbour Ian Armstrong, himself in for aggravated assault, claims to have heard the faint sound of retching. The cell door has been opened and closed a few times. A man two cells down claims he has heard Lyall's voice and the governor's. They are not sure what the clanking of mop buckets could signify, however. In the morning they will be told that Ratcliff was taken ill and carted off to hospital. The men on outside fatigues will say that they thought he looked sicker than a whole flock of parrots.

Ratcliff will never come back. He did not have any friends, and more pathetic still, no traceable relatives on the outside. One or two of the prisoners might note that a young guard who was kinder than most, probably because he was young and almost idealistic, seems to have left. Lyall is just trying to work out what accident could have caused this to happen to a body. Something has got to go on the death certificate and he does not think that swallowing a bomb will do.

CHAPTER ELEVEN

Whenever the screws were nervous they started throwing their weight around. It was typical – Jim's first real sight of the sky, of outside, for almost three weeks and the bastards had ruined it.

In the exercise yard the men liked to walk in groups with their friends. It was seldom enough they got out these days and the time allowed for socializing was being gradually cut down – it all ate into man hours. That meant that when they got out into the yard they split up into groups, some walking slower than others, some stopping completely, and swapped news or just enjoyed the sense of openness – and air which did not smell of tar and urine – in companionable silence. But today the screws weren't having it. They kept everybody moving at the same speed – or tried to – and tried to stop people talking.

Half-way round his second circuit Jim felt himself being pushed to one side. A man was crouching down, trying to get up to a small group of three or four men who were talking without moving their heads. One of them was Randall, and Gorgeous George was walking alongside him.

The man in front of Jim moved, bunching up to the man

in front of him to hide the other man's movement from the guards. Jim now saw that there were three or four men doing the rounds, saying a few words to people here and there, then dropping back or moving forwards. The screws knew that something was going on but did not know what.

'What's going on?' Jim spoke more out of hope than expectation.

'Wish I knew. Someone said something about a bloke topping himself.'

'When?'

'Yesterday evening. They're searching the cells wing by wing. That's why we're out.'

'Do you know who?'

The man did not answer. Jim saw that he was looking hard across the yard, watching someone very closely. They passed a screw – nobody Jim recognized. There had been a lot of staff changes recently.

'They're saying something like Rattiff. I think it's a name. Screws. Beat him up. Killed him. Someone saw a bucket full of blood or something. Can you believe that?'

'Not very easily. Are you lip-reading?'

'Learnt it off a bloke in the Scrubs. Comes in useful.'

'So that's why the screws are all looking so shifty.'

'They're trying to pass it off as suicide,' the man said.

'Or one of us – if they're searching the cells they're probably looking for a weapon,' Jim said. He looked up at the sun and tried to breathe deeply but his chest felt constricted. Suicide or murder? How many people had he sent to prison to die? How many convictions?

Suddenly he bumped into the man in front of him, and felt the man behind him move up against him.

'Here, watch it!'

'Can't help it mate, sorry.'

'What's going on?'

The guard by the door was talking urgently into his walkie talkie. Jim craned his neck. A group of men about five yards in front of him had sat down. One started shouting: 'Protest lads. Everyone sit down.' Another shouted: 'Protest against brutality!'

A mutter ran round the yard. Jim looked quickly round. Randall was standing. Very few people were sitting.

'Come on! United we stand, divided we—'

'You bloody well sit,' someone shouted back.

There was a ripple of laughter. Jim did not know what to make of it. A demonstration was a pain in the neck. He'd been on the 'Ban the Bomb' marches back in the sixties as a red-faced young constable, his shaved neck prickling with embarrassment at the good-natured and not so good-natured insults from the marchers.

But then again, if it were true that someone had been beaten to death … Why hadn't Lyall told him?

Randall was not sitting down. In fact he was shaking his head and looking wise and sorrowful and it seemed that most of the prisoners were taking their lead from him. Suddenly the doors to the yard swung open and twenty guards ran out. The protesters were lifted to their feet and carried off. The rest of the exercise period was cancelled. As they shuffled inside Jim felt something sharp prick his back. His back stiffened.

'Don't stop walking,' a voice said. 'Don't look round. Randall wants to talk. Be ready. Be steady. Be good.'

The pressure relaxed.

'I don't get it,' Jim said that night to Joe. 'Why didn't we all just join in? I mean we've got enough reasons for fuck's sake.'

'Perhaps there's a time and place.'

'What could be better than then?'

'What's the point of a demo?' Joe asked.

'To get a point across.'

'And to think you were a highly regarded copper. Publicity you moron. Publicity. And who's going to hear about a sit down protest in an exercise yard. The screws? They don't need telling what's going on. They know a damn sight more than any of us.'

'But if a man was killed—'

'*If* a man was killed.'

'Are you saying we do nothing?'

'If someone important decides to do something, you'll hear about it.'

'But you're saying we do nothing.'

'I'm saying ... keep your head down or you'll get it knocked off.'

'So nothing gets done, ever. This whole stinking system—'

'Spoken like a hardened old lag. Sorry, spoken like a little spiv wet behind the ears. The real old cons just get on with it.'

'And that's it?'

'Don't shout and Uncle Joe will tell you a story. Are you lying comfortably? Then I'll begin. It happened to a chap my old man knew, a jeweller called Petrie. Now he did have a narrow escape. Done for murder, set up job of course, and condemned to hang.

'Anyway, the day before the execution, they check the old gallows. You know, make sure the pulley's working properly, tie a new knot, and check that the trap door opens when you pull the lever. Everything fine and set up nicely for the morning.

'Morning comes, the prisoner's woken up, given his hearty breakfast, and it's time for the hangman to make sure that everything's working to his satisfaction. So just before the poor old sod's brought in, our patriot hangman pal, as the *Sun* might call him, slings a sack of sand about the same weight as the victim on to the trap, stands back, and pulls the lever.

'Nothing happens.

'He tries again. Nothing. By this time Petrie is out there waiting and they're wondering whether it's time to put a hood on him. They send a bloke in to ask, but the hangman's in a fair state. Every time he pulls the lever, nothing happens.

'So he asks the guard to help him check the mechanism. Now under the old gallows there's this pit that the body falls into with a tray to catch the drippings. When you pull the old lever it simply releases the bolts which hold the two halves of the trap together. Body falls. Neck breaks. Justice done. So he tells the guard that he'll go into the pit, and when he shouts "now", the guard is to pull the lever.

'Anyway, he goes down, but the guard sees the sack of sand, and being a cautious sort of chap, takes the trouble to move it off, not wanting to kill the hangman when twelve stone of sand comes thudding down on his head. As it happens, it's just as well that he does. The hangman shouts "now", he pulls the lever, the traps open and one of them catches the hangman in the eye; proof positive if proof was needed that it's all working.

'They call in Petrie. Close the trap, tie the old sack on his head, put the noose round his neck, pull it tight, but not too tight for comfort, hangman pulls the lever—

'Nothing happens. Consternation! They take Petrie out, and go through the whole thing again. Again the trap opens, and this time the hangman gets a nasty bang on the back of the head. They bring in the victim, bag on head, noose on neck, pull the lever.

'Nothing.

'What next? Third time lucky? It's getting late now. About eleven. They decide to get the carpenter in to give it a really thorough overhaul. Take the damn thing to pieces if need be. But the carpenter's out on a job and won't be back till three.

'Petrie gets taken back to his cell and demands a hearty lunch which he is duly given. Three o'clock the carpenter turns up. He goes over the mechanism. Nothing wrong. He tries it a few times. Nothing wrong. People are getting a bit edgy now. Suppose it hath been decreed that my dad's mate wasn't meant to hang? Hangman doesn't like that and suddenly has an idea. He throws the sack of sand on the trap, gets underneath and tells the carpenter to pull the lever.

' "Suppose it works," the carpenter says.

' "It won't," the hangman says.

'It doesn't.

'The carpenter has an idea. He has a close look at the trap door and what he finds is that the planks that it's made of are green wood, and they've all bowed up in the middle, ever so slightly but enough so that when someone stands on it, the wood flattens and jams the whole trap solidly in the frame.

' "I'll have to replace that," he says and calls the timber yard. Timber yard's closed. He looks at his watch. Five o'clock. Time for him to go home, but he promises to fix the trap the next day. Oh no, the next day is Saturday. Have to be Monday then.'

'Well, what happens then?'

'Oh, there's a phone call from the Home Office. Petrie's appeal's been upheld. He's out of prison in two months and goes back to his old job.'

'What's the point then?' Jim asks. 'What's that got to do with fair or not?'

Joe paused. 'As a matter of fact I'm not entirely sure if it's anything to do with it at all. It just makes me think that life is probably a concatenation of loosely related accidents.'

'Life's a what?' Jim asks.

'You've really been wasting your time. Me, I try to learn at least one new word a week.'

'Just what are you trying to prove?'

'Life's a bitch and then you die,' Joe said. 'And accidents will happen. Good night.'

Jim did not sleep for a while. He wondered where they had hanged men in Long Barrow prison.

CHAPTER TWELVE

Jim picked up a pile of books and began sliding them into the shelves. *Car Maintenance for the Expert* – fine if your car was a Morris Oxford, vintage *circa* 1964. *The Kontiki Expedition* – Jim slid that in next to the other seven editions of it. He had glanced at the photographs of bearded sunburnt men adrift on a glittering carpet of sea and thrust it away quickly.

The man who had died was called Ratcliff and his cell was on the ground floor of D Wing – Jim had found that out at breakfast. Another dead man, except this time Lyall had not asked him to find out about it, which either meant he had stopped trusting Jim or he did not think that the Rat's death fitted into the pattern. Or both.

Tindall was looking at the shelves with an air of pride. They were gradually filling up with books, more and more of the floor was clear, the end was in sight.

'Yes. Real progress at last. I must say, it really gives one a sense of achievement. Soon we'll be ready to start distributing them. Oh, by the way, another load of books have come in – they're somewhere in the building. I told one of the guards that you'd be along to pick them up some time this morning.'

'That's fine, except I don't have privileges. I'm not meant
to go anywhere apart from this room, and it's got to be
locked as long as I'm in it.'

'No, no, that's all been taken care of. I had a word with
Mr Lyall this morning. Someone will be coming for you in
a few minutes. I do hope that's all right.'

Ten minutes later the guard opened the door and stood aside
for Jim. The books had been left in the main prison reception
area, inside the main gates at the other side of the grilles that
separated the cells from the administration wing.

It was the first time Jim had been outside the main prison
block for four years. Four years. The trolley wheels
squeaked over the shining linoleum floor. He felt his heart
begin to thump. Jim saw a window on his left and saw sky
through it, a pale watery blue sky.

'What are you staring at?' the guard said.

'The sky,' Jim said.

The guard shrugged.

'Get a move on,' he said.

Jim led the way across the central hall, trying to control
the movement of the trolley which had a life of its own. The
books looked like the contents of a primary school library,
but there might be some learning-to-read books in with
them. The prison had once had a literacy programme but
it had been cut: not because there were no takers, nor
because there were no teachers but because the admin
budget had been cut and there was not the staff to arrange
it any more.

A shrill scream whistled from the landing on D Wing,
quickly shut off. Jim jumped, then realized that it was only
the sound of a kettle boiling. A guard appeared on the
landing. He looked down at Jim's escort and made a T with
his two index fingers.

The escort nodded at Jim and shrugged. The guard on the balcony jerked his head at the row of cells on the ground floor. The escort shrugged, then smiled.

'Slight detour,' he said gruffly. 'Take ten.'

He pushed Jim towards an empty cell, closed the door behind him and locked it.

'At least you'll have plenty to read,' he said.

The tarry stench of prison disinfectant hit him immediately, and prickled his nose. Everything was wet and stank of the stuff: the walls, the ceiling, the door, even the bed frame. He looked around him. The cell was empty apart from the bed frame. The walls glinted in the dim light – it was too much to expect the guard to have turned the light on.

He put a large book called *Mitten the Kitten* on the springs and sat on it gingerly. He tipped backwards and as he put a hand out behind to steady himself, he saw four parallel marks in the paint by the side of the bed. They were just off the vertical, angled slightly towards the head. As if something had been dragged down and across.

Empty cell in the middle of D Wing. This was Ratcliff's cell. It had to be. His stomach turned over and his heart began to beat faster.

He moved his hand over the wall, feeling its lumpy smoothness. His fingers came to the four parallel score marks. He spread them, crooking them slightly so the nails touched the wall. He lay down gingerly on the bare springs. His fingers fitted into the marks. He pulled his hand down and across. They were scratch marks made by finger nails.

He tried to scratch the walls himself but could not make an impression on the paint, let alone dig into the plaster. He spread his palm and beat the wall softly, then stood up. *Well done, Inspector. Let habit take over. A man died in here. How? Look for anything now, anything.* He moved quickly to

the window and felt the bottom of the bars. No string. The
men sometimes hung things out of the window tied to
string, like Ray Milland in *The Lost Weekend*. In the bars?
No, they weren't loose. In the bed? No mattress. In the
frame somehow.

The frame was bolted to the floor. Jim slid under it and
ran his fingers along the under edge of the struts. The metal
was cold and beaded with water. It was possible, just
possible that they had not scrubbed under the frame.
Possible, but in fact they had. It was all wet and clean. He
rolled on his side and ran a finger along the angle of the
floor and the wall. He looked at it. Spotless.

His face was six inches from the wall. Jim was looking at
a chip in the paint about two inches from the floor and on
a level with his eye. It was hidden by an irregularity in the
wall. The chip in the paint was bright and white, deep
enough to show the red brick underneath. He looked more
closely. There was something in there, actually embedded
in the brick. He fished a ballpoint out of his top pocket and
began to probe gently round the hole. It was easier than he
thought. There. It was rocking in the hole now. The plaster
around it was rotten.

Loose.

It dropped to the floor, a flash of white, and hard. It took
Jim some time to realize that he was looking at a human
tooth, a molar, torn out by the roots. There was a worn
filling in it and over the smell of disinfectant Jim caught a
slight odour of rotten food.

He picked the tooth up – it was so much larger than one
imagined, then looked at it and the wall. It had gone in at
an acute angle from the floor. He laid his cheek on the cold
concrete and slid it up to the wall until his nose was
pressing against it. He turned his face this way and that,
forcing it lower, then tighter into the wall. He opened his

mouth and tried to bite the bricks.

It was impossible.

He slid out, and sat on the end of the bed. Something had happened in here. But what could force a tooth from a man's head and sink it into a wall? What? There was no way his tooth could have got there. He couldn't have been hit, he couldn't have banged his head, or had it banged for him, not in that confined space, not that close to the floor.

And the scratch marks on the wall . . .

He sat on the edge of the bed and tried to hug himself to keep warm. The door rattled. Terror started from him in sudden beads of sweat.

'Stinks in here, doesn't it?' the guard said. 'Come on, let's be getting you back now.'

Jim nodded and began to push the trolley away. He could feel the tooth in his breast pocket, cold and hard against the skin.

There was a rumour going around that night that the Rat had found a way of escaping from the prison. He called it the Ghost Train. He had told someone about it weeks back.

No one knew how the story had started, or where it had come from, which was just as well, because the rumour was growing that whomever the Rat had told had reported it straight to the screws and the screws had killed him while they were trying to beat his secret out of him.

Jim was told over tea by Mother Skinner's friend. The other news was that Skinner was about to be transferred from secure hospital back to the sick bay and then probably back to his cell.

'It's criminal,' the friend said, spearing a potato and opening the conversation up to the rest of the table. 'Him an epileptic as well.'

'Is that what it was then?' Jim asked. 'Epilepsy?'

'Well, you saw.'

'I saw something. I thought it was more serious than epilepsy.'

'My point exactly. They've got no right to put him back inside.'

Jim looked at the man closely and tried to work out which of them was mad. Outside the prison walls, the world flowed by with a semblance of normality. But on this grey island, stranded in the middle of the stream, nothing made sense at all.

CHAPTER THIRTEEN

'Welcome to my parlour, Mr Carroll. Sit down, take the weight off your feet. There. That's better. Now George, Georgie Boy, wouldn't know what to do without him, Georgie Boy will pour you a drink, won't you Georgie Boy? Or perhaps you don't drink on duty.'

The last words were whipped out savagely. Jim felt Gorgeous George, Randall's lieutenant, slide into the gap between him and the door. George was massive and young and horribly impassive. His neck was as wide as his head which made it look like a bulb on top of a thick stalk. His shoulders sloped down like the sides of a volcano, all the angles filled and swollen with muscle. Blond hair sat in tight curls on his head. He had the old bad boy's tattoo across the knuckles of his big pink hands: TRUE HATE. He probably had a T-shirt with the words 'Yea though I walk through the valley of the shadow of death I shall fear no evil because I am the meanest motherfucker in the valley' written on it in blue biro. The lines would slope and the spelling would be off in a couple of places but it would not bother George.

Jim did not think he was gorgeous at all. He was not the sort of person you wanted to have standing behind you while you tried to beard the monster in its lair. He heard the prison on the other side of the door. In the next door cell someone shouted, 'Snap'!

He gave what was supposed to be a faint smile and said: 'I'm not on duty, Randall.'

'He's not on duty, Georgie Boy. Get the man a drink, give him a serviette. He's sweating enough. Give him a bath. He stinks.'

Jim watched Randall carefully – he was average height, hair cropped short, buzzing with energy. Close to and from a distance it was impossible to tell how old he was. His skin said forty, his eyes, which seemed to be held in a net of wrinkles, said sixty, seventy, eighty. He had a slight tan – Jim saw the sun-lamp by the bed, next to a copy of Machiavelli's *The Prince* and a big black bible.

His mattress, which was thinner than most, lay on a hardboard base. Now that he looked at Randall, Jim saw that his movements were curiously stiff, as if the vertebrae on his lower back were fused together. Like an insect. The effect was compounded by the way he held his arms: slightly bent with elbows out. Perhaps he wore a corset. Some people said he had a Kelvar waistcoat. He was often confined to his cell with Georgie Boy and he did about three spells of solitary confinement a year with seemingly no effect. The screws would not have him on the punishment wing any more because he was too negative an influence on the other prisoners.

Randall never left his cell unless he was surrounded by at least four of his men. At meals they sat at the end of the long table nearest the door, one man on either side of Randall, two facing him. Outside his cell he never talked and seldom even looked up. Considering the extent of his influence, very few people actually had anything to do with him, apart from his small army of followers of which George was the worst.

'What are you then, Jim, Jimmy boy, James James Robinson Robinson Wetherby George Dupree? The mountain coming to Mohammed, or Mohammed coming to the mountain? Still it was clever of you to come. George, give the man a cigarette.'

'I came because you told me to, actually.'

Randall lifted an eyebrow. 'Good,' he said. 'Please Mr Carroll, relax. I am not a Hannibal Lecter. People seem to think that I am. Some people even need to think that I am. It does no harm. But I am a business man.'

He sat down opposite Jim, cupped his face in his hands and stared into Jim's eyes. His eyes were pale and set very far apart, and there was a slight cast to one of them. Jim found that he was constantly looking from one to the other. It made him feel shifty.

George put a glass of pale amber liquid and a packet of untipped Players down on the table next to Jim. The whisky smelled sharp and golden. Jim's mouth began to water. *Control, show some self-control.* He took a cigarette and tapped the end.

'Take the packet,' Randall said.

Jim smiled and shook his head.

'Hit him,' Randall said.

The blow came from nowhere and was like a hand grenade exploding in his ear. The chair rocked sideways. Blackness swooped in on him, stars furred one side of his face. He was lopsided, one half of his head was swollen and spongey with pain. He must have been hit with something flat and hard.

'Take them,' Randall said.

Jim swallowed blood. The inside of his cheek was rough and bleeding.

'Hit him,' Randall said.

This time it was the other side. Again, so unexpected

that the chair rocked. The world sang. From very far away
he heard Randall say 'Take them'. He was looking at his
arm down the wrong end of a telescope. It was long and
thin and hard to control but it made it all the way to the
flat packet and closed over it.

'Mouthwash.'

A plastic beaker appeared on the table. Jim took a gulp,
looked around for a basin, realized that there wasn't one, and
was about to swallow it. Randall leaned forwards and looked
into his eyes. Jim spat the mouthful back into the beaker.

Randall smiled. 'Now you understand me, Mr Carroll, we
can talk.'

Randall leant his elbow on the table and in a curious
gesture squeezed his forehead with his thumb and index
finger. A large ring with what looked like a garnet in it
sparkled in the light. 'I've been watching you, Mr Carroll,
you see, I like to watch you. You are a dissimulator, but
you don't realize that you are deceiving yourself. You are
finding something out, I suspect for Mr Lyall, and I suspect
I know what, but I want to hear it from you.'

'I won't—'

'George.'

'All right,' Jim said. Randall was sitting with his hands
hovering slightly above the table, like antennae. His head
was pushed forwards on his neck and he was very still.
Only his jaw moved up and down. Jim was mesmerized and
listened.

'You see prison allows me unrivalled opportunities for,
shall we say business – more in some ways, than life
outside prison. Provided that is, the rules are followed. And
the rule in prison is to ensure a measure of stability.
Nobody wants trouble in prison. Certainly not the governor, certainly not the guards. Certainly not me – it is
upsetting for everyone. The more stable the society, the

more trade will flourish, the harder people will work for their little luxuries, their tobacco, their drugs, their radios. And the harder they work, the happier they will be, and the greater their sense of dignity and worth. Occasionally people need to be punished – for the greater good of all. Because people are punished, the better everyone else behaves. The better they behave – you catch my drift?'

Jim nodded. 'I see,' he said. He pushed a loose tooth with his tongue.

'Of course you see. You were a policeman. Police understand these things. But I can see that you're not really convinced. You're pretending to be, but in fact you think I'm a nutter. Right?'

'No,' said Jim. 'I think what you're saying is—'

'Hit him.'

This time he half-turned. The wooden paddle crashed across his face. He felt the skin split over his cheekbone. A shadow came down.

'Oh Jim. You should take your punishment like a man. Georgie Boy's an artist, but your moving like that – well it's making things difficult for him. Now if I say that thing again, you won't move will you? Hit him.'

'NO!' Jim threw his arm up. Nothing happened.

'Control, Mr Carroll, is all. Now we can get down to business. You are working for Jack Lyall. You will tell me in what capacity.'

Jim felt numb. Randall knew that he was working for Lyall. Technically that made him a grass, and as a grass his life was not worth anything. He thought frantically. If he told Randall, that might give him a measure of protection, but he would have to play it cleverly.

'The suicides,' he said thickly. 'Four of them: Campbell, Burroughs, Masters, Powell. Lyall doesn't think they're suicides.'

'He thinks they're murder?'

Jim shrugged.

'An unnecessary question. Why does he not think that they are suicides?'

'Their necks were broken.'

Randall tilted his head on one side and appeared to consider.

'A prison officer?'

'Apparently not.'

'Why do you say that?'

'Because if Lyall had had any suspicions whatsoever that it might have been one, he would never have brought me in.'

'Good.' Randall nodded. 'Your theories?'

'None at this stage.'

'New evidence?'

'It seems that all four men were into the occult, and all four claimed they were innocent.'

Randall sniffed. 'Interesting. Anything else?'

Jim reached into the breast pocket of his tunic and dropped the tooth on the table. It lay like a prehistoric artefact on the Formica. Long. Yellow. Curiously decorative.

'Not the sort of thing I would choose to carry around with me. Can you explain?'

'It's a tooth.'

'I can see that.'

'I found it in what I think was Ratcliff's cell. It was embedded into the wall so deeply it might have been fired from a gun. It was also too near the floor to have got in unless—'

'Unless, Mr Carroll?'

'I don't know. I can't think how it got there.'

'Unless?'

'Unless he was lying on the floor and his head exploded.'
Jim tried to sound dismissive.

Randall did not laugh. His face stayed completely blank.

'And that is the kind of information that you have been passing on to Mr Lyall.'

'Yes.'

Randall rubbed his hands briskly together. 'Well then, kindly do not pass on anything more. From now on you are working for me. Lyall is only worried because when the privatization plans come through, he wants to be part of a team in the management buy-out, and thinks that rumours of strange and unnatural deaths might prejudice his position. He is a pawn of the governor's. You will find on the other hand that working for me affords you certain privileges, not the least being that instead of people avoiding you, they will talk, because I tell them to. Meet me here tomorrow evening. We will continue then. Good night, Mr Carroll.'

Jim muttered, 'Good night.'

Along Randall's landing, down the stairs, across the central hall.

The wardens did not look at Jim; the prisoners did not look at Jim. He dropped on to his bed like a dead man.

CHAPTER FOURTEEN

'This,' Randall said the following evening, 'is Mr Soper. He's got a very boring nickname so I always call him Mr Soper.'

George pushed Jim into the cell. A man, looking more relaxed than he should have done, strictly speaking, gave Jim a big smile. He had floppy blond hair and teeth like tombstones.

'Hi,' he said. 'How are things?' He sounded like a public school boy who had refused to grow up. He turned to Randall. 'So this is the filth, right?'

Randall looked at Jim. 'Mr Soper is labouring under the delusion that he and I have struck up a rapport. I apologize for his rudeness. Mr Soper is not here because I like him. He is here because he served time with Burroughs in Maidstone prison some four years ago, and then shared a three man cell with Burroughs and Campbell two years ago here.'

'Right,' Soper said, still smiling inanely. 'Burroughs, Campbell. Right.'

'So tell us what you know.' Randall's voice was ominously low.

'Well, what do you want to know?'

'Everything,' Randall said.

'Oh now wait a minute, matey. What about my side of the bargain?'

'Your side of the bargain.' Jim noticed that what might have sounded like a question from anyone else invariably sounded like a statement from Randall.

'You know, the old quid pro quo. You don't get anyfink for nuffink in this old world. Am I right, gents?'

Jim cringed.

Randall nodded. 'You are right,' he said. 'George, give him something.'

Soper spoke quite well for someone with a broken finger. He held it out in front of him like a dog with a thorn in its toe, staring at it occasionally in disbelief. The finger itself was as fat as a courgette, the colour of an aubergine, and stuck up from the hand only a few degrees off the right angle.

'I hardly knew them, honestly,' Soper said. His eyes darted from George to Randall to Jim. 'I mean I don't know if anything I say will be any good. I—'

'Mr Carroll will be the judge of that,' Randall said. He raised his eyebrows at Jim.

'Which one did you know best?' Jim asked.

'None of them.'

'Keep your voice down. Now, that's not answering the question. You shared a cell with Burroughs, twice. You spent time with Campbell. You probably knew Masters and Powell. Now which one of the four did you know best?'

'Why do you want to know?'

'You don't learn do you,' said Randall. 'George?'

'I'm just asking! Oh my God don't hurt me again. It would help me.'

'We're asking because we want to know,' Jim said. 'Not

to help you tailor your answers.'

'Campbell, as a matter of fact. I spent more time with Burroughs but he never spoke much. I mean they were like this.' He hooked two fingers together, winced from the pain. 'I mean that's cool as far as I'm concerned. It was all the other stuff.'

'What other stuff?'

'They were so stuck up. Wouldn't associate, especially Burroughs. Convinced he was innocent. Wouldn't talk to anyone else – apart from the other three. He was an academic so perhaps he just thought he was naturally more clever. I don't know.'

'What did Campbell do?'

'Campbell? He'd been the leader of some dodgy cult church on the South coast. Made a fortune ripping off OAPs, then got done for fraud and embezzlement, I think. That's what made it all so unlikely.' Campbell had been to see the chaplain, Jim thought. Campbell was a grass.

'What?'

'The fact that he trashed the library. A year ago or so.'

'Campbell did that?'

'Of course. Him and Burroughs were working there – in the end they blamed it on Burroughs. He did a spell on the punishment wing, then time in solitary.'

'That's different?'

'It's a special cell, in the join of B and C Wings. Right?'

'That's right, Mr Soper,' Randall said.

'Well I think that's what turned his mind. Sent him, you know, haywire. He was always the ring leader of those four, you know, the one they all looked up to. He came out and even Campbell stopped talking to me. I started feeling like a stranger in my own cell. Then one evening I caught them.'

'Yes,' Jim said, trying to sound bored. Soper licked his lips and shot a sideways glance at Randall.

'They were planning to escape. It was one evening. I walked in. The four of them were huddled in the cell, and I heard one of them, I think it was Powell, say: "Well, if that's the only way out, I'll do it." But he didn't sound or look happy. In fact I'd say he looked terrified. I asked Campbell about it the next day. He didn't say anything at first, but eventually he did.' Soper paused deliberately. 'When I asked him straight out if they had a plan to escape, you know what he did? He smiled. Said they'd found a way to get out. By train.'

'By train?' Randall looked ominously at George. He sat down on the bed beside Soper and took his hand.

'Honestly. Honestly! I'm just telling you what he said.'

'Hang on to him, George. Carry on, Soper.'

'And it wasn't an ordinary train either.'

'What was it? The Orient Express?'

'No. The Ghost Train. He said he was taking the Ghost Train. He said he'd got his ticket.'

'All aboard for Loonytown,' Randall said equably.

Joe had not spoken to Jim for two days now. He had taken on the air of a hippopotamus with a grievance. It did not suit him. It made the cell claustrophobic. Joe was making a point: namely that Jim was making a mistake. He should keep his head down, keep *stumm*, play out his time. Jim knew that it had all gone too far for that now.

He still kept the tooth in his pocket. It was the one piece of solid evidence that he had, but there was still so much to piece together.

Lights out. Jim listened to Joe's breathing for a while then decided he could stand it no longer.

'Joe. Listen . . . Joe, I need your help.'

The whole structure of the bunk shifted as Joe rolled on to his side.

'Joe, I've got myself into this thing – it may not have been the best idea I've ever had – but I've got to see it through now.'

A pause. Jim could practically hear the big man think. Eventually Joe spoke: 'You may like walking around with a face like a squashed melon. You may like sitting in cells while Gorgeous George tortures information out of middle-class drop-outs with no more sense than an empty bread bin. You may like it but I don't, not one little bit. And what's more I don't like sharing a room with someone who does.'

'Whoever said I liked it?' Jim protested.

'Don't try and kid me, Jim Carroll. You love every minute of it. Back to the old police routine: hard man, soft man. Come on sonny, you can trust us. Shacking up with Randall like that shows me what you're really like.'

'Joe, it's not like that. Being perfectly straight, in a way I suppose I do like it. It's given me something to think about.'

'What has? Cuddling up to psychopaths?'

'Randall is not—'

'He is and you damn well know it!'

'If I could only explain—'

'Explain what?'

'It's not just Randall who wanted to find out. It was Jack Lyall as well!'

'WHAT? Jim, that means you're working for both sides at the same time.'

'They both want to find out the same thing. For different reasons, but they both want to find out about the deaths in prison. It's like a police enquiry, Joe. I couldn't say no. These four men died last year. No one knows how. Either there's a very clever murderer walking round the Barrow, or else—'

'What?'

'Who knows?'

Joe took a deep breath.

'Who knows? That's all you've got to say?'

'At this stage, what else can I say? I'm completely in the dark.'

'All right,' Joe said after a pause. 'I still think you're crazy.'

'You'll help me?'

'I'll do nothing of the sort.'

'Have you heard of the Ghost Train?'

'Only when I was a kid. Well, no. That's not strictly true. Some people use it as slang to describe moving between prisons. You know – getting on the Ghost Train to go to the Scrubs, but—'

'As a means of escape?'

'No, not at all.'

'It's just that one of the dead men said he was escaping by it. It doesn't make sense. He trashed the library, and was so disruptive on the punishment wing that they banged him into solitary.'

'You have to be pretty desperate to do that. I mean if you wanted to get into solitary that's what you'd do. Was he disruptive normally?'

'Quite the opposite, from what I can gather.'

'Perhaps he was sick of his cell-mate.'

'No, they were good friends.'

'Perhaps he wanted some peace and quiet,' Joe said pointedly.

'He certainly got that.'

'No need to be so sarcastic. I'm just trying to turn the thing around. Instead of trying to work out why he would behave like that, think of him doing it for a reason. We all have reasons for our actions.'

'You mean there was something to do with solitary that he wanted to find out about?'

'Stupid idea, I know. Sorry,' Joe said.

'No, no. It's a great idea. It just leaves me with a problem.'

'Which is?'

'How to get into that cell.'

There was a pause, then Joe said: 'Listen, Jim, I think I was wrong. I still don't like the idea of you having anything to do with Randall, but if you're trying to find out about this, honestly, then I can see it's important. And I'll try and help.'

Jim smiled into the darkness. 'Apology accepted,' he said.

CHAPTER FIFTEEN

The guard came for Jim the next morning after breakfast. He led him into the hall, along some narrow passages which smelled of cabbage and cat food, into a small annexe. He unlocked a heavy, oak door reinforced with metal bands, pointed at a small hallway and locked the door behind him. There was another strong door opposite and a smaller one on his left. After five minutes the second door opened and Lyall walked through. He unlocked the big door, and asked Jim to shoot the bolts.

Daylight poured in through the open door. Jim heard a car alarm go off. Outside was that close.

It was a raw morning. A wind sighed above the prison walls and gusted fitfully in the yard. A sheet of newspaper skidded down through the air, swooped over their heads and was slapped against the perimeter wall. Grit stung Jim's ankles. The flags in the yard had been lifted and stacked against the perimeter wall.

Jim shivered. His eyes stung. He rubbed his arms but it did not make any difference to the cold that was creeping through him.

'Know what this place is?' Lyall asked.

'No idea.' Jim's teeth chattered.

'It's the old gallows yard. The door you came through was called the Hangman's Gate. The condemned man was led from his cell – always the same one – down the steps and out here. There would be benches set up in ranks against those walls for the rich spectators – and scaffold on the other side of the perimeter for the yobs. It was a spectator sport. They'd hang the man, let him down, a doctor would certify he was dead and either sell the body on to the local hospital or fling it over there into a lime pit. Just there where the roses are growing. Roses like lime, I suppose. These flag stones that have been lifted – we had a work detail do that the other day. The men uncovered one of the holes where they fixed the gallow's supports. Ratcliff, the man who died recently, was working here with them. They said he had a sort of fit over there – by the bushes. I'd like you to have a look.'

'I thought all the activity went on in his cell.'

'A lot did,' Lyall said blankly.

Jim walked over to the wall. A great rose bush lay half out of the ground. Its main stem was the thickness of a man's wrist and covered with wicked, curled thorns. Near the bottom they had little shreds of dark fabric hanging from them.

The air wrinkled. Became heavier and stiller. A sound emerged from the thick silence – a distant clacking, broken and discordant, the sound of wood on wood. Jim wheeled round. The prison shuddered. Each window was a port; each port a mouth tonguing the sound at him. A movement dragged his eyes downwards. There, in that cell set in the angle of the building something was passing back and forth, a head rocking backwards and forwards. Darkness was framing his vision, crowding out the light. Secrets curdled the air. It was crawling with them, infected. He could hardly see. The day wrinkled all around him.

Something scratched his ankle. He almost screamed. A thin stem from the rose was trailing across his bare ankles. A rose is a rose is a rose. A rose by any other name would smell as sweet. Not this one though. Calm down.

'Learn anything?' Lyall said. Jim blinked and shook his head. 'Now don't tell me you're coming over all strange.' The air was clear. His head was clear. 'That's what they said happened to Ratcliff,' Lyall continued, his face pinched by the cold, but under control and looking closely at Jim. 'Turned a funny colour. I wondered if you'd spotted something.'

Jim looked up at the window where he had seen the head moving backwards and forwards. 'What's that cell, there?'

'I told you – it's the old condemned cell. Or did I? We use it for isolation these days. Nice in there. Decent bed. Those who are about to die, we salute you.'

'Who's in it now?'

'Today? No one. Empty.'

'I saw somebody in it. A head moving in front of the window.'

'Probably a cleaner.'

'You didn't really get me out here to show me the old yard, did you?' Jim asked.

'No, not strictly speaking. I came to apologize. I was hard on you last time. I – er, was going through the personal effects of the men who died, those things the relatives didn't want to take, and came up with this. I think it was Campbell's. It's from your library – one that those bastards didn't burn. I suppose it must have been in one of their cells.' Lyall squinted up at the sky. 'I need answers, Carroll. My time's running out. My men, the officers, are getting restless. They know there's something wrong. I have a feeling this old place is going to explode soon. That'll be bad for everyone.'

Jim took the book. He knew that Lyall was right, and knew too that it did not matter who he was working for: Randall, the Governor, himself. All he had to do was get to the bottom of the mystery before something else happened. 'I'm making progress,' he said. 'Powell and his friends were all trying to escape. If you lot knew, that's a motive for stopping them—'

'But not killing them, surely.'

'No. That leaves the other alternative – that one of the prisoners killed them, but that's not likely either. Randall didn't know about the escape plan. He's the only one with enough screws in his pocket to kill four men, but if he didn't know . . .'

'Back to square one,' said Lyall.

Jim looked up at the grim prison walls. It was filthy, blackened by the smoke of the town. Or perhaps the filth was seeping outwards from the grey cells within.

'No,' Jim said. He was shaking with cold now but went on, trying to burrow for the truth and follow a new idea. 'You never get back to square one. You never even go round in circles. It's time you see. Ever tried to peel an apple in a long strip? It comes away in a spiral. So you always come back to the same place in one dimension, but not in the other. A spiral, not a circle or a square. The trick is to look back, and see what's changed.'

'Mr Carroll, you're a bit of a philosopher.'

'Not a philosopher: a prisoner. It means you can always be somewhere new just by standing still.'

'Like back in the library?'

'I'll try anything once.'

Tindall was at his most petulant and irritating that morning, fussing that they had not made enough progress, looking at the books that Jim had arranged and complaining feebly that he could not make head or tail of how they were organized, grumbling about his back, his chest, his neck that he had cricked, and the smell in the room that he ascribed sniffily to drains.

Rather than truss him up and drop him in the corner with a gag in his mouth, Jim strained his mouth into a smile and suggested that he made labels that actually described the categories and then stuck the labels to the shelves.

'With what?' Tindall asked.

'Glue!' Jim said, trying to hold his voice down. Tindall thought about it, agreed but then insisted that he would have to cut the cards up himself because Jim was not to be trusted with a pair of scissors.

While Tindall painstakingly measured the width of the shelves, Jim flicked through the book that Lyall had given him. *Men of Their Time* it was called: *Studies From The Age of Endeavour*.

The age of endeavour was the beginning of the nineteenth century, apparently, when 'the seeds of genius took root and spread into mighty structures.'

Jim flipped the pages to see where they opened. 'Thomas Loveyard: the man of cloth.' Thomas Loveyard was a weaving magnate, no less, who set up the mighty mills that powered the nation's commerce. Jim's eye flicked over the turgid, heroic prose, and stopped at an all-too-familiar place name. So Thomas Loveyard had lived in the town, and had made his fortune there. So Campbell had been interested in local history. So what?

Thomas Loveyard had married. He had moved from the mill town to a great house he had built on the edge of the moors. There was a picture of it, a pretty engraving.

Jim flicked past it. Frowned. Stopped. Flicked back. It

looked awfully familiar: a regular, many-windowed house, three storeys high, square and very symmetrical.

He skim read. Cragside House. Edgerton on the Moor. Thomas Loveyard moved there with his beautiful wife, and lived there happily for thirty years. At the bottom of the page was a footnote.

Edgerton was the home of the notorious Mad Weaver, William Lestrange, the Murderer of the Moors.

Jesus! Jim sat up so suddenly that he knocked the chair over behind him. He stared at the embroidered blanket hanging on the wall. His eyes widened as if to take in the import of his discovery.

The house. The house in the book was the same as the house on the blanket. Someone had embroidered Loveyard's house on to the blanket. Not only that, he had embroidered the whole village. That was Edgerton on the Moor, with its houses, inn, church . . .

Graveyard.

William Lestrange.

The biggest grave.

This was the murderer's blanket, every stitch made while he waited to hang. That was his tombstone – he must have run out of space and abbreviated the name.

William Lestrange.

Strange.

But he was never buried there. His body had been sold to a hospital, or been thrown into a lime pit in the shadow of the gallows, under the wall where the roses grew.

Strange. Jim reached up and touched the fabric. *How did you kill?* he thought. *Who?*

He moved closer to it. It was hard to see; perspective put some of the tombs behind others so the words were half hidden, but he thought he could make out some of the names on the tombs.

He drew closer. The blanket smelled of earth and something richer, thicker, sweeter, a cloying fug that entered the head. He could see more clearly now. He could see grass growing between the graves, a dog-rose spreading along the ground.

Names. So many names, ten, twenty – how many could he fit onto the rug? Thirty, forty?

His heart thumped; his breath caught in his throat; his nerve ends began singing. Four names stood out, four ordinary names but they turned Jim's blood into ice:

Powell.
Burroughs.
Masters.
Campbell.

And there, on the tomb behind:

Ratcliff.

Jim rocked back on his heels, unable to take in what he saw. He looked back at the other names – all of them gone, all of them dead. His brain raced. This was something Lyall had to see. This was a record of – what? Death? Murder?

He turned, and in so doing missed something.

He missed the way the thread twitched in the corner of an unmarked tombstone, set back against the graveyard wall. He missed how the thread moved like a slow, thin worm, arching above the fabric, painstakingly, blindly questing for a gap in the weave. He missed how it dropped through, twisted, turned, worked its way up again and made a tiny running stitch. And then another. And another.

He missed it. He was hammering on the door, yelling for Jack Lyall, and not caring who knew about it.

CHAPTER SIXTEEN

They locked Jim in his cell and it was four o'clock before Lyall came to see him.

'What the hell are you playing at?' he asked.

Jim just said: 'Trouble. It's in the library.'

'I looked in earlier. Tindall was just packing up. He says he's got flu. I couldn't see anything wrong and according to him you started to yell and scream, and insult him rather personally.'

'Just take me there. I'll show you what I found. And bring a torch. The light's going.'

Lyall raised an eyebrow. Jim led the way out.

'What do you think it means?' Lyall asked when he saw the names.

'What do you think it means? At the very least it suggests that someone is getting in here and filling names in on the grave stones. That to me suggests a degree of organization.'

'Tindall?' Lyall said. 'No. And I suppose we can rule you out.'

'I – I can't see it,' Jim said. 'Not Tindall. I mean why?'

'Why would anyone do it? If there is this organization, why draw attention to it?'

'It must be some sort of death cult,' Jim said. He felt his voice trail off. It sounded so limp.

'Don't be—'

Jim pointed at the grave with 'Strange' on it. 'Well, that's one person we know died here at least. Strange must be William Lestrange, known as the Mad Weaver. He was a murderer. This is the village he lived in. My guess is that he did all this embroidery while he was waiting to hang. There are five more names that we know died here. And look at all these others. Look! What I want to know is when they died. This blanket had been wrapped up in the cellar for years.' Suddenly the colour drained from Jim's face. He moved back and supported himself with a hand on the table. Lyall thought he might be about to faint.

'Where's Joe Cohen?' he asked, his voice a hoarse whisper.

'Cohen, I thought that was what you wanted to see me about, actually.'

'What?' Jim spun round.

'I'm used to you behaving like a madman, but for Cohen to go off the rails like that. I mean a red-band and everything.'

Joe's gone off the rails. He knew they were important but the words would not make an impression on him.

'—couldn't get him into the punishment wing. He's a big man and still quite a puncher. They stuck him in the isolation cell until he cools down. He'll be out by now.'

Jim found he could not speak. All he could do was point to a grave in the corner of the graveyard with the word 'Cohen' wriggling across it in white thread.

'I said he'll be out by now,' Lyall repeated, but his voice had lost its confidence.

The men who opened the door could not understand what

had happened at first, so much of what had been inside Joe was out of him: soft tissue, organs, bones. He had been gutted, then filleted. There was so much tissue and blood in the cell that it looked organic itself. All that had been left inside him was his skull. His mouth was smiling. In all the confusion that followed, no one noticed the rope burn around his neck and it did not show up on the Polaroids that Jack Lyall forced himself to take.

Unnoticed too at first was the way Joe's empty fingers, trailing in the puddled gore, had smeared a word on the old stone floor. There was a great big foot print in the middle of it which did not help.

'Angela?' one of the guards said, after the body had been taken away.

'Angel more like,' another said. 'Perhaps the poor fucker was thinking of heaven.'

Part Two

CHAPTER SEVENTEEN

The bus crawled up the last half-mile to her stop, belching black smoke from the exhaust. As it climbed, the hedgerows gave way to fences, fences to mossy drystone walls, then they too turned sharply off to left and right and suddenly the moor poured away to the horizon, a vast, dun sweep of land, dimpled with shadows, burning with the soft glow of the sunset.

Angela White felt the sun warm on her face through the dirty glass and thought about the history project. Telegraph poles, hedges, the odd cottage flashed past her face. Further from the bus the landscape wheeled more slowly. No inspiration there. What was that irritating phrase Mummy always used when she asked for seconds? Things always come to those who wait.

Funnily enough she had not said it for some time. *Perhaps they're changing. Perhaps I'm changing.* For a second she felt that she was on the brink of a momentous discovery, and that a whole world of inspiration was about to open up in front of her. The feeling disappeared. Gone with a whispering pop like a soap bubble. *Hormones,* Angela thought. *Who'd be twelve and a quarter if they could be any other age?*

The village lay beyond a low ridge crowned by a trio of wind-sharpened trees. Angela stood up and walked down the central aisle of the bus, stooping low and peering out of the window, trying to time the moment to press the stop request button. Too late and the driver would not stop – he was a right old meanie and had once taken Melanie on to Witherly and she had had to call home to get a lift. Too early and she would be left standing in front of THE MAN who had stared rather too long at her when she had climbed on outside the school. She had been hoping at every stop that he would get off, but he was still there, chain-smoking, dropping the butts on the floor and grinding them to shreds with the heel of his training shoes. She pulled her skirt as far down her knees as she could, put her nose in the air and made her way down the bus.

The driver grunted goodbye as she got off. She watched the bus slowly gather speed, glanced behind her to see if there were any cars which might stop and give her a lift, then with a resigned shrug she turned left up the single-track road to Edgerton on the Moor.

It was two miles to her home. The road climbed up a low ridge, dropped again into the shallow Snare Brook valley, crossed the stream on a stone humpbacked bridge then rose along the shoulder of moor where the village lay.

The sun was low behind her, just lighting the upward slope, but it would be dark in the valley and by the time she climbed up the other side the light could well be gone. A white fertilizer sack, snared on a barbed wire fence, snapped a black mouth at her. She shied two feet sideways like a startled pony.

Angie White
Had a Fright
In the Middle of the Night

Oh forget it. You're twelve and a quarter; you're in your thirteenth year. Far too old to be bothered by that kind of thing.

Am I really?

Yes, she told herself firmly, the days of Angie White are over. I'm Angela now. Angela. And people don't tease me any more.

She began to march up the hill. She knew she was tired but her legs felt strong. An hour's drama practice for the school play – she was the only girl in her class to be cast as one of the fairies in *A Midsummer Night's Dream* – followed by swimming training was a lot to get through three times a week, not forgetting the homework, but it was worth it. She could do it, she knew she could. She was just beginning to test the extent of her abilities.

But a year ago things had been very different. A year ago, after her father had left the police force and they moved from the town to the country, nothing, but nothing had gone right. She had been a clumsy, awkward, freckled-nosed, pale-faced, green-eyed freak. A nobody – but a nobody nobody could ignore. A hateful bouncing mat of flaming red hair saw to that.

It all started when Miss Steadman had asked her to read her weekly essay out in front of the class.

It had been called *Night Fears (But Now I'm Not Frightened)*. Angela thought that the title sounded rather sophisticated – like a Genesis song – and the essay was the best thing she had ever done. She had actually been proud to read it out.

It was all about how when she was a little girl, all of two years before, she had never been able to go to sleep because she had been so frightened of the monsters that lived in her room.

There had been Mr Black: twig-thin, feet racked into

terrible high arches and a face like boiled dough who lived in the wardrobe. And Mrs Flat, a flapping wide-backed monster who rose each night from between the floorboards and hovered above her head, dropping dust on her face. Under the bed there was The Basket Man, a strange, hybrid creature with a head and body of wicker and hands like swollen crab claws. Strange balls of dust lived in the corners of the room that could enter the body through any little cut you had and turn your blood to powder. The ceiling light was a gigantic feather-soft moth with huge tombstone dentures and eyes like ragged black pools . . .

Each night they danced around her bed. Each night they took it in turns to wait, to wait, to wait. They inhabited every shadow, they caused every creak. Only the sound of her parents going to bed, the reassuring rush of water in pipes as one of them ran a bath could soothe her to sleep.

Then she told how she had conquered her fear of them.

It had been a particularly bad night. Mrs Flat had risen from the floorboards like a dry manta ray and hovered above her bed, dropping dust from underneath her leathery armpits. Angela knew that the light would brush the dust away – she called it night dust – and sometimes, when it piled upon her face in soft, itching mounds, she had to turn the light on six or seven times. But that night, as she stretched her hand out to the bedside light, she heard the Basket Man begin to stir. She heard him rustle and creak from under the bed, getting ready to reach out with his terrible red claw and grab her arm . . .

She screwed her eyes tight shut, lay the pillow on its side so that when she put her head down it covered both ears and pulled the bedclothes up above her head. The bedroom door was only five steps away but she could not make it. She knew she could not make it.

Terror built up in her. She wanted to scream but was too

frightened, she wanted to move but was paralysed with fear.

Somebody help me, please, she whispered in her mind. PLEASE.

And something happened.

It was as if a shadow, no, not a shadow, *her* shadow lifted itself from the bed. She could see in her mind's eye another Angela, just like her but shadowy and insubstantial, move through the room.

And fear had gone.

She had lost her fear because she was not really there. She was a part of Angela and apart from her. She was her shadow self, her brave self, a beautiful hard-armed warrior queen.

She walked through the room fearlessly. She looked in the cupboard. It was empty. She looked under the bed. There was nothing there. She squeezed between the floorboards. No Mrs Flat. She sat in the middle of the floor and said: 'It's all right. I'm here. You need never be frightened again.'

Angela opened her eyes.

No Mrs Flat. No Basket Man. No Mr Black.

Brave Angela had done it. She crawled out of bed and joined Brave Angela in the middle of the floor, laughing with relief, but feeling very solemn and important as well. She watched the darkness and thought.

If you became a part of whatever frightened you, you were no longer frightened. If you understood it, you were suddenly on its side and it was no longer frightening. If she loved the darkness, it could love her. That was how her essay finished.

Immediately there were muffled giggles from the back of the classroom.

Angie White
Had a fright
In the middle of the night.
She's a git
Scared to shit
Can't have a crap 'cos her arse don't fit.

They'd started chanting it as soon as school was over and
it had lasted a year.

She learned a lot during that year. She learned that most
people were easily frightened, so that if she began to make
friends with someone, it was all too easy for that someone
to be persuaded that they should not really be talking to
Angela.

Rumours began to build up out of nowhere. That she wet
her bed. That she would take her knickers down for a
sherbet fountain. That her mother was a tart like Lilo Lil.
And because the rumours came from nowhere, she realized
that in some ways what was happening to her was a sort
of game. People do not need to hate in order to be cruel;
they were cruel creatively, cruel because it was fun, cruel
because in some weird way they needed to be. The fact that
she was the object of their spite was largely irrelevant.
Horrid but irrelevant.

She learned that grown-ups did not necessarily give the
best advice. Her father told her to stand up to them: bullies
were cowards at heart. But when she tried to stand up to
them she found out that they were much stronger than
her. They were enjoying what they were doing; courage
was no protection from pleasure.

Her mother told her to ignore them. 'Show them that
you're above all that. They'll respect you for it.' But of
course they did not. They just called her a stuck-up, snotty-
nosed bitch along with everything else.

The only true thing her mother said was that it would all be over one day. And one day it was.

One morning the whole world seemed to hate her, the next it had completely forgotten that she was meant to be the bed-wetting daughter of a notorious local prostitute whose father was the Yorkshire Ripper, most likely.

Suddenly nobody teased her, nobody really noticed her. Those in her class who had felt sorry for her began to be friendly. She got on to the school swimming team. People cheered and clapped her when she won a race. She was accepted. She was even popular, and would have been more popular if the scars of the previous year had not taught her to trust almost nobody. It did not really matter. People liked her now and she could decide whether or not she liked them.

It taught her that people have short memories.

She paused at the top of the valley. It was all right. She could still see the stream and the bridge which meant that if she hurried there might still be just enough light to use the short cut when she got into the village.

She trotted down the hill. A track branched off on the left across the valley floor to a small disused granite quarry where the villagers dumped their old fridges and mattresses. Nothing there, although the hard black emptiness of the quarry bothered her.

Darker now. She crossed the humpbacked bridge, unable entirely to rule out the possibility that a giant crayfish was lying curled up in the gloom, ready to snap at her legs as she walked past.

Sheep were lying down, grey mounds on the heather. Long heads with yellow eyes followed her as she passed. It was darker than she thought. Her legs were feeling hollow as she forced the pace up the slope. Tired. If only she could make the short cut it would save half a mile, but then what was the point of saving half a mile if you knackered yourself in the process?

At the top of the hill she slowed down. Lights, at last! Only another mile and she would be home, able to stretch her hands out in front of the fire, sink back in the armchair with the telly on. It was her father's turn to cook, which meant something elaborate and filling because he had this theory (which she thought made good sense) that if he *had* to cook, he should do something special – sort of make it an exception every time. It seemed to prove a point to him.

One of the stars that glimmered in the sky started to flash. The light on the radio-mast ten miles away. It was a clear night. That meant frost.

The village straggled along a small road which crossed the T on the lane from the bus stop. The houses were laid out to the left and right of the junction, with a small village green in a sort of triangle to the right, and the church set in the angle of junction to the left.

As she looked the lights went on in the pub – just on the right of the junction. Her house lay at the other end of the village, the last one in fact, if you did not count Cragside House, but that had been empty for years. She knew that because her mother was an estate agent and was always grumbling that the house would not move. No one would buy it, it being riddled with dry rot, whatever that meant.

Here was the problem. If she followed the road she would be walking two sides of a right-angled triangle. The advantage of that route was that it was lit by street lights. The most direct route involved cutting across the grave-yard that lay in front of the church in the left hand angle of the T. You got in through a kissing gate and you could easily scramble over the wall on the other side. The advantage of that was that she would be able to knock ten minutes off the walk and maybe catch the end of *East-Enders*. But it was looking rather gloomy . . .

She switched her school-bag from one hand to the other and decided to see how she felt when she got there.

Then she heard a noise. It was no more than a slight crunch of something slipping on gravel. A sheep? Too heavy for that.

She willed herself to look over her shoulder, down into the valley. It was quite dark now. Was that white shape a stone or a face? It didn't move. But she must be silhouetted against the skyline. She swallowed and willed herself not to run.

What was that song her mother always sang?

Just your imagin-a-tion, running away with you.

Running away. If you ran, IT ran. What ran?

It was getting cold. *I could run to keep warm*, she thought, and began to trot.

For a minute or two she heard only the creak of her bag, the rustle of clothes and the rush of her breath.

She stopped suddenly.

Silence.

'Hello?' Her voice sounded as thin as cotton.

She heard the stream, a motorbike far off on the main road. Nothing else.

She squinted into the gloom again. Then began to walk, looking over her shoulder.

Crunch, crunch, crunch, but these were her footsteps, surely. She gasped as a white shape rose suddenly on her left and blundered off on to the moor.

A sheep. Just a stupid old sheep. They were all sheep. The thing to do was get off the road. The road just gave an illusion of safety.

She liked the phrase 'an illusion of safety'. It sounded nicely rounded off and very grown-up. If she were off the road, anything on it would miss her. She would be able to see it, but it would not be able to see her.

A wall on her left. That was the field below the graveyard. But ahead there were lights. This bit of the journey always seemed to take the longest.

At the graveyard she paused, closed her eyes and forced herself to count to ten without looking. Pressure built up in her. Her limbs began to feel lighter and lighter.

Eight – nine – ten.

She crashed through the kissing gate, pushing it forward, slipping round the side. But as she turned, she did see something. A little shape had hissed past, thin arms seeming to stream behind it.

It missed her. Angela stuck her fist in her mouth and ground the knuckles against her teeth and tried to shrink down into the thickness of the wall. The gate clacked, metal and metal.

The thing stopped. Turned. It seemed to be made of patches of moonlight – a girl, no a dead and mottled thing, just hovering on the road, with a blunt, blind head that was lowered and thrusting this way and that.

Angela screamed, then she was through the gate, wriggling like a little eel, legs stumbling over the grave mounds, cold winter grass whipping her shins.

The gate banged shut.

Oh God, Oh God. WHICH WAY?

She looked around. Stumbled and fell as a mound rose up like a trap in front of her. The fall was soft, but her head glanced off a tombstone, a word smearing against her eyes.

Stunned she lay still, not breathing, lungs like acid and rusty razor-blades under her tongue.

A hand reached down from behind.

'Aha! I thought I heard something. Come on. Up you get.

Up you get. I'll not have – goodness me! Angela!'

She stared up at the vicar's face.

'Angela, what are you doing? Is this a game?'

'Oh Mr Arnold. I thought, I thought—'

It sounded disrespectful to say that she had been planning to take a short cut through the graveyard. She looked hurriedly behind her. It was too dark to see now. The vicar put a hand under her armpit and lifted her up.

'My dear girl, it's only me. I was just on my way to lock up. Look, here's your bag. But what *were* you doing?'

When they had moved to Edgerton the vicar had come round to talk to Angela. Her mother must have asked him. He had been very kind and told her that Jesus loved little boys and little girls and was careful to watch over them when they were asleep. She had not thanked him for this image of another face in the dark, this one with a billion eyes, able to see every child in the world, but she understood that he was trying to help. She could not tell him that she had been trying to make herself scared. It sounded rather shameful.

'Poor old girl. Just come back from school?'

She nodded. 'Swimming and drama.'

'Jolly good. Jolly good. No more – ah – funny dreams? No? Good. Imagination's a funny thing. Runs away with us sometimes. Parents all right, are they? Good. Here, take my arm. Make an old man happy.'

He crooked his elbow and made his eyes twinkle. Angela gave him a weak smile and walked uncomfortably with him out of the graveyard.

CHAPTER EIGHTEEN

Her father's Vauxhall Cavalier with 'Orion Security' painted in fancy letters on the doors was standing on the gravel outside their house in a different position from the morning. That was good. It meant that he might have been called out. For some reason work had not been coming his way recently and although it made him bad-tempered, at least there was less argument now about Angela's mother working, which was a good thing.

She paused, surprised to see a car parked in the street outside the sitting-room window. They did not usually have visitors in the afternoon. Did not usually have visitors at all, ever for that matter. A beaten up Austin Princess. She did not know anyone with a car like that. After her fright she felt particularly vulnerable and shy and was reluctant to meet anyone. If her father was trying to impress someone – a new client for example – he would either look daggers at her or be falsely chummy and call her 'old girl'.

She paused in the back porch, straining to hear voices. The radio was bleating a pop song. She opened the door a crack. No one.

She was welcomed by the warmth and light. The kitchen

looked as if a bomb had hit it, but then it always did if Dad
was cooking: a dirty protest, her mother called it.

Angela snapped off the radio and looked at the big colour
cookery book lying open on top of a pile of meat trim-
mings.

'*Boeuf Bourgignon*, creamed potatoes, caramelized baby
carrots ...' Good. She was starving, even though her
mother would complain about how much it was all costing
them. If you spent the time looking for work that you spent
cooking ...

She wandered through the kitchen, all the time getting
closer and closer to the door which led into the living-
room. She heard her father mutter something, then
another voice say quite loudly: 'Well, that's the message. I
can only repeat what he told me.'

'But I told you—'

'Look. I'm not comfortable doing this. I don't like it. Have
you any idea how few convicted criminals admit their
guilt? To hear them talk in there, it's not a case of
miscarriages of justice. We're talking abortions. Nine times
out of ten, ninety-nine times out of a hundred, nine
hundred and ninety-nine times out of a thousand—'

'You've made your point.'

'—I don't believe them. But Jim Carroll is a good man.
I'm convinced of that. He convinced me.'

'So now you think you're Lord Longford,' her father
said.

Angela had never heard her father talk like this before.
It was the way kids talked in the playground at school –
silly and sneering. But then she also thought that the other
man sounded rather false as well. Jim Carroll – she
remembered him from years back when she had been quite
small. A big square man, quite quiet, quite funny. He had
done that trick with his thumb, holding his hands flat-

backed towards her and making it look as if one of his thumbs were stretching. It had amused her but her father had gone and ruined it by showing her how it was done. Jim Carroll had always been with his father. That was it, he was Dad's boss. Then he stopped coming round, and that was that.

There was a pause, the creak of chairs, the rustle of trousers.

'Doing well for yourself as a consultant these days?'

'As well as any other days.'

'Well, I've said my piece. I'll be off.'

Angela heard the front door open, turned the radio back on, then went and looked out of the window. A grey-haired man in an anorak got into the Princess. He had a battered, dull-skinned face. He looked as if he were on the point of saying something to her father, even to the extent of winding down the window. Then he shook his head and drove off.

She walked into the living-room. Her father, with his back to her, must have picked up the phone as soon as the other man had left.

'Yes: Chief Superintendent William Fairley. Oh. No. No message. Wait a minute. Tell him Brian White called for him but I'll try and reach him tomorrow.'

It was odd watching people when they didn't know you were looking at them, she thought. They become different – younger, somehow. She knew her father liked to pretend to be stricter than he really was.

'Oh, you back?' Her father turned and saw her.

'Mm. Who was that?'

'What, on the phone?'

'No, I saw someone driving away in an old car.'

'Oh, just some joker asking me about work.'

Angela glanced at the kitchen clock. She'd missed a good

twenty minutes of *EastEnders*, but then it didn't make much difference if you missed twenty minutes or twenty episodes. Nothing ever happened. Nothing ever changed.

'I thought it was darts on Thursdays, anyway.'

'That was yesterday.'

'But you were in last night.'

'It was cancelled,' her father said. *He stayed in to meet that man*, Angela thought, both impressed and rather frightened by her ability to see through words to what people were really thinking.

'Oh. Have I time to do some homework, then?'

'Plenty, depending on when your mother gets home.'

The phone rang. He jumped on it. From what Angela could gather her mother had been showing someone a house quite late but was through now and would be back in half an hour. Half an hour would give her time to get through her homework with any luck. She left with her father shouting down the phone about women estate agents always having to work in pairs.

The Whites' house was an old stone labourer's cottage. It had been extended by the previous owners and again by the Whites when they first moved in. The kitchen and living-room of the original cottage had been knocked through to make a large living- and dining-room and a two-storey wing added at a right angle. This housed the kitchen on the ground floor and Angela's bedroom above it.

The floors were connected by an open staircase that led up the side of the living-room. As she walked through she noticed that her father had been looking at his old photographs again. The box was on the battered old dining-room table and the big group picture that usually lived on the bookshelf next to the West Midlands soccer championship trophy was lying by it, face downwards.

The photograph had always fascinated her and she knew all the faces in it intimately. There had been a time when she could never tell which one was her father. Next she had been shocked that he could ever have looked that young. Now she saw the greaser haircuts that must have only just been inside the regulations and wondered how anyone could ever have trusted such a rough-looking mob. Your friendly neighbourhood bobby. They all looked thin in the way that people in old photographs sometimes did. Perhaps they were thin. Perhaps people had been poorer then.

She rifled through the pictures in the box, past her parents' wedding, past far too many of her as a baby, then came to one she had not seen before: a picture of her father with two other men. They were all dressed in holiday gear, very flash with odd, old-fashioned sunglasses, signet rings, and terrible shirts. On the back was written 'Blackpool, 1959. Brian White, Bill Fairley, Jim Carroll'.

Bill Fairley, Uncle Bill, was her father's oldest (only) friend. Good old Bill Fairley, he called him. Trust old Bill Fairley not to forget a mate.

Her mother liked him too, and Bill Fairley made a fuss of Angela in a sort of flirty way that her father did not mind at all. In fact he seemed rather flattered by it.

Angela liked Bill even though he was a bit flash. She liked him because he never seemed worried by money, never let anything worry him, and always gave the impression, when he talked to you, that you were the most important thing in the world. Of course you knew you were not – he had not got to be Chief Superintendent, on the fast track to Chief Constable, by being nice to his friends' children – but as her mother always said: Who cares when it's fun?

She put the photograph down and peeked into a red

cardboard folder. A sheaf of photocopied papers, stapled together in the corner. Take them out and have a look? She got no further than reading the first page.

Interview 1: James Carroll.

Then her father moved suddenly in the kitchen. She shoved the papers back in the folder and closed it neatly.

'Homework done, lovey? Everything all right? Oh, I feel I hardly ever get to see you these days. I miss you.' Her mother turned from the kitchen sink and the washing up and gave Angela a soapy hug.

'Is Dad worried about something?' Angela asked. Her mother went back to the sink.

'Oh, he's upset today because he was called out to a job and the price they offered was so low he would have lost money on it.'

'He thinks what you're doing is dangerous, doesn't he?'

'Now Angela—'

'Mum, I just want to know. You treat me like a kid. If I don't know what's going on—'

'Oh believe you me, you don't want to know what's going on. Enjoy being young, lovey. And you know that you get – easily upset. I don't want to bring you up thinking that there's a maniac behind—'

'If you don't tell me things, I'm going to think it anyway.'

'Well, we just want you to be happy, that's all.'

Angela polished a glass and looked at her mother through it. It stretched her neck out and made her body float. She put it down quickly. 'Why did Dad retire from the police?'

'He thought he'd enjoy himself more as a security consultant.'

'What's a recession?'

'Questions, questions, questions.'

'I have a naturally enquiring mind,' Angela said.

Her mother laughed and blew soap suds at her. 'You are getting too big for your boots – and too tall for that skirt. The rate you're growing!'

'Minis are back in. Lucky for you. Can I go and see Melanie, please?'

'All right. Half an hour only. I want to see you before you go to bed.'

'Oh, why?'

'Because you're growing up fast and I want to talk to you. And we're out tomorrow night.'

'I know. See you.'

She hung up her drying-up cloth and ran out.

Melanie was Angela's best friend and nearest neighbour in the village. She went to a private day school in Witherly.

'She's upstairs,' said Mrs Frobisher who was reading in their sitting room. Angela trotted up to Melanie's room, feet sinking into the heavy beige carpet that lagged the floors, corridors and staircase of their old farmhouse.

Melanie's room was a startling contrast. She lived for pink. She had a pink counterpane, pink walls, pink school files, pink soft toys on the bed (mostly pigs), and a pink lightshade. When Angela walked in she was lying on the floor, head propped up in her hands.

'Listen to this,' she said. 'Tom's mother asks him to go to the greengrocers and buy two pounds of pears and three pounds of apples. On the way back he's to drop the pears off at his grandmother's house and she will pay him for them. But when he gets there he finds that he's forgotten what the price of the apples and pears was, though he remembers he's paid £1.20 for them.

'"Don't worry," says his grandmother. "Last week I was

shopping with your sister Ruth and we spent £1.03 on one pound of apples and three pounds of pears. Does that help you?"

'Question: How much money does Tom's grandmother owe him and how did he find out?'

Melanie frowned. 'Do you think it's one of those lateral thinking questions when Tom just goes back to the shop and asks the greengrocer?'

'No. It's variables. Simultaneous equations,' Angela said.

Melanie looked blank. 'But you still can't work it out. I thought it all through. I mean if you don't know either of them.'

'You can. Look. You do it like this. You just multiply the bottom one by three, and that makes the apples the same. Then you subtract this from that.' Angela went through the calculation.

'Wow!' said Melanie. 'It's like magic, sort of. I mean it's done but you don't know how. You're a genius!'

'It's probably wrong,' Angela said quickly.

'Oh, I bet it's right.'

'I like working things out.'

'I don't,' Melanie said. 'I wasn't meant to be a mathematician. I was born to dance.'

She leapt to her feet, put a pencil between her teeth and tangoed across the floor with Angela in her arms.

'You gotta relax baby if I'm gonna sweep you to paradise and back. That's my Humphrey Bogart voice, incidentally. He's brill.' She pulled her T-shirt down tight. 'Look – my tits have grown again. I hope they never get as big as Mum's. She says I'm sex-obsessed. Hey baby, what's wrong?'

Angela felt as if she were going to be sick. She sat down suddenly on the edge of the bed. The pink room swam around her. She was shivering with the cold of the moors;

the cold had seeped right into her and was wrapping itself around her bones, bringing with it a regurgitation of night and terror.

'I just gave myself a fright this evening, coming back from the bus stop.'

'You're mad to do that. I never would. They'd never let me.'

'I don't think there's ever anything, it's just if you think there is—'

'Your dad should pick you up from school.'

'He hates doing it.'

'Why? Has he told you?'

'I can tell. He thinks it's what mums do.'

Melanie shrugged. 'Sexist pig,' she said decisively. 'Anyway Mummy always says that the older you are, the more frightened you get.'

'Why?'

'Because you know more, I suppose.'

'Oh no.' Angela thought that sounded awful. 'I can't tell my parents because if I do they'll just tell me I'm highly strung.'

'Did you see something?' Melanie asked. 'I mean really see something?'

'I think so.'

'Like a what? Like a man?'

'No, nothing like a man. More like a girl. Except it was floating.'

'Wow! We could sell it to the papers.'

Angela thought back to what Melanie had said earlier. It worried her. You were supposed to feel less frightened as you got older, weren't you? Melanie sat down on the bed beside Angela and patted her lap. 'Sorry Piglet,' she said. 'Come to Roo.'

Angela made a face. With Melanie you sometimes felt

like a machine that she used to give her hormones a work-
out. 'I know,' she said. 'You can help me. I've got to come
up with an idea for a crappy history project by tomorrow.
I don't know what to do.'

'History? What – you've got to do a folder and things?'

'That's it. They like pictures and maps.'

'Don't I know it.'

'I mean it would be nice to choose something simple and
obvious. Like – I don't know.'

They looked around for inspiration, then out of the
window. Cragside House was a black cut-out against the
night sky. A shape without stars.

'Hey!' Melanie said. 'That's it!'

'What?'

'Do that.'

'What?'

'That – Crag House. It's so big it's bound to have been
lived in by someone rich and famous. Dad was talking
about it the other day. Apparently it was empty when they
moved in and that was an age ago.'

'Yes, but—'

'It's probably not lived-in because it's haunted. It'll be
fantastic.'

'It's riddled with dry rot,' Angela said dubiously. 'I heard
Mum say. I think they were trying to flog it to a Dutch
businessman.'

'And your mother'll have a set of keys. I bet you
anything you want in the whole world. Come on.'

Melanie's eyes were alight. Angela had seen that look
before. She would have forgotten all about it by tomorrow.

There was a knock on the door.

'Hello you and hello you,' said Mr Frobisher. He smiled at
them. 'My my. It looks like a Shanghai love-nest in here. That
was your mother on the phone, piglet. 'Fraid she wants you

home. Says she's tired and going to bed. And bed for you in
twenty minutes,' he added, looking at Melanie.

'Da-ad.'

'Yes, sorry old thing.'

'Night then.'

'Night.'

Angela walked down with Mr Frobisher, leaving Melanie
pouting.

At the front door, Angela paused. The coldness and
darkness joined and seemed to swim around her like bitter
water. Anything could be out there. Anything. She listened
and heard night noises. A bird flapped its wings in a tree.

'Mr Frobisher?'

'Hmmmm?'

'I'm sorry. You couldn't just see me to the road, could
you? I'm sorry, I'm just a bit—'

'Why yes. Yes of course.' Was it her imagination, or did
he glance quickly into the sitting-room where his wife was
sitting?

He too seemed to think it important that Angela link
arms with him. Different from a grown-up holding hands
with a child somehow . . . somehow.

'Cold night,' he said at the end of the drive. She pulled
her arm from his. 'Okay.' He managed to make her seem
rather rude for doing it. 'I say, look at the stars.'

Out of politeness she said: 'There's Orion,' and pointed.
But when she looked back down, Mr Frobisher was looking
at her, not the constellation. She ran the twenty yards back
to her house, with the cold air making a long white plume
of her breath behind her.

Bill Fairley's black shining car was standing outside their
house when she got back, its windows and roof dusted with
frost.

She opened the kitchen door quietly, meaning to slip past them, but her father was in the kitchen, getting a couple of cans of Websters out of the larder.

'Angie, come and say hello to Bill. He was asking after you.'

Bill Fairley was sitting in the big armchair.

'Angie baby,' he said. 'How's my girl?'

'Oh fine.'

'Still swimming?'

'I'm in the team. I had practice tonight.'

'Whoops, here we go,' said Angela's father.

He pointed the remote control at the television. The sound came up.

'—on this bleak, lonely, wind-swept corner of this desolate moor, the police pursue their gruesome task—'

Angela moved round to Bill Fairley's side so she could see the screen. He patted the arm of his chair for her to sit on, then put a comfortable arm around her waist.

'Chief Superintendent William Fairley, heading up the investigation—'

And there he was in a dark coat, the wind ruffling his hair. In the background a shelter made of bright blue plastic, wind-torn clouds, the moor. A microphone was waved around his face.

'Yes, I have decided to take personal charge of the investigation, and no,' an easy, slightly rueful smile, 'no I am afraid that I can't comment on this discovery in connection with any other crime committed in these parts.'

Cut back to a studio.

'Damn right,' Angela's father said. 'Well said Bill.'

'It's ever since the Silence of the bloody Lambs. All they want to talk about is serial killers. Oi you,' he squeezed Angela's hand. 'You don't want to listen to this talk.'

'What's it like being on telly, Uncle Bill?'

'Like being on radio,' William Fairley said. 'But with pictures.'

'Be off with you William Fairley. And you – off to bed,' her mother said.

Angela trudged up the stairs. She paused at the top and looked down into the room. Her father was slumped in his chair, a beer can perched on his little pot-belly. She thought he looked terrible compared to Uncle Bill. Her mother caught her staring. 'You,' she said. 'Bed.'

Angela

She glanced up. The voice had sounded far away. She thought it had come from the other side of the window as if it had been blocked by glass.

Angela

Far away, but clear. She looked at the grown-ups. Her father smiling emptily, her mother looking pleased but nervous, as she always did when Bill came round. Bill looking as if he were interested in everything.

Angela

She looked up, half-expecting to see Melanie's face on the other side of the window. But it hadn't been Melanie's voice. None of the grown-ups had spoken or moved. The voice might have come from inside her head. After swimming, sometimes her ears did funny things.

'Angela, didn't your mother say bed?' her father asked.

'Everything all right, Angela?' Bill said.

'Sorry. I thought I heard someone outside.'

'On a night like this? I'm sorry for them. It's cold out there.'

Cold out here

It was like Bill's voice, but an echo.

'Angela, you've walked mud into the carpet,' her father said suddenly. 'Now honestly. Can't you wipe your feet?'

Angela looked at the carpet. There were a few traces of mud on it by the door.

'It wasn't—'

'Brian, she's meant to be going to bed,' her mother said.

Suddenly Angela realized that if it was not her who had brought the mud in, it was Bill, and it would be embarrassing for him to have to admit that he had walked mud into the room, and embarrassing for her father too.

She ran downstairs, ignoring her mother's protests, fetched a dustpan and brush from the kitchen and started flicking the mud from the carpet up into the pan. It was an odd, reddish clay but seeing as the carpet was brown, it didn't really show.

'Bed time now, my girl,' her father said.

'I should be off too,' Bill said, pushing himself up.

'Finish your beer man,' her father said.

Angela waved to them as she ran upstairs. She saw Bill take a long swig from the can.

'Brian,' he said in a voice that suggested he had said it many times before, 'I'm running late, but there's honestly nothing to worry about.'

Her mother looked brightly from man to man as if she did not understand what they were saying.

Angela's bedroom was big and oblong. The white melamine bed with its bright red duvet was pushed against the far wall. There was a desk against the inside wall, and a cheap music centre on a hardboard stand beside it. On the floor, underneath the radiator, were a couple of bean bags.

She pressed her nose against the cold glass. Moisture beaded on it instantly. There were condensation runs on the wooden window-frame. The light in the room made the darkness opaque even though it was clear out there. Cold always meant clear, and clear always meant cold.

Cold out here. Cold out there. Bill had said cold out there and she had heard the echo: *cold out here.*

Cold but not clear. She drew the curtains, pressed her hands against the radiator until the heat began to hurt, then got ready for bed.

CHAPTER NINETEEN

er parents both overslept and she was the first down the next morning. She felt light-headed and heavy-bodied and had a dim but very big memory of a nightmare, that lingered faintly in her mind like a stale, cheese-sweaty smell.

What was it? A chase? Grass – outside somewhere – and blue sky, then darkness. Somewhere dark ... no, that was not quite the important thing. Somewhere cold. That wasn't quite it. The cold place. The cold room. The memory slipped irritatingly away from her.

It was early-morning cold in the kitchen. She went to the window and rubbed a clear patch in the frost that blurred the glass in sharp, surprising patterns, holding herself against the radiator that was just warming up. Outside it was half-way between morning and night. Away to the west the sky was dark blue over the plain, growing lighter as it swept up and over. Over the moors it was the finest oyster pink.

She filled the kettle, turned on the radio and began to lay the table for breakfast.

'Another blow for the region's economy as Loveyard's lays off another forty workers from their main mill—'

Lay for two or three? Two. Dad was bound to be late

down if he didn't have anything to do today.

Cornflakes, sugar above in the cupboard. Bowls, spoons
underneath. Side plates for toast? Flora and Golden Shred?
Homework. Have I done my homework? Yes. Where is it?
In the bedroom.

'This latest murder victim seems to be fitting into a grisly
pattern—' the radio said.

Swimming things in airing cupboard: costume, towel,
goggles.

'—possibility that we have a serial killer—'

Cornflakes or Weetabix? Cornflakes. Splosh on the milk.
Lots of sugar. Crunch crunch crunch. *Cereal killer*, she
thought and returned to the radio.

Just my imagination, running away with me . . .

'Oh darling, you've got yourself up and laid the table.
You are good.'

Her mother appeared in the doorway, looking sleepy and
smiling. She went to her bag, and started rummaging
around in it for something, taking the big clump of keys out
at the same time.

Keys to the door. Cragside House. She thought about
Melanie's idea from the night before. She could take
pictures of it, maybe scrape together some old prints of the
village. If she could get inside and see how much had
changed over the years . . .

Her mother kept more keys in her desk underneath the
window in the living-room.

'Now there was something I had to tell you – Oh yes.
About this evening.'

'You're out, that's all right. I'll go over to Melanie's or
something.'

'Will you pet? Are you sure? I don't like to think that –
Oh never mind. It's better than you being on your own.
You are all right?'

Angela pushed her cornflakes around.

'Fine.'

'It's just that we don't get the chance to talk so much these days. Everything seems such a palaver when you live out here.'

'It's not a problem, Mum. I'm fine. I've been on my own before. I don't know why you worry.'

'It's just—'

'I know, I know. You never seem to get a chance to see me. It's all right. I'll survive.'

She stood behind her mother and gave her a hug. Her mother squeezed her wrist and looked up at her.

'I know you will.'

Her mother wandered out again. She heard the steps creak and her shout impatiently: 'Brian come on wake up!' then walk on into the bedroom.

Angela nipped into the sitting-room. In the second drawer from the bottom, smelling of ink and paper, she found four bunches of keys. They were for Vacant Possession houses in the neighbourhood, kept here to save her mother the trouble of having to drive down into the town to pick up keys from the office.

'Cragside House' was written in ink on a little disc of cardboard. She put the keys in her pocket, just as she heard her father stomp from the bedroom to the bathroom. Then:

'Has anyone seen my dratted signet ring?'

Same as usual. It was always by the bed or on the ledge above the sink.

'I'm off, bye!' Angela called and left the house for school. There was an early morning bus that passed through the village. Miss that and she would have to get a lift from her mother, and it seemed that all she wanted to do these days was to tell Angela how much she had changed.

*

It was odd walking into the empty house, after school. It made her feel that there were all sorts of things that she could do, like go through the jewellery and try on bras and things, but she knew from past experience that they were never as much fun as they should be. She looked outside. It was afternoon light. Melanie would be back in ten minutes or so and then maybe she could persuade her to have a look round the big house with her.

But Melanie was reluctant, which was typical. 'Let's watch a video instead,' she suggested. 'We can watch *Pretty Woman* for the seven millionth time or *Basic Instinct*. Then afterwards we can pretend we're mad and we're lesbians.' She knelt on the bed, arched her back and shook her head. 'Do you think they really do it?'

'What? Stab people with ice-picks?'

'Oh, right yeah. No, stupid. I mean *it*. Sex and things.'

'Things. Definitely,' Angela said, trying to imagine. 'Lots and lots of things.'

Angela threw a pillow at her and stood up. 'Come on. We're going to see that house,' she said. 'And if you're not coming, I'll go on my own.'

'Oh no you won't,' Melanie said. 'But I'll come anyway.'

The door set into the high stone wall did not creak or groan; they did not have to push back last year's autumn leaves with it. The latch was well-oiled, the door opened to a gentle push.

'I expect Mum keeps it like that to try and impress people looking round,' Angela said.

The high wall went all the way around the house, except right at the back where a rocky outcrop formed a natural barrier. The ground sloped. To the right it swept upwards to the high moors. To the left it fell away. Set into the ground where it began to rise was a small, low building that seemed to be half-buried. Stone steps cut down through the grass. The top of the door was only two foot or so above ground level.

Around the house lay lawns and flower-beds which had run completely wild. The grass lay in great, thick matted swathes; the beds were crowded with tall brown weeds, seed heads rustling in the gentle breeze. There were rose bushes, hollyhocks, shrubs, banks of hissing iris leaves. A pergola completely smothered by a stringy fog of honey-suckle.

The girls' shadows stretched away from them on the wet grass.

'Anyone at home?' said Melanie.

The door was set in the middle of the symmetrical front. On either side were three high sash windows, blinded by the shutters that were kept shut to discourage vandals. There was a row of six windows on the floor above, with the middle one filled in, above it another layer of smaller windows, then a sort of low parapet and what looked like dormer windows in the roof.

By the side of the door the bell-pull was set in a scalloped saucer. Melanie pulled it. A second later there was a deep clanging inside the house.

'Sorry,' she said. 'Just letting them know we're here.'

Angela nodded. Her first thought was that they didn't want to wake anything up.

The front door was locked by a Yale and a Chubb. It was wide, and stuck at the bottom where the frame had swollen. Angela kicked and pushed it with her foot. It shuddered open.

The hall was very dark. The only light came from a window half-way up the stairs. The walls were panelled in dark wood, the floor was herring-bone parquet, swollen by damp and uneven underfoot. Leaves had crept in and rustled under their feet. Melanie closed the door.

'What do you think?' she whispered.

'Don't start whispering or we'll never stop,' Angela whispered back. They giggled quickly. Angela pushed open a door on her right and stood in the doorway. Melanie looked over her shoulder and grunted dismissively.

Light fell through the gaps in the shutters on to a patterned wooden floor. The room was completely empty. No dim white mounds of dust-sheeted furniture. No ancestral portraits with glaring red eyes. Nothing in fact. Dullsville. Angela felt her excitement begin to drain away. Melanie had wandered on. She paused at the bottom of the stairs, then turned into a room off to the right. Angela followed. It was lighter in here, thanks to frosted glass panels in the door. A kitchen, disappointingly modern with black and white lino on the floor and an electric cooker.

'The last person who lived here was a football manager, or something,' Angela said. 'He ran off with the house-keeper. It was years ago.'

'Very historical.' Melanie rolled her eyes and looked bored. 'We better go upstairs.'

The upstairs landing was wide and gave on to a short corridor on either side. The girls no longer left shadows; the sun was far below them. A rose petal had blown in from somewhere and skidded across the floor in the draught. At one end of the hall was a small table with dusty estate-agent particulars on it. The floorboards seemed to bend under their feet. They stood still. Silence fell around them in prickly folds. Melanie walked down the hall; Angela pushed open the door in front of her.

Light burnished her face. The sun was slipping behind a band of slate grey clouds. She moved through the doorway into a great bedroom. In front of her was a window; on her right a huge, mahogany four-poster bed, its mattress propped up beside it. There was a cheap wash-basin plumbed into the wall. Mirror tiles at wonky angles. Mould staining the wall next to the U-bend.

Angela was drawn to the window which stared over the garden, the wall and the moor. Down on the plain the town smoked and glittered in the dusk.

A movement in the garden. Angela's heart leapt. She moved to the window, aware suddenly that the room smelt unwholesome. Riddled with dry rot. What did it mean? Ivy had broken through the rotten window-frame and a long, muscular arm had begun to creep across the wall.

Angela felt the chill of outside on her bare knees. She strained her eyes.

The garden was dark. There was a figure against the wall; slim, small, standing very straight, facing her and looking up.

Tricked by reason, she thought it must be Melanie. She raised a hand, then realized that it could not be. She could not have raced down there to stand so still in the shadow of the wall. Her heart leapt into her mouth and she stepped to one side, out of sight, her hand still raised in greeting.

She turned to the door. It had swung shut silently behind her. Her breast hollowed. Her heart fluttered.

'Melanie,' she hissed, trying to peer around the corner of the window and keep an eye on the door at the same time.

No answer.

The room was darker. She saw a band of light slip up the wall into the shadows of the cornice. The bed loomed.

'Melanie.' More urgently. She hung in time, unwilling to move.

Angela

The word fell into the air like a leaf dropping on to still, dark water.

It had come from behind her. The hair on the back of her neck crawled. She could feel the window now, the glass, the emptiness behind her.

'Melanie.' Her voice was a thin bleat. Somewhere a floorboard creaked.

[*Angela*]

'Melanie!'

Terror grabbed her. Jerked her legs on a puppet string of fear. Across the floor. Hand on door, she yanked it open, felt it push towards her, staggered backwards, saw a black shape fall on to her.

'Angela!'

Light washed her face, blinding her.

'Angela White! You will explain yourself young lady!'

Her mother staggered back, smacked Angela's hand from her cuff which she had grabbed in her terror.

Angela opened and closed her mouth. She could not speak.

'Angela, I will not have you coming in here! Now you get up off this floor this instant! Yes, and you too Melanie Frobisher – I saw you, I know you're there! Come out. Come out young lady!'

Melanie stepped into the room, looking defiant. Angela felt herself deflate. Had it been her mother out there in the garden?

No. It could not have been.

'Now you two girls, you come with me now. You come with me, out of this house and we go straight home. Yes. Straight home this instant. To think – oh look!'

The torchlight wavered across the floor and stopped on

the bundle of keys, lying where Angela had dropped them.
'Now. Out!'

'And thieving as well,' her mother said.

'I wasn't thieving.'

They were in the kitchen. The fluorescent lights were welcome for once.

'Well, if I had taken something from my mother, something my mother had been entrusted to keep safely, it would have been called thieving. And I would have been sent to bed without supper.'

'Spare me,' Angela said. 'Anyway,' she said, feeling subtle, 'I thought you and Daddy were out tonight.'

'You thought, you thought, well it just shows that perhaps we can't go out, thinking you're grown-up enough to be left.'

'Perhaps you shouldn't have left me then,' Angela said. The television that her father had turned up roared with laughter.

Her mother sat down suddenly, and buried her face in her hands. Angela who had been trying to play on her mother's guilt, suddenly felt stricken by it.

'I try,' her mother said. 'I try. I work, there's a recession, I try and bring you up, I try and – I try to do everything. There's your father—'

She looked at Angela. Her face was lined and the tears glistened in the wrinkles.

'Oh, I don't know. I just don't.'

'I'm sorry,' Angela said.

'Please promise me, darling, please promise not to go into that place. It's dangerous, honestly. It was getting so dark and if it hadn't been for Janey and Tim pulling out, well, I dread to think.'

'I think, I think I saw someone else in the garden,' Angela said.

Her mother walked to the freezer and pulled out three chicken tikkas. 'Just one of the village children, I expect. There isn't much we can do about it. I think they'd be doing everyone a favour if they burned the place down. But do not go into that house ever again. Understand? I know it was your history project, but honestly you had no right just to take matters on like that. I'm sorry darling, but I can't allow it. Understand?'

'I understand.'

'Promise?'

'Promise.'

'Then give me a hug.'

CHAPTER TWENTY

W et Saturday. Boring, boring telly. Father watching Rugby League with his four-pack of Websters, cheering or groaning when freakish men with huge bottoms and tiny shorts grabbed each other or fell over in the mud, seeming to drown in the armchair in between his shouts. Mother grumbling that he looked like a cliché – whatever that meant – and marching like a martyred sergeant major through the house with armfuls of dirty washing, clean wet washing, washing from the dryer, washing that needed ironing, things that shouldn't have gone into the wash, shouting at Angela to help, Angela guessing wildly and shouting back that she didn't want to be a cliché, mother yelling incoherently at Angela and almost bursting into tears. Angela putting on the dark blue cagoule that always provoked Melanie into sticking two fingers down her throat, and walking out into the rain.

The history project nagged her. Mr Appleby was threatening to take all the projects in 'just to see how you are all getting on'. Panic in the streets. Sickness in the stomach. Thickness in the throat. She was convinced that she was going to fail; that she could do nothing, that she would be ridiculed in front of the entire school. At assembly. The

head teacher saying: 'And now Mr Appleyard has something to say,' and Mr Appleyard standing up and saying:
'She really is a moron, and you all know who I mean'; and
the entire school shouting: 'ANGELA WHITE'.

She stood in the storm porch and fought back the tears.
It was starting again: the terror and the teasing. They
always seemed to go together. First the terror, being chased
down the road by a ghost, then seeing something in the
garden, then hearing the voice. Then the teasing. The
sneers. The pinching. The whispers. The—

'No.'

She surprised herself by speaking. The teasing had not
started. She was making that up. Mr Appleyard was all
right. No one had teased her for ages. She swam now. She
was in the team. She acted. It was fine. As for the terror –
she had just scared herself on the road, imagining monsters, filling her mind with demons. The faster you ran, the
stronger the fear; the stronger the fear, the faster you ran.
She knew all about that lurching, swooping downward
cycle of terror, but understanding it like that made her feel
courageous.

Confidence washed through her.

The figure in the garden? Just one of the kids from the
village, probably as scared as you were, dummy.

The voice? Melanie's voice, muffled by walls. Her
mother's voice, confusing her because it was unexpected.

Fine. The rain had just stopped. Blue sky was spreading
over the moor, pushing the dark clouds away. There was
a rainbow over the town.

Feeling happy again, she stuck her head into the kitchen
and asked her mother if she wanted any help.

Later, they were all sitting around the kitchen table. Teapot
on a trivet under a tabby cat cosy, chocolate fingers on a

plate in the middle. Steam on the windows. A real family tea.

'Do you know if anyone's lived in the village a long time?' Angela asked.

'What's this about?' her mother said.

'I'm still trying to find a history project.'

'Oh, heritage stuff and all that,' her mother said vaguely. Her father unwrapped his hands from his mug and suggested they go and have a look at the prints in the pub, but her mother said she was not having her thirteen-year-old daughter go into a public bar on a Saturday afternoon. Her father said, rather sulkily, that if you asked him, nobody in the village had lived there more than a few years; Edgerton was a dormitory village. When Angela asked him what a dormitory village was, he said it meant that the whole bloody village was asleep.

'That's not what it means, pet,' her mother said, looking coldly at her husband, 'it means that people work in the town and come back here to sleep. Honestly Brian. How is the girl going to learn anything?'

'It was a JOKE!'

'But the houses are old, aren't they?' Angela asked.

'Well, some are, yes,' her mother appeared to think, then added quickly: 'Now you're not thinking about Cragside again, are you?'

'No. I promised, didn't I? Anyway, I don't see why just because somewhere's big and empty, it's automatically interesting. I should just take any old house and see who lived in it.'

'That's nice,' her mother said. 'Why not get some fresh air now the weather's looking up? But mind you don't go bothering people. You're not a little girl any more.'

Angela could not quite see the connection but let it pass.

*

The land rose at their end of the village and she could look down over the houses, spread out messily along the side of the road as if they had been dropped there by someone who did not really care. At the other end of the village, beyond the church, stood the new close of modern box-like houses, built in a tidy circle around a tarmac loop. That was different, she thought. That was how they did things these days. Compare that to the Frobishers' house, which was all on different levels and had funny old corners, and you saw the contrast.

Lights went on in the house across the road. She could see the yuppies, as her father called them, moving around in the brand new kitchen which her mother envied. They had bought the house a year ago from a friendly couple whom her father had called the hippies. Angela had never been able to work out whether the hippies were young or old. They had tried to run the place as a vegetarian restaurant, the Old Forge they called it, but nobody ever ate there and they had been forced to sell up. Angela had rather liked them and had always hoped that she could be a waitress in the holidays and make some extra money.

The old forge. The old farmhouse.

'Ting,' she said. Of course. All those names were clues to the past. The old forge had actually once been a forge with horses having their shoes made there, a chimney belching out black smoke, a big man with a bright red face and a leather apron pounding away at an anvil. The Frobishers' farmhouse had once actually been a farmhouse with cows and horses where Melanie's parents now kept their Range Rover and the Suzuki jeep that Melanie had been promised on her eighteenth birthday.

But what did that show? First that there was no longer any need for a blacksmith and his forge. Why? Because the farmers no longer needed horseshoes and things, and anyway, if you needed anything metal you would go and buy it in a shop and find that it had been made in a factory. On top of that the farmers had gone because the Frobishers lived in their house, so that must say something too.

All the lights were on inside the old forge and she could see the sitting-room. It was very empty with a pale polished wooden floor and a black hi-fi on a black metal stand. That was where the hippies had stuck a few forlorn looking tables, garden flowers in jam jars, rickety chairs.

A light came on above the yuppies' back door and a moment later Mrs Yuppie appeared carrying a miniature vacuum cleaner. The light was automatic, her father had told her bleakly one evening, adding that he could have sold them one just the same except he couldn't compete with the mail order companies. The yuppies seemed to have a lot of gadgets like that. Encouraged by the sight of someone doing something as ordinary as cleaning out their car, Angela crossed the road.

Mrs Yuppie was dusting the dashboard of her smooth black car and watched Angela approach, her face darkened by the windscreen. She stuck her head out of the car.

'Hello,' she said. 'Who are—?'

'I'm doing a history project,' Angela said. 'I wondered if I could ask you about your house. I just live across the road.'

'I see. Well ...' The woman looked rather blank. 'I suppose it is quite old, this house, but we haven't discovered anything about it, I'm afraid.'

'Do you know which bit did what, I mean when it was a forge?'

The woman shrugged. 'Didn't know there was anything in it really.'

She was pretty, Angela thought. Quite made-up. Tight jeans and stockinged feet in little black shoes.

'Look around outside if you like,' she added. Her husband stuck his head out of the door.

'It's the little girl from across the way. She's doing a history project. Wants to look around.'

'History eh?' the man said. He went back inside and looked at her through the window. Angela looked self-consciously at the building, then wandered off round the corner.

There was nothing to see. At the back of the house they had knocked a huge hole in the wall and had installed sliding glass doors – a security risk (oh shut up Daddy). There was a raw scab of red earth in front of them where the ground had been levelled for a patio and stacked by it was a huge mound of blackened stones. It took her a bit of time to realize that the stones had once been the chimney. Now she could see a scar running under the whitewash all the way up the wall.

She felt a quick spurt of sadness, followed by anger. What right had they to do that? Nobody owned the past – so how could they change it so carelessly? Horrid, horrid people.

She turned away.

The forge was surrounded by a small, neglected garden, bounded on all sides by a low bank of earth which was probably a collapsed dry-stone wall. The garden sloped down from the house to the moors below the village. On a clear day you would be able to see for miles – what her mother called a good prospect. No, this might even qualify as a delightful or even outstanding prospect. She blinked away a drop of mist that had gathered on an eyelash. It was as if a thin shutter had come down. The air was suddenly darker and she began to feel stupid, as if someone was watching her, judging her. She looked around furtively. The grass was long and wet. There were a few apple trees dotted around. Big deal.

Above the roof of the old forge she could see the top floor

of Cragside House, the windows looking very black. Something made her dislike the idea of walking round the old forge under Cragside's empty windows. She turned back, but then realized that it would mean walking past the woman. Fear of the big house and fear of embarrassment struggled within her. Fear of embarrassment was the stronger impulse and she carried on round the house. An overgrown vegetable garden forced her away from it towards the collapsed wall. There was a short row of outbuildings which jutted out from the forge here, and behind them was a dip in the ground.

In the dip stood a ruined cottage.

It was tiny. The roof had long fallen in and the walls were slowly dissolving under a mass of climbing plants. In all, the whole cottage could not have been much bigger than their kitchen at home. She'd never seen it before because she had never been around the back of the forge and it was well hidden from the road, but even when the roof had been on and the chimney smoking, it must have been nearly invisible. A secret. History. Secret history. Who lived in you, house?

Feeling intrepid she walked slowly down the slope towards it.

The cottage had been more or less square. Rotten door posts stuck up through the ivy from the middle of the wall facing the village. At each end pointed gables rose sharply against the sky, with a chimney set into one of them. The roof must have collapsed under the weight of the foliage. Inside, the plaster and stone work was green and the floor was thick with nettles which marched out of the door and around the house: nettles three, four feet high, like guards. Moss grew in chinks in the walls. The fireplace sprouted brown bracken. The nettles swayed together. The greenery rustled and dripped.

Angela felt a mixture of fear of sadness. Who had lived here? she wondered. Why was this cottage left to fall down? Her boot caught in something. She looked down and saw it was held in a snare of bramble. She bent to untangle herself. No, it wasn't bramble. It was a climbing rose. That wasn't ivy then crawling all over the cottage, it was a gigantic rose. The cottage had been taken over by it. It had crawled all over the building, smothering it, weighing it down, slowly flattening it.

The ruin hunched its shoulders at her. It was so sad, so forlorn that she wanted to leave it, but – Authentic Detail, remember – perhaps she would discover something of interest inside.

Angela

She whipped round anxiously.

An—ge—la

Her mother calling her.

Angela

That voice was not her mother's. She turned slowly back, feeling the same scratch of hair on collar that she had felt in the bedroom of Cragside House. The voice had come from the cottage. This time.

Not again. Not outside. A soft voice. A little voice. A girl's voice, sibilant but with the gentleness of petals, airless. A voice from the roses. The cottage and its thick sprawl of roses trembled.

Angela

Inside and outside now; the voice was all around her. She saw now that the giant rose bush that covered the ruins was dotted with rotting blooms, big ones like artichokes, small, tightly furled buds, blasted and frost browned, nodding in a breeze that came from nowhere.

The cottage seemed to grow. Out of nowhere she heard a strange rhythmic clatter start.

Oh, stay with me, Angela, stay with me.

She turned and ran blindly away from the cottage.

Angela

The voice was following her. Her foot caught again. She stumbled and fell. Thorns dug through her jeans, piercing her knee with the dull sharpness of a needle. The rose bush had spread this far. It lay tangled along the ground, running through the grass. She scrambled to her feet and ran again, her feet sliding on the wet grass.

Angela

Even here she heard the voice. She risked a glance over her shoulder, saw nothing, missed a sudden dip in the ground, twisted and fell heavily, one knee bent under her and thumping hard into her stomach, winding her.

Angela

A voice in her ear, small, soft and rotten. She had landed on a tiny head of blooms, hardly opened, blotched and browned. The soft edges of the petals loosened, curled back

into lips. A tiny mouth, thin and limp and layered, opened
in a rose bud.

Angel—

She yelped and jumped away from it. The ground was
rising now towards the big house. Here, where it stood and
faced out towards the town was a steep cliff of black rock
topped by a wall. She looked up and saw, or thought she
saw, a strange pointed roof, just poking out above the wall.

AngelaAngelaAngelaAngelaAngelaAngelaAngelaAngela

The ground was broken here, dotted with boulders that
lay tumbled at the foot of the cliff. Hide. Hide.
The voice seemed to be coming closer. She forced her
legs to push her up, over boulders. On her left the wall
suddenly dropped in height. She jumped on it, slipped on
the greasy stones, momentum carrying her over. She
tumbled down a sloping rock cliff, dank with ferns and
mosses, dripping with water where a small spring broke
from the moor. Smacked floppily into the ground. Winded
again. She was inside the wall now, away from—
She looked up. A horrid head of tight little buds bobbed
above the wall, dark against the grey sky.
Angela screamed. Picked herself up and belted for the
house, her single instinct to get something, anything
between her and – it.
The back of the house was messier than the front. There
were outbuildings here. A concrete shed. She rattled the
door handle. Locked. A door in the side of the house – the
back door into the kitchen. Glass panels.
By the door was an old, cast-iron boot scraper. She
picked it up, not even noticing its weight, and flung it at the

glass panes. The scraper smashed through the glass and
glazing bars. She put her hand through as quickly as she
dared and felt for a key. Found it. Turned it. Pushed the
door.

It did not open. She sobbed in frustration, kicked it,
thumped it, kicked it again, felt something give at the
bottom, kicked and thumped and pushed, and then suddenly it was open, the frame splitting with a powdery snap.
She closed it behind her in time to see, out of the corner of
her eye, a shape, dreadful and ragged in the twilight,
bouncing, scraping along the ground, arms like tendrils
held out, head so loose. Whimpering, she ran across the
kitchen, slammed the door behind her. Heard it boom
against the frame. Bounce open again. Caught that stiff,
jerky movement through the frosted glass.

She staggered up the stairs, aware for the first time how
tired she was, how her legs were just levers, how they could
not push her up any faster. Her spit was like metal. The
razors were back, rusting under her tongue. She ran down
the corridor, looking for the back stairs.

At the end of the corridor was a narrow door. She pulled
it. Pushed it. Thin steps wound upwards but it was too late
to go back now. Fear had made her an idiot. She was
trapped. The house was narrowing into a funnel. She
dropped on to all fours and scampered up. Light dropped
dimly on her from a dirty skylight. She rounded a corner.

The scale of the house changed. The ceilings had
dropped; the corridors narrowed. Two ancient bathrooms
on her left, the baths set in narrow, wooden cells. The
servants' quarters. The windows were half-blinded by the
parapet. A pigeon exploded into life outside, whacking its
wings to freedom.

Angela panted, tensed. In the hoarse stillness of rasping
breath and pumping heart she felt a terror so extreme that

it was a sickness flooding her in a loose, bitter wave. She screamed. She screamed. Screamed. It seemed to make the terror less, blew some of it from her. She paused, panting. Breathing space.

Join your fear. That was what she had learnt in the nightmare time. Join your fear. Take it on. The thing is coming for you. Go for it instead. Or if not, just face it.

A rustle on the steps. The stench of rotting roses, a rustle, the scratching drag of briars.

She turned to the stairway and began to back very, very slowly down the corridor. The dreadful sound grew louder. *I would rather die than see it again*, Angela thought, *I'll jump over the parapet.*

She turned and opened a door at random. A small bedroom, the ceiling barely clearing her head. Something brushed against her scalp. Instinctively she knocked it away, a white tendril like a cross between a spider's web and a root. She saw now that it hung in ghost clouds over the window, was festooned from the ceiling, had crept along the walls, was under her feet.

She took another step. Felt the room was elastic; the boards were bending and suddenly the floor was powder beneath her and she was falling.

No time to think.

Her arms flew out. She felt them hit the floor on either side of her falling body. The floor held for a second, yielded, then suddenly gave. Her outstretched, grasping fingers touched something almost solid that fluttered like a thin bird in her hand as she fell.

Falling. Landing. Something that gave. It did hurt like hell, but she was lying on her back, half on a mattress covered in rotten wood and plaster, looking at the dust spiral through the hole in the ceiling, framed by torn lathes.

She felt hollow and dazed. Still holding the thing she had clutched she ran from the room, down the stairs and out into the evening.

She now knew what 'riddled with dry rot' meant. The thought made her laugh so much that once she was through the door in the high wall, she collapsed on the wet ground, and started to shake. Nothing followed her.

CHAPTER TWENTY-ONE

Her jacket was ripped. She began to slip it off. Dully she tried to force it but it kept on sticking on something in her hand. She looked down and saw that she was holding a stiff, leather-bound book, secured by a locked flap across the front. It looked for all the world like a Filofax except it was harder and the edge of the paper was marbled. She slipped the book into her pocket and hung the jacket up, then opened the back door as quietly as she could, and began to tiptoe across the floor. Something was under her feet. Mud. The treads of her training shoes were caked in it and she had left dog pallet prints of strange, reddish clay on the carpet tiles. She grimaced and sat down on the floor of the kitchen to tug her shoes off.

Her mother was suddenly standing above her.

'Angela White. What have you been doing?'

Angela said nothing. She looked up. Her mother put her hands on her hips. Angela began to shake, tried to talk but found that her jaw was juddering and her whole face trembling.

'Angela, what is it? Angela? Your clothes are – your face is all scratched, and what's this in your hair? It looks like lumps of plaster.'

Her mother knelt down, sensing now that something was wrong. It was too much.

'I was chased,' Angela said in a tiny voice. 'Something called me and started to chase me. I fell through a ceiling in the house. It was riddled with dry rot. I fell through a ceiling and then I ran out again. It's chased me before. I thought it was my imagination but it's not, really. This isn't dreams. This is REAL!'

Her mother and father carried her upstairs. Her father ran a bath for her, and then took his torch and went out to Cragside House. Angela sat in the warm water, being sponged by her mother, something that had not happened for years. Half-way through, the door bell rang. Her mother went to answer it. When she came back, she said: 'It's the police. Well, it's Uncle Bill.'

Angela looked horrified. 'I can't talk to him! It was a ghost! What do you think I've been saying all this time?'

But her mother had become brisker. 'No more of that, darling. Now just pop out of the bath, I've laid clean clothes out for you, come downstairs and tell Bill what happened.'

'What's all this I hear?' Bill Fairley said. 'Improper use of a boot scraper to effect illegal entry? Assaulting a ceiling? Or to put it another way, GBH on some innocent floorboards that just happened to be lying around?'

Angela made a wry face. 'Hello, Uncle Bill,' she said.

'You can Uncle Bill all you like,' her father said. 'That was some hole you made in the back door. Now it's an honour having a superintendent coming to interview you. Very special treatment.' He looked ugly and proud as he spoke. And a bit shifty.

'Tell me about it, pet,' Bill said, ignoring her father. Angela noticed how clear his face was, how definite the features. His eyes were blue ringed with brown.

She told him how she had crossed the road, and spoken to the yuppies.

('So the husband actually saw you go round the back?'

'Yes, I suppose so, I can't be sure.')

She'd seen the cottage in the dip and gone to have a look. Bill was interested in the kind of voice she had heard: high or low, male or female; and the direction it had come from. Angela could tell that the answers she was giving him were not quite what he wanted to hear.

('It was a sort of breathless voice.'

'Like the person was wheezing or was panting?'

'No, like the person did not breathe.')

Things got even more embarrassing when she came to describe the person. Big or small, child or adult, jacket, trousers, shoes, hair, face, expression?

She had shaken her head. 'It wasn't like that. It was more a thing than a person. One of the roses spoke to me.'

'Oh for goodness sake!' her father exploded.

'Steady on matey,' Bill said. 'The girl's had a terrible shock. There was someone after her, you can tell that by her state. I'll chat to the people across the way, then have a shifty round the grounds. We'll send some lads to give the house the once over, and then do a proper search when it's light.'

He turned to Angela and smiled: 'All right, pet,' he said. 'You're a very brave girl but next time, run home. All right?'

He patted her on the shoulder and got up to leave. Her parents followed him into the kitchen; Angela could hear their muffled voices through the door.

Her mother opened the door. Framed in the doorway she saw Fairley, on the point of leaving, stiffen, look down, before disappearing into the night.

'Well,' her mother said. 'That's that.'

Angela yawned. She was so tired that her head started to sway on her shoulders. She thought that she might be scared but by the time the light was out, she was asleep.

CHAPTER TWENTY-TWO

Her father was on the phone when she got up, ordering sheets of hardboard from a timber merchant. The clock on the sitting-room mantelpiece said five past ten.

Five past ten. It was Monday. She was late for school. Her father winked at her and put the phone down.

'Thought it best to let you lie in. Take the day off, that's what we decided.'

'But it's rehearsal tonight, for the play.'

Her father stood in front of her and put his hands on her shoulders. The gesture made Angela feel awkward. 'You went through a lot yesterday,' he said, looking hard into her eyes. 'I'm taking you down to the hospital this morning for a check-up, X-rays and such, then lunch in town, and back here this afternoon. By that time the police will have had a chance to take a proper shifty around and Bill might want to ask you some more questions. All right, pet?'

'I feel fine.'

'I'm sure you do, but that's the plan for the day. I promised your mother. Now have your breakfast and then get ready for popping into town. We won't be long. We'll have a pizza or something. How about that?'

'Great, Dad.' She shuffled into the kitchen. Come to think of it, she was sore all over.

In the hospital a nice woman doctor with bobbed blonde hair and efficient looking glasses shone a little torch in her eyes and made her look all around. Then she was walked up to another floor for X-rays, and finally asked to strip to her pants and bra and lie on a bed while the doctor felt her limbs in a brisk, disinterested fashion. Angela was glad she had put on her new panties; the doctor's hands were cold and soft as they kneaded and prodded her abdomen, back, shoulders, legs.

'What's this?' the doctor asked.

There was light scoring across the top of Angela's thighs, pink graze marks on the smooth white skin.

'It's a graze. I must have done it when I fell,' Angela said. The doctor pressed down on the fleshy part of her inner thigh, hard.

'Ow!' Angela said.

'Sore there?'

'Yes. No. You hurt me.'

'Is that a bruise?' The doctor pointed to a yellowish purplish mark on her hip.

'Yes.'

'How did you get it?'

Angela said: 'I bruised myself when I fell through the ceiling and when I fell over the wall.'

'And nobody caught you,' the doctor said.

'No,' Angela answered.

The doctor seemed to be making up her mind as to whether Angela was telling the truth or not. Then she pursed her lips and told her to get dressed.

After the hospital they went to The Pizza Place on Green

Street. It was on the ground floor of a big, newly cleaned brick building. Rows and rows of windows marched the length of its three storeys, except on the ground floor where arched windows had been knocked into the brickwork for the shop units that lined the street. Half the shops were empty. Their blank windows held displays advertising other shops or concerts at the Old Exchange concert hall.

Above the main doors was a plaque set into the brickwork: a T with an L curling around it. There was an outer lobby with a plate glass wall at the other end, letting you look into Office World, a place where all lights shine upwards, all seats are black and all plants are at least six feet high. Inside the restaurant, while they were waiting for their food, Angela read some text written in fancy writing, hanging in a picture frame by their table.

> 'Loveyard's Main Mill. This restoration was carried
> out with the help of generous grants from the Local
> District Council. The mill closed down in 1985 and
> the building was saved from dereliction by converting
> it to mixed use offices. It is a fine example of
> early nineteenth century industrial architecture.'

The waitress came with a Coke for Angela and a beer for her father.

'What's a mill, Dad?'

'A factory really. Why?'

'The plaque says this used to be a mill.'

'Well then?'

'What did they make here? It says it was Loveyard's Main Mill.'

'Loveyard's eh? That would be textiles. Weaving and such like.'

Angela felt something stir inside her. Sweat bloomed on

her forehead. She was suddenly very cold, but sweating, and she was seeing everything through the wrong end of a pair of dirty binoculars.

'Don't know what happened to the Loveyards. Big family here they were. All dead now I suppose and the business been run into the ground. Can't compete, that's the trouble.'

Angela felt fine again. The sickness had passed through her, which was just as well because their pizzas arrived and she was starving.

As soon as they got home she went up to her room to rest, but almost as soon as she flopped on to the bed her father came pounding up the stairs.

'Come on, love. You're wanted.'

'No, let her rest.' Bill Fairley's voice.

She sat up, her heart quickening, no longer tired.

'It's all right, Dad. I'll be fine.' She glanced in the mirror on the way out. She looked like a fright mask: face as white as paper, eyes as dark as—

dead girl's tongues

Angela shuddered. She had not meant to think that.

'Well, how's the girl?' Bill said. 'Looking tired. Are you sure you want to go through with this?'

'Of course,' Angela said.

'I mean retrace your steps. It may be important. It may not be. It may jog your memory. You were pretty hazy last night if you remember. Shocked. I do realize. I mean if you'd rather not—'

'No, that's fine,' Angela said quickly. 'I'll just get my jacket and shoes.'

She slipped her jacket on, feeling something heavy bump

against her hip. Her fingers touched the book that she had
put into her pocket the night before. Until now she had
forgotten all about it.

'Your shoes,' Bill Fairley said. 'I'm afraid we had to take
them away to have a look at them. Why not put on the
wellies? Here, you sit there. Come on, give us a foot.'

Having her wellies put on by a superintendent made her
giggle, especially when he looked up and gave her a wink.

'Come on,' he said. 'Let's get this over with. You know
it's very brave of you to do it.'

As soon as they got outside, Angela regretted it. Retrace
her steps. The first step she took meant that she would end
up in the house, falling. Would that – thing – wake up
again?

No

'No what?' Bill said.

'I didn't say anything,' Angela said.

They crossed the road. There were uniformed policemen
standing outside in capes. They all looked curiously at
Angela. Bill was wearing corduroys, green wellies and a
Barbour.

Round the back of the yuppies. Question: Could the man
see you? Answer: I don't know, but I felt someone was
watching, although that was later.

Question: When was that? Answer: Down here, by the
ruined cottage.

The cottage was small, hunched, depressing. Too sad to
be menacing.

Question: So you think someone might have been in
here?

Answer: I don't know.

But as she said it, she knew she was lying. She knew the

voice had come from the roses, and now, seeing them
writhing all over the little cottage, she knew she was going
mad. You couldn't tell people about things like that. If you
did, they teased you.

She heard Bill Fairley order some men to clear all around
the cottage.

'I ran this way,' Angela said, thinking that if she took the
lead, he might not ask her questions.

They followed the route she had taken as closely as she
could remember, along the wall, then up on to the rocks
where the wall grew lower. Angela could not remember
where she had got over exactly so she guessed. Bill Fairley
got over first, jumped down then held his arms out for her.
He took her round the waist and funny things happened in
her body, an emptiness in her stomach, a tiny ache in her
breasts.

'Here?'

'Yes,' she said. He started looking very closely at the
ground, parting the grass, touching the black earth.

'Sure?'

'Yes.'

'Then what?'

'I ran for the house.'

'In a straight line?'

'I think so, yes. When I got near I zigzagged around a bit.
I thought I could hide in a shed. But they were all locked.'

'So you just picked up a thirty pound lump of cast iron
and heaved it through a door?'

Angela could not tell if he was joking or not. She was
worried about the door. She swallowed.

'I'm sorry about that,' she said. 'I'll pay for a new one.'

Bill Fairley put a hand on the back of her neck. It was dry
and warm. 'Pay for it? Goodness me, the door was rotten
as a bad apple. The whole house is. It's a bloody death trap

if you ask me and it's a miracle someone hasn't been hurt
before. In my opinion you've done the community a
service. You've shown what a mess it really is. They'll have
to condemn it.'

They walked to the back door where Angela's father was
driving five-inch nails through a sheet of hardboard, cut to
the size of the door. All the way, Fairley was casting around
on the ground, pressing the soil, looking at it.

'Well,' he said, looking at Brian. 'That's it.'

Angela wondered exactly what 'it' was.

'We better get this young lady home,' Bill said. 'She looks
ready to drop.'

She made herself a mug of hot chocolate and took it up to
her bedroom, then remembered the book she had grabbed.
It was only when she thought about it that it struck her as
odd. A book under the floorboards – didn't that mean
someone must have lost it, or hidden it? More hidden
history. More secrets. She ran downstairs; the men were in
her father's study, talking in low voices. She tiptoed down
the stairs, ran lightly across the living-room to the storm
porch and retrieved the book from her jacket pocket. Half-
way up the stairs her father stuck his head out of his study
door.

'I thought you were resting,' he said.

'I was. Am. I just wanted a book.'

She bit her tongue. Her father looked at the book in her
hands. In the gloom he would not be able to see that it was
leather-bound. He nodded. 'Well you just take it easy. Have
your cocoa. Your mother will be furious with me if she
doesn't like the look of you.'

The book was in better condition than she was. It smelled
a bit but those awful white strands, which her father told

her were the dry rot fungus, had not got into it. The cover was cracked and filthy.

She rubbed it with her fingers. There was a pattern embossed in the middle of the binding. She blew on it, then took an old hairbrush from her drawer and rubbed away, spat on it then rubbed some more.

It took her some time to recognize the pattern. The letters T and L writhing together on a shield – the same insignia she had seen set in stone above the Pizza Hut door. What had that been called? Loveyard's Main Mill. L for Loveyard. T for something else, but L for Loveyard almost certainly. And the same sign turning up on a book in a great house at the end of a village. It must have been the Loveyards' house, and now she thought about it, hadn't she seen that same pattern above the front door?

If that was their house, and that was their sign, this then was their diary. And she had a history project to write.

She opened the book and began to read but felt her eyelids growing heavy after the first page. She hid the book under her pillow and went to sleep.

CHAPTER TWENTY-THREE

She started to feel strange half-way through the morning, during history. Mr Appleby was a real enthusiast, always smacking his hands together and rubbing them, though how anyone could get enthusiastic about local clog manufacture she could not imagine.

Only ten minutes to go. Her head had stopped aching but she was terribly tired.

'Right now. Projects.' The class groaned.

'Oh no,' Mr Appleby said. 'Oh no. Now, you're to tell me what they are and I'm going to give you a prep to get them under way. Come on, come on, you've all had some time to think about them, so let's see now. Mark, you start.'

He called through the class in alphabetical order. Two of the boys wanted to do the Falklands war, and another the history of the motorcycle. The six wives of Henry VIII were popular. Someone wanted to do the Great Train Robbery, and two others thought it was such a good idea that they asked to switch. Angela was asked last.

'The Loveyard family,' she said.

'I'm sorry. Who?'

'The Loveyards. Who started the mills.'

Mr Appleby raised his eyebrows. 'Well, no shortage of

local material. Yes. Yes. I think that's a very good idea.'

Angela thought so too. She felt incredibly happy, as if someone inside her was stroking her with a soft little hand.

Then the sickness started, a horrible full feeling as if she had swallowed something large and bad. It sat in her stomach, but at the same time there was the pleased, happy feeling which somehow combined with the sickness. It was like eating far too much of something nice, but more than that, it was like eating something you liked, and then discovering that in actual fact you hated it and just wanted to be rid of it.

'Right then,' Mr Appleby said, smacking his little pink hands together once again. 'Let's have lots of observations, interviews, photographs. You may find you just want to base it on interviews, for example. Or perhaps you could find some old records. You never know. Talk to people. Remember, the past is all around us. We just have to look and listen.'

After lunch there was gym. Up until two terms before they had to wear black pleated skirts for gym, but now, if they wanted, they could wear shorts and tracksuits. Angela still felt sick and the queasiness had somehow crept into her bones, so that wet little worms of coldness gently squirmed in her marrow. She dawdled until she was almost the last girl in the changing rooms, then slipped her sports shirt on over her vest and put the tracksuit on top of that. They weren't allowed to do it – it was unhygienic, but with any luck Mrs Hay would not notice. She joined the other girls in the gym.

But Mrs Hay was in a bad mood.

'Heavens above! I don't think I've seen such a miserable bunch of stick-arounds. No wonder you look so cold. Come

on everybody, off with those tracksuits and we'll try and
generate a little bit of good old-fashioned body heat.'

There was a chorus of groans. 'Now I mean it. Off with
those suits – you'd think we were in Siberia, Angela White,
from the way you're all hunched up – and twice round the
gym. Come on, come on! Open up those frowsty old lungs.'

She leaped in the air a couple of times, clapping her
hands above her head.

'Ready now—' She blew her whistle.

Angela was still struggling out of her tracksuit bottoms
when the whistle went. 'Come on Angela. Last one in, last
one to get moving. What's the matter? No pushing there.
Come on speed up or you'll all go round again.'

Angela set off. When she was about half-way round Miss
Hay called out: 'Last five girls have to climb the ropes.
Come on come on come on.' The ropes hung from a bar at
the end of the gym. Climbing them was agony with
everyone staring.

Angela began to run a bit faster. She heard her breath
whistle through her mouth, heard the thump, thump
thump of her feet on the floor. The other sounds receded.
Thump THUMP thump. Her breath came a little faster. She
looked over her shoulder. Silly, no one there, only Mandy
Tong sticking her tongue out as she lapped her. THUMP
thump thump. She tried to go a bit faster, then faster still,
but she was tired, so tired from the night before. Silly, what
did you do last night? THUMP thump thump.

She ran a little faster. Funny, it was getting colder in the
room, not warmer. She felt something swoop down behind
her, looked over her shoulder and screamed because
behind her there was no gym, no red sweating faces of her
class mates, just nothing.

Nothing.

No colour. No texture. It crept up around her, a shape,

a feeling, and suddenly she was overtaken by a terrible
sense of sadness so intense that she gasped. Not hers, not
hers. Someone else's. The sounds of gym swirled away like
water down a drain pipe, and very clearly in that blank
emptiness, a girl's voice said:

'Run. You must run. The ropes!'

'Why? Where?'

'Run. Just run.'

Swimming had made her fit. She kicked like a sprinter,
she felt the blankness begin to slip away from around her.
Yes. It was like accelerating out of a cloud of vapour. The
gym began to materialize around her, very faintly, then
more clearly. The harder her feet hit the floor, the clearer
it became. She heard voices shouting Angela! Angela! and
suddenly she was back, running, running—

She saw the wall too late. Behind her she heard a faint
gasp, she swerved, flung her arms out. Slipped. One
shoulder crashed into a climbing frame, her feet shot out
from under her, her head plummeted down and smashed
on the floor of the gym.

Blinding darkness. A great gong drove a wedge of pain
into her head and darkness flooded in.

'Angela White. Angela White. Are you all right?'

'Oooh, do you think she's dead Miss?'

'Angela White. Get up!'

Angela opened her eyes. A world of polished wood
stretched away from her nose.

'Angela!'

Why didn't Miss Hay just leave her alone?

'Maybe she's swallowed her tongue Miss.'

Angela sat up. She had a headache but otherwise felt
fine.

'I will not have ragging like this in my gym. Screaming

like a little street urchin. Now is your head all right?'

Angela rearranged her legs which were at a strange angle and hurting her, then got to her feet, wobbling a bit. 'I think so. I've got a headache though.'

'Now into the shower with you, and report to me after school. We'll have words, young lady.'

'But suppose she's concussed?' someone asked.

'Are you concussed? Are you concussed Angela?'

Angela thought not. Miss Hay conferred with the head teacher and between them they decided that it would be for the best if Angela was sent home.

She put a record on, lit the gas fire and settled down on the sofa with the diary.

The first thing she discovered was that it had not belonged to T Loveyard (T stood for Thomas) but to his wife Eliza. It was obviously one of a series because it did not begin with the paragraph that you always found at the beginning of diaries that went: 'Hello, I've decided to write a diary. I'm going to be completely honest in it and if YOU are reading it STOP or you will die.' Or words to that effect.

In Eliza Loveyard's diary you got a very full description of what she did, and the money she spent doing it, but no idea of what she thought unless she had found it hilariously funny.

Angela flicked through, skim reading and occasionally dipping in for a page or two, usually where the exclamation marks started coming thick and fast. There was a report about a chambermaid going red every time she or her 'beloved Thomas' entered the room; there was a comment on how badly certain houses in the village smelled and how could she beneficially discharge her duties of occasionally visiting the sick of the village if that duty made her sick. She described a house party, and how much they had all

laughed: how a maid had injured herself – bruised her arm
and head – so that she was unable to work for a day and
how inconvenient that was. Angela closed the book, held
it by the spine and let it fall open.

17th October
A picnic! A surprise for my beloved Thomas, though
alas, too much of a surprise for he set off early this
morning and was deaf to my entreaties to stay. Still,
the day dawned bright and fair, as if the Gods were
smiling on our endeavour. I took the opportunity to
spend much of the morning in bed, so as not to tire
myself out overmuch, and also so that our guests
would not tire of me by having my company
throughout the morning hours! An irritation when I
arose: Margaret, my personal maid had left! Quite
disappeared though we later discovered her to be
living in a next door village, apparently married to a
great ruddy-faced pigman who unbeknownst to us
had been courting her outside Cragside's walls. This
left me to train the idiot Fitt girl in the arts of hair-
brushing and ladylike toilet. I also ordered her to
attend the picnic at which point she was near
overcome with a fit, or FITT! of shaking. However I
misjudged her – misjudged her idiocy. So terrified
was she of this that not only did she fail to attend the
picnic, SHE disappeared too, no doubt to take her
swinish pleasures in the arms of some stout yokel.

What a pig she is, Angela thought.

   Picnic: ham, chickens, good muttons, potatoes,
champagne and ales, jellies, etc. All fine. From the
rock we gazed down over the town, its mighty spread,

its fine smoking chimneys, and even within sight of Cragside, fancied we could hear the tumult of its factories. Rapt as we were in contemplation, imagine our surprise, our delight, on seeing my beloved Thomas appear over a small rise in the land, much dishevelled I might say, and furious to be discovered in such a state. When asked if he had arrayed himself up like an American Indian warrior for our benefit (his clothes and face were streaked with reddish mud), he snorted then tried to make light of the matter, claiming that he had been testing a young cob of Mr Smollett's of Netheridge farm which, being imperfectly broken, had thrown him and dragged him.

Poor Thomas. He seemed quite distracted.

Angela flicked back and forth. Now it seemed that dear Thomas was being bothered by agitators at the mill who were stirring up trouble, now he was setting off on a journey. Now Eliza was complaining about the cost of ribbons; now she was in tears. *Why?*

One of her maids had been discovered dead. Murdered. Angela read on:

Sensation! Horror! The Fitt girl was discovered by some shepherds, whose dogs, alerted by the stench, discovered the body hidden in one of the natural caverns under the moors. The poor child's shift, quite torn and bloodstained, was found under the bed in the weaver's cottage. Oh horror! Oh justice! Oh how plain it should have been, that he, having no sense of decency or propriety even living under our very windows, a thorn in our side, that vile man, that agitator should be a damned murderer. He will be taken to the prison and there he will be hanged!

Angela stood up and walked to the window. She felt something like a pain in the middle of her chest. The poor girl. Angela wished that she had not carried on reading, but she had not been able to stop. A murder. Here, in the village. She had walked the same floorboards as the girl – it did not matter that it had been so long ago. Did not matter at all.

And the murderer so close, within sight of Cragside House. Angela's heart started to thump in her ears; and the room seemed to be advancing and retreating. Evening had crept up on her while she had been reading. Lights were on in the village; the yuppies' house was dark. By pressing her cheek against the window she could just see the bulk of Cragside House, and below it, in that little hollow, the ruined cottage.

She felt sick. It had to be. That was the weaver's cottage, overlooked by the great house. That voice, that voice she had heard was the girl's: Fitt, she was called. Angela Fitt. An Angela had been murdered here and she wanted to talk. *It's not my imagination*, she thought. *It's not. There really is something out there.* Suddenly she felt full of pity. A village girl, her age. Dead. Murdered. It wasn't fair. It simply wasn't, and that awful woman had been horrid to her right up until the morning she had been murdered. Somehow that trivial detail upset her more than anything else.

Behind her she heard a rustling. She felt a light draught, as light as a baby's breath, stir her hair. Her body tingled. Her back was alive, electric. If she turned, if she turned . . .

What would she see? A murdered girl. A dead girl. Riddled with rot – suppose that happened to people as well as buildings . . .

yes-s-s-s-s-s-s s

It was the slow gathering of dust, a fall of leaves, the dry rustle of dead skin.

'Leave me,' Angela said. 'Please.'

help

'Oh, no, not that, anything but that. Not help. Scare me, haunt me, but don't make me help you—'

But she could feel its need, touching her with relentless, freezing pressure. Cold and rot. Decay and want. And in her bedroom. Terror washed over her in slow shuddering waves of understanding. Here, in her room. A thing in her room, a cold stranger. All that sickness she had felt earlier in the day. Had that been the stranger too? Inside her? The cold grew stronger, and in the cold the dreadful smell, like the stench of a filthy fridge, thin, damp, musty, frozen rot and—

Lights outside. They swept up the road and described a wide arc on her bedroom ceiling as the car hit the ramp in front of the house.

A sudden rustle. Tissue paper on hard steel. Angela felt the presence leave. She exhaled. It was as if she had been strung up on fishing hooks. She felt her back soften – she had been tensing it like a shield. She whimpered and ran to the light switch, then froze, her hand reaching up to her mouth, as if to stop her heart jumping out of it.

The pages of the diary were slowly turning. One, two, three. Around the bed hovered a thin cloud: a delicate thickening of room's atmosphere. Angela could see yellows and greys and pinks in it, the colours of her body, her breath, her sweat, her dust, taken by the ... thing. Five, six, seven, the pages flicked over.

Then they stopped. There was a flurry in the room, the air rushed inwards with a tiny pop. The book was open at the seventeenth of October, the place marked with a single rose petal.

The back door slammed downstairs. 'Hello-o, I'm home,' her mother shouted.

The terror had gone with the ghost. She just felt mangled now and limp. She walked noisily into the bathroom, ran a basin of warm clear water and sluiced her face again and again and again. Then she went downstairs to see her mother.

Her mother gave her a hug. 'How are you pet? You're sopping and trembling. The school phoned and I came just as soon as I could.' She put a hand on Angela's forehead. 'Mmm. Temperature's all right. Sit down.'

The kitchen table was covered with supermarket bags that were collapsing sideways and spilling their contents: wine bottles, meat, vegetables, fruit.

'What's going on?' Angela asked. 'Are we receiving Royalty?'

Her mother touched her fringe with a finger. 'No dear, just supper. Oh,' she added casually, 'and Bill Fairley's dropping round, so it's early bed for you.'

'Mum. I'm nearly thirteen.'

'And you're not well yet after that shock. You don't look yourself at all. I wonder, should I take the day off work tomorrow? Things are ever so quiet. Well, we'll see in the morning shall we? No arguments, and you can help me if you like.'

'Gee, Mom. Thanks,' Angela laughed. 'Just like in a real functioning family!'

Her mother laughed a bit wildly and threw a J-cloth at her.

As it happened, by eight o'clock Angela was numb with tiredness. She made herself a Cup-a-Soup, gulped it down

and staggered up the stairs to bed. Her father was fiddling
with wine bottles, and the bathroom was still warm with
steam from her mother's bath. She brushed her teeth like
a zombie, and lurched into bed, just as she heard Bill
Fairley's car arrive.

She heard the grown-ups make greeting noises, voices
rising and falling in unison, then a pause, then the sound
of someone walking quickly up the stairs. A knock on the
door. Angela sat up.

'And what's my favourite person been up to this fine
day?' Bill Fairley said. He sat on the edge of the bed and
asked her how she was, adding that he thought she looked
as if she needed a good rest. A holiday somewhere.

'Some hope,' Angela said. 'Anyway, there's school.'

'How's that going?'

'Oh, all right I suppose. We're all meant to be doing a
history project. I think I've got something for mine at last.'

'Oh yes?' Bill Fairley raised an eyebrow.

'It's to do with the Loveyards – they built Cragside
House.'

'I'd have thought that was the last place – anyway,
haven't you been barred from there?'

'Oh, I don't have to go there again. Something that
happened there,' she went on. 'I think I'm the only person
who knows.'

'Would you like to tell me?' Bill Fairley asked, cautiously.
Angela looked at him. If she began she would have to tell
him more about the ghost, the thing. She knew she could
not. She so wanted him to respect her, or at least not to
laugh at her. He was looking sharp and interested now; she
could just imagine how his face would change. *I think I've
seen a ghost. Pathetic!*

She shook her head. 'I can't,' she said. She lay back on
her pillow. Bill Fairley leaned over her. For a second she

thought he might kiss her goodnight. But instead he just stared very hard into her eyes, as if he wanted to look behind them and see what was going on in her brain.

'We're all watching out for you, Angela,' he said. 'But we've got to know what's on your mind.'

His breath smelled of peppermint. Then he touched her on the cheek with a knuckle and said goodnight.

CHAPTER TWENTY-FOUR

The rest of the week passed in a blur. She went over to Melanie's but felt distracted. The voice spoke to her at odd times: sometimes just a single word.

Angela

and sometimes

help me

Anywhere away from home, and the voice was always accompanied by an unpleasant feeling of fullness and sickness in the stomach and throat. She was losing weight and felt out of condition, like a dog without its Vetzymes. Her mother was involved in some tricky negotiations involving two floors of a modern office building just off the ring road and was in late and out early. Her father was increasingly depressed and spending more and more time away from home. Angela always knew he had been out because he would leave his muddy boots in the middle of the storm porch and she would have to scrape them against the door step to get the worst of the mud off them, then tidy them away.

On Saturday morning she heard her mother get up at

around nine and drive away in her Fiesta. Her father got up shortly afterwards, as if he had been waiting for her to leave. She heard his footsteps on the gravel outside, heading in the direction of the moors.

'Good riddance to bad rubbish,' she said. She ran a bath for herself, read her mother's *Hello* magazine until her fingers went white and wrinkly, got dressed, made herself some toast, and called Melanie. She felt like having a lazy day, lying on beds, chatting, watching a film, even watching sports on TV. The wind panted outside and spat gusty gobbets of rain against the window.

'Oh, Angela,' Melanie's mother said. 'How are you? No, Melanie's just gone into town with her father. What a pity you missed her. I wasn't expecting them back until tea time. Bye bye, poppet.'

That really only left one thing for it. She would have to do her homework, or research, as Mr Appleby insisted they call it. She had books on weaving, local industry and the history of the town. She put them down on the kitchen table and wondered how to begin.

It was really out of a sense of curiosity that she turned to the back of the book on weaving and looked in the index for reference to Edgerton. Nothing. Plenty of references to Loveyard but none to the village. Oh well.

She picked up the second book. There. Edgerton on the Moor.

She scanned the page, disappointed that there did not seem to be any reference to Thomas Loveyard, just a lot of stuff about working conditions and strikes. Agitation. That rang a bell. In the diary upstairs Eliza Loveyard had talked about an agitator – that was it. She ran upstairs to get the diary, and back in the kitchen she flicked through it. She found the reference shortly after the description of the picnic.

... a thorn in our side, that vile man, agitator should
be a damned murderer. He will be taken to the prison
and there he will be hanged!

There was no reference to Edgerton on the Moor. She
turned the page and found it, half-way down. '... William
Lestrange, a self-employed village weaver, lay preacher and
agitator. He gathered a considerable following by holding
vast open air prayer meetings, "under the watchful eye of
God", railing against the conditions inside the mills and the
living conditions in the town, which he claimed gave rise
only to "gin-drinking, promiscuity and all forms of beast-
liness". His simple message of good and evil, a vengeful
God, and a rural Utopia found a ready audience in the
dispirited mill-workers, many of whom were themselves
country folk, forced off the land by the collapse of the rural
economy.'

Angela's head spun. William Lestrange. The name
sounded odd to her, and the thought that she had passed
by his very cottage somehow terrifying. Her eyes scanned
the page again, stopping at a name which stood out:

... he was later found guilty of murdering her, Angela
Fitt, a servant girl at Cragside Hall, Home of Thomas
Loveyard. Much was made of this fact at the trial, and
the implication that the girl had in some way been
coerced into spying for the man, although no evidence
was presented. After the trial the weaver's cottage was
left empty, and for a while became a popular tourist
attraction for day trippers from the town.

Fitt. Angela Fitt. Angela White furrowed her brow and
thought: So perhaps when I heard that voice say Angela,
she wasn't calling me. She was announcing herself. She

was telling me who she was. Oh, what's happening?

Angela felt that she was going to burst. The diary had been hidden. That meant that there was something secret in it. But what could that have been? The page the ghost had opened it to, of course. The day of the picnic.

She found it hurriedly, still marked by the rose petal. A picnic. And a place. A place where you could see the town *and* Cragside House. The picnic had taken place on the day of Angela Fitt's disappearance. Oh God, the day she was murdered! A day the foul Mrs Loveyard ate chicken and jellies, a day Mr Loveyard got thrown from his horse and covered in mud.

So, there was a place described in the diary and it was a place that she was going to find.

She went into the storm porch and put on her cagoule, then her fell boots, which were waterproof up to a point and should give better grip than wellies on the wet moor. Her father had dumped his size ten monsters on top of them, she noticed. She put her boots on. Her heel landed in something soft.

Yuk.

She looked. There was a sort of patty of mud that must have fallen off the tread of her father's boots, still glistening with wet. She pulled it out. It was heavy clay, the colour of red brick, horribly sticky. She chucked it on to the drive, wiped the boot out with kitchen towel and set off into the rain.

Red clay. Red mud. What a coincidence. There must be a seam of it somewhere on the moor that Dad had walked through. A thought, buried but alive, began to stir in her mind. Something to do with mud. Possibly.

A gust of wind threw stinging rain in her face. She blinked the water away from her eyes. Cragside House loomed above her, the ground sloping down to the left where the town lay, hidden now by marching ranks of dark rain clouds.

A movement caught her eye. The gate through the wall into the grounds of Cragside House was open, banging gently in the wind. That was wrong. Suppose one of the kids from the village had got in somehow, and was trying to break into the house. The next person to fall through the floor might not be as lucky as she was. She would not actually go in, just look through. If she saw someone she'd shout; if not, she'd just close the door. She was poised on a razor's edge of curiosity and fear, the fear adding spice to the curiosity.

Peering through, she saw nothing, just the garden looking sodden and depressing, the tall weeds, those that had not been knocked flat by the wind and rain, nodding quickly as gusts shook them.

Then – in the corner of her eye – movement.

There, again. Movement. A head bobbing by that odd little building that seemed sunk into the ground, hard up by the wall. Her skin shrank around her bones.

Then she remembered that steps led down through the earth to the doorway. Still, that meant someone was trying to break in. She decided to shout 'Oy!' then run.

She opened her mouth. The head reappeared, turned towards her. Then smiled.

Angela raised a hand. What on earth was he doing there? Did it explain the mud?

She was beckoned over impatiently. Closing the door in the wall behind her she walked across the grass to the man.

CHAPTER TWENTY-FIVE

I t was her birthday. Her parents had promised her a picnic with chicken, jellies and ham. It was meant to be a surprise but she had surprised them in the middle of it all, but that was all right.

She was given chicken but it stuck in her throat and she spat it out in a solid lump that tasted of mud. Then someone had suggested that they play hide and seek and someone else, it was probably Melanie, thought it would be more fun if they all took their clothes off. Angela was shy about doing that in front of her parents and Uncle Bill. Underneath her clothes she was wearing a bloodstained shift.

Because she was the birthday girl, Angela was told to hide.

For some reason everyone was sitting on her parents' bed, which they had brought along with them. Melanie had got under the covers with a strange boy with an old soft face. They began to count. One. Two. Three. Four.

They would stop when they got to thirteen. That was the important number. She had to find a hiding place before they reached thirteen. She ran from them. The only place to hide was Cragside House.

Five. Six. Seven. Eight.

Her birthday cake stood on a table in front of the door in the wall. Above the door the letters T and L had been joined by a peculiar looping S. The candles on the cake were burning. Angela walked quickly past the cake, careful not to bump into it. The smell from the candles was like Sunday roast when Mummy cooked pork, except the smell was more oily and sooty. The next time she looked the candles had become little girl's fingers, blue with cold, or pink because they had been skinned.

Nine. Ten. Eleven.

It was cold inside the wall. She ran to the house, but the door was barred to her, blocked because her father had nailed it up. She turned. The only place to hide was that funny little building, half hidden in the earth. There — someone she knew was beckoning to her, urgently.

Come here. Angela. Come here

She was cold and sweating. Underneath the shift she was wearing a coat of sweat that the moonlight lay on and made white. She heard laughter behind her. Somewhere in the distance a man was singing happy birthday.

Twelve. THIRTEEN. COMING!

Melanie's voice was dark and stiff like prickly tweed. Angela heard footsteps behind her. She could not look. On they came. She flattened herself against the wall.

They mustn't catch me. They mustn't catch me. Somewhere inside her a tricky little voice said: Don't worry. It's only hide and seek.

But it did matter. She was hiding. They were seeking. If they found her . . .

She poked her head around the edge of the door and saw them. Their feet were naked and trailed on the ground like thin pink fronds. Their necks were swinging like seaweed, and on top of each neck, that had been stretched and kinked, a tiny dead head, blank, white and stinking, swaying, searching, seeking.

They rushed through the door, turned and fanned out. Angela ran, crashing through the line, saw them turn, lunge at her with little mouths and tongues like thick ropes, spitting blood. She battered her way through to the door, threw it open and fell into light.

Blinked.

Light.

Blink again.

The first thing she saw was a candle, burning so close to her face that she could feel its warmth. The first thing she heard was her breath, hissing sickly in her ears.

She was lying face downwards on a slab. Its coldness sank through her jeans and sweatshirt and flattened and deadened her skin. The sharp edges of her hips hurt. The corners of her mouth burned where a band of tape holding a plug of fabric in her mouth cut hard. The plug pressed against the back of her throat, causing a solid lump of nausea to sit there, bobbing up and down like a cork in a bottle.

She moved her head slowly to the right, squinting against the glare of the candles. She could see almost nothing except darkness, and the glare of the candles stopped her eyes adjusting, but she thought that she could make out rough brickwork on the other side of a small room. The floor was earth. She turned her head. Rock, then bricks. She could not see ahead. Everything was hidden by the light of the candle; its warm, protective light made a cocoon of blackness around it.

Movement in the darkness. Someone was moving

around out there. She knew she was scared, but in a funny
way she felt calm. There was that thing they always said on
nature programmes when the antelope or the wildebeest or
the zebra was brought down by lions or dogs or cheetahs.

They don't feel a thing. They go into shock. They think
that they're just dreaming it.

A blob of wax balled under the flame then ran suddenly
down the side of the candle.

I'm not dreaming this. It's too real.

Different sounds now came from in front of her. Something was being dragged over the floor. She arched her
back and tried to raise her head above the flames, holding
the position until her muscles screamed. She could just see
a back hunched over something on the floor. Beyond that
was a darker hole in the darkness, a door or a corridor? It
was so cold and dark in the room that she was sure she was
underground, so the steps had to be leading upwards.

What time was it? Were her parents back yet? If they
were, they would see that she had gone. What would they
do then? Come looking for her? No, they would assume
that she had gone off to Melanie's. They wouldn't worry
until her bed time. Oh my God. They would never find her.

Thinking of home made her want to cry. A lump rose in
her throat to meet the terrible pressure of the gag. She felt
tears in her eyes.

Oh God. What's happening to me? Oh please someone
help me.

hands

The voice was so deep in her ear a fly might have been
talking. The thing was back, talking to her. She struggled
to turn but could not see anything.

hands

Something repellent, cold and soft brushed against her wrist. She gave a little scream deep in her throat. It was behind her. She could not see. Cold and soft. The voice was cold and soft too. She wanted to get away. Anything. Even attract the attention of the man in the cave.

She began to struggle. She writhed. And as she struggled she felt the rope around her wrists give a little. Stretch a little. She lay still, trying to flatten herself against the stone like a snake. The rope was loose! She could work at it. She had small hands – everyone said so.

They were tied wrist to wrist. By linking her fingers into a sort of hinge she found that she could exert quite a lot of pressure. The rope bit hard. Still she strained. She felt the knot slip fractionally and give her a tiny amount of movement. She tried to compress the bones in her hand and then rub them against each other to slip the rope over one. Every time it stuck where her thumb joined her palm. If she moved her thumb under her palm, it forced the wrists apart, thus tightening the rope that way. She continued to rub and strain. It was hopeless.

Then she froze. The figure at the end of the room had risen. She closed her eyes tight, heard footsteps walk quickly over to her, then stop. He was bending over, checking her bonds. His breathing sounded odd and Angela risked one peep.

She saw his head, looked up at him and just thought: Why? The sickness of betrayal, the incomprehension that he—

He even looked sorrowful. So why? Why? WHY? Her body began to shake. She sensed in him a massive indifference, that the sorrow was part of an act, and somehow he had to act to himself. She closed her eyes and was shaken by dry sobs.

*

When she looked again the candle had burned down a quarter of an inch.

It was easier to see past him now. She saw his hunched back, his elbows and arms working as if he were threading something.

She flexed her hands again, wincing because the raw wounds had stiffened in the few minutes that she had lain still. She was used to the pain now, knew what to expect and resolved not to let it stop her. If the blood made the ropes wet, they might give a little. She worked away, the pain building in waves until she thought she could bear it no longer, but she found that if she did bear it, if she did go through the barrier, it lessened slightly. It was like swimming training. When you hit that black wall of tiredness, you didn't stop, you climbed it into the light.

light

The voice was so sad. Again she tried to look round. Nothing. No one.

He had stood up now and was moving with greater purpose. He moved to the middle of the room holding something.

A stone attached to a thin piece of string soared up into the darkness.

What was he doing? She bent her neck backwards again, forcing it further than she had managed before. The roof of the small room was domed and full of floating darkness, but across the space was a beam. And hanging from the beam was a hook.

Long ago they had used the hook to swing the great blocks of ice up on to the shelves that lined the walls. There, packed in straw, they had sat out the hot summers, sweating slightly, shrinking slightly, filling the air with damp coldness until the servants had come with their chisels and mallets and chipped the ice for iced tea, ice creams, sorbets and cold drinks.

Angela watched as the stone swung through the air three times, and on the fourth time, sail over the hook and drop on the other side, suspended like a spider a few feet from the ground. The candles magnified its shadow and against the wall she saw a dark shape, girl-sized, swinging and twitching above the void.

The man held the stone and began to pull. Thicker string began to snake up from the floor. Then rope. Then a noose.

She was as mesmerized as a monkey by a python. The thick loop of rope jerked up slowly into the air, and hung there, swaying slowly from side to side. Angela felt her strength evaporate. Her hands stopped working the rope.

Her neck could no longer hold up her head.

My neck. My head.

Oh Mummy oh Daddy oh Mummy oh Daddy oh—

blow

Mummy Mummy Mummy Mummy Mummy

blow

Mummy Mummy Mummy Mummy Mum— What?

blow

It was the voice again. Different now, stronger and higher. Not exactly more urgent – it was too airless, too blank for that – but insistent. She was too limp to be frightened. It was just another thing.

Then whump.

All the air was suddenly expelled from her body. Everything was expelled from her body. Something dark seemed to pass through her, hit the stone beneath her then coil in her belly. It burned through her, grew, forced its way through the sphincter in her throat, up to her mouth and stop. Threads of smell worked their way around the plug of cotton in her mouth, lay on her tongue, trickled up her nose. The stench was old, wet, rotting: a compound of earth and bone and flesh and—

It started to push like a little hand, a little hand that came from a little body that was trying to crawl up out of her throat. Angela wriggled, anything to get it away. Her tongue worked behind it, tasted it. The plug shifted and her body began to spasm in a last tremendous convulsion to expel the invader.

Strength burned up her arms. She felt the rope shift and at last begin to slip.

The noose gave a last twitch and the man emerged from the shadows, took a step towards her, saw what was happening and paused.

It was all Angela needed. The ropes slackened suddenly, her hands snatched the gag, and her whole body coughed out a sudden wave of darkness. It flew from her mouth, gathered around the candle and smothered it.

Darkness. Sudden darkness.

She rolled from the slab, and crashed to the floor, crawling away as soon as she hit it. Her hands were useless, dead. She supported herself on her wrists. She heard the rustle of a leg pass her head, hands groping where she had been lying and ripped desperately at the rope around her feet, forcing it past her heels, tearing her

shoes off in the hurry, then skipped away, her ⌐
blindly in front of her face.

The man behind her fell, swore, then stood still. She
heard him move slowly away from her, his arms swishing
the air. He was cutting her off, moving to stand between
her and the door. He would move towards her now, slowly
and methodically.

She wanted to spit. She knew she had to move.

Opening her eyes wide to try and draw in any light she
could, she stretched her arms out and tried to think where
she should go. Past him? Wait until he was almost on her,
then dart between his legs and dash for the door? But what
was on the other side?

She closed her eyes, squeezing out a tear, then whispered: 'Help me, whoever you are.'

She almost screamed when she felt the tiny thing fall
into the palm of her hand. It was small and damp and soft
as petals, a rose bud. It lay still in her palm a second,
trembling slightly in the warmth, and Angela closed her
hand.

It guided her gently, pulling her this way and that . . .

Angela followed blindly. Behind her she could hear the
man beginning to advance. She was being led away from
him. The hand pulled her down. She crouched on all fours.
Air eddied around her face. Air! That might mean a tunnel.
A tunnel leading under the moor.

She heard the figure shuffle towards her. Her hand was
being pulled through a tiny gap, actually behind the slab
she had lain on. She squeezed and strained, grunting,
oblivious to the noise she was making. Her arm was tugged
down. There was a gap in the floor. She worked her
shoulder through, then her head. Jammed. Wriggled a bit
more, feeling her legs beat the wall, feeling a hand close on
her ankle. She lashed out desperately and suddenly she was

through. The hand gripped her ankle but her weight pulled it free and she was slipping, then falling through deeper blackness, a long slide of terror with the mud slick on her face, and hidden things brushing her hair, roots catching and teasing her, rocks embedded in earth like little teeth, onwards and downwards so that even the thought of the terror up there diminished, became faint compared to this rushing black slide into hell.

Then she stopped, smoothly, quickly. Her shoulders were wedged solid in a narrow, sticky throat of mud and her head was in a shallow puddle. Her nostrils were full of mud, her legs were thrown back over her head, cricking her back. She could not see a thing, and when she tried to raise her face, her head hit earth. She inhaled water and began to choke.

Panic surged through her in a wave. She coughed the water out, felt a vacuum build in her lungs, desperately twisted her head then sucked in – air. A thin stream, charged with cold. Her head dropped again and her nostrils filled with mud, but by twisting around so that it lay on its side, half in water, and lifting every time she breathed, she could take in air.

She tried to wriggle backwards but her body was caught in a right angle, bent upwards, and she could not get the purchase to move back. She humped her hips, moved forwards, but her shoulders only wedged themselves more firmly against the slick, sucking walls of mud. Her head dropped. She lifted it. Dropped again. Lifted it. Skewers of pain speared her neck. Dropped it. Lifted it, but it was shaking so much that she could hardly get it clear of the water. Dropped it. Lifted it.

Her muscles screamed at her. Then gave up.

She felt her strength going but with pounding red waves slamming in on her head from all sides, instinct took over.

Instead of trying to reach forwards with both hands into what felt like a void, she slipped one arm underneath her body, back behind her so her shoulders met the tunnel at a slope. There. The free hand moved. Again. She wriggled desperately, felt herself slip forwards an inch, then another, then just enough for her feet to grip on the wall behind.

She pushed.

Stuck.

Pushed again.

An inch.

Pushed again.

Two, three inches. Four, five, then suddenly her body passed through the neck of mud, and she was free, lying in a bitter void, and too weak to do anything but breathe.

Time passed. Angela's body started to shiver. Mud dried slowly on her face and began to itch. For a while she lay there, then she lifted her hand and scratched her cheek. Mud flaked. She picked mud out of her ears and the world became quieter as the dull rushing of her blood subsided. She rubbed mud from her eyes but she still could not see anything.

The movement triggered a trickle of thought. If she itched she could scratch. It followed that if she was not stuck she could move, but the thought of movement disturbed her. She felt more comfortable lying in the wet darkness, subsiding slowly into the earth that cradled her.

no

She waved the word away. The mud was warming up. It was her bed. If she moved all that would change. If she stayed still her body would sleep and the discomfort would go.

live

That voice again; the dead voice, the dead girl's voice. To drift in a net of flowers through the moonlight, to feel neither hot nor cold. To ignore the pull of the earth and the pull of the sun, to float in endless limbo, neither dead nor alive, just being. No work, no worry, endless, endless dream life. She was through with being frightened. She would rather stay here and dream.

you will die

Oh, but this voice was persistent. That was the point, wasn't it? But dying was putting it too strongly. She was falling into an earth sleep.

She felt something prick her legs and kicked out angrily. Her ankle hit the roof. A lump of earth fell heavily on it. The tunnel seemed to writhe around her and she felt something slipping above her head.

She screamed and wriggled forwards. The roof gave behind her with a sound like a sack falling. She pulled her legs free from the fall, turned round and sat up.

She was in utter blackness in a place that had never known light. She began to breathe in panicked spurts. She felt earth on either side of her, in front of her nothing. She imagined pale things, bleached by darkness, eyeless and soft-skinned that slithered through these tunnels. She thought of earthworms, eight foot long and as thick as her leg, gliding through the soil. She thought she felt the wall move and shrieked and pulled her hand away.

The earth killed her voice. She began to shiver in huge, shuddering waves but she did not feel cold. More by instinct than anything else she began to crawl, keeping her right shoulder pressed against the wall to remind herself that she was going forwards, touching the left hand wall for reassurance.

She had hoped to keep the walls of the tunnel close by on either side of her but found that the tunnel was widening. Soon she could only feel the left wall by stretching out her arm. Then she could not find it even if she stretched both arms out. She struggled on, hands plashing down, knees sliding forwards.

It dawned on her that she had not felt her forehead brush against anything for a while. She stopped and waved a hand above her head. Nothing. She rose into a crouch, touching the wall for support, then pushed herself up. She straightened her back, and arched it and took a tentative step forward. Unused to being upright and with nothing to give her any sense of up and down, she felt herself overbalancing. For a sickening instant she thought that she must have taken a step over the edge of an invisible precipice. She threw her hands out instinctively and felt them smack into the mud. After that she stayed on all fours and only moved into the upright when her tortured muscles forced her to stop and stretch.

She was aware that the wall she was following was veering off to the right before she felt the ground beneath her change.

Her hands, so used to sliding forward, stopping, gripping, taking the weight, did so of their own accord now. Suddenly her palms were on rock, not earth. She registered this, tried to stop but her hand slid forward of its own accord as the rock loosened and gave way.

She lurched again, desperately tried to lean back but her centre of gravity was too far forward. She teetered for a second, then fell.

Again she did not fall far. She struck the water almost immediately. Her head went under, hit rock, her feet

followed and forced it down. She kicked out wildly, righted
herself and found her footing precariously on a round,
slippery boulder.

The water was freezing, agony on her legs. She began to
shiver and took a tentative step back to where she had
fallen in. The ground levelled out slightly and she found she
could wade; the water came about half-way up her thighs.
She took four steps and realized that she should have
reached the edge.

What had happened? She had fallen, twisted, pushed off.

Perhaps if she turned left and took two steps. Nothing.
Her waving hands met nothing. She stopped again. Now if
she retraced her steps. Turn around. Two steps, turn right.
Try again in that direction. Nothing but blackness and
freezing water; two layers of cold.

She was utterly lost in the void.

'Oh God oh Mummy,' Angela whimpered. She struck out
in what she thought was a different direction, took ten
paces, turned and ran screaming in another. She stopped
and beat the water with her fists. The sound rose into space
and echoed flatly around her.

She shouted again to crack the silence and tried to think,
putting on her mother's practical voice.

'Well, young lady, we won't get anywhere like this.
Either you can decide to stay here and freeze, or you can
pull your socks up and make a bit of an effort. It won't
matter what direction you go in. The point is unless you
try, you won't get anywhere.'

Angela whimpered again. She strained her eyes, popping
them wide with finger and thumb to try and gather any
light there was against the retina. She held her breath and
tried to listen, straining the silence for sounds however
faint or distant.

At first she could hear nothing but the dull muttering of

her body, then she heard a plink. She thought of a huge canopy of earth above her, the water and the damp, and how a single drop of rain must have fallen, trickled through the soil to land, plink, in this underground lake.

Surely it could not just be the odd drop that had filled it. She tried to find different levels of silence, in the way her father had told her to find different levels of taste in the odd mouthful of wine he had passed her.

And then she heard something, a sound that was so faint it seemed to run under the silence. A distant, thin murmur. Running water.

She turned her head to the left and right, and made off in what she thought was the right direction, pushing through the water, feet feeling for irregularities, her arms waving in front of her face. She would slip and fall, recover her footing and push on. She knew she had to try and find the sound again but now, when she stopped and tried to stand still, she overbalanced. There was no sense of vertical or horizontal in the darkness. She had been in it too long. She squatted down until the water was up to her neck, tried to stop her teeth chattering and control her breathing that was whistling through her teeth.

There. She got a fix. Stood up and walked on. The darkness was in her now; skin is waterproof but Angela knew she could not keep the darkness out. Fear had ceased to be a matter of earthworms and ghost train ghouls. It was as big as the world she was in now – something boundless in this darkness. It was something like cold – all around her. It was something you withstood as long as you could.

But the darkness was killing her. She could feel it seeping in through her pores under pressure, staining her body, the stain creeping in and through. Her skin was darkness now, and it was finding a way past the white cage of her ribs to the soft, working jewels buried deep inside her. She waded on. She no longer felt like a single being. Instead she was just a jungle of parts: of limbs, of feelings, of sensations, of thoughts. All were connected to the mind, all sent little messages of pulsing energy through to it like little generators. But one by one the component parts were shutting down. The lights were going off.

The sound of water grew stronger. Now she could hear it over the sound of her clashing teeth; the sound of her breath, the sound she made pushing the water in front of her. It was a small waterfall trickling and chuckling over a ledge into the lake.

Immediately below the waterfall the lake deepened. She lost her footing, plunged forwards and went under. She came up, hands grasping, and felt the water falling on them. The rocks underneath were smooth as bone knuckles. She slipped off, was pushed by the gentle current to one side, and found rougher rocks. She climbed up and lay on a shelf of stone, her body trying to shiver itself to warmth.

After a while the body picked itself up. Keeping one hand in the stream for guidance, it crawled against the current. Where the tunnels seemed to fork, it would pause, sniff, and an ancient little-used area of the mind decided in which branch of the tunnel the air smelled right. The fingers gripped the soil, assessing slope, moisture, fed the information to the brain. The hands slapped down on mud and stone, the knees, almost open to the bone, scraped after them. The head moved from side to side. The hands moved. The knees moved. Angela's body pressed onwards.

The tunnel opened. A breeze, winding its way down through the dark, stirred the still, dead air. The head lifted. The nostrils widened. Some other smell was threading through the deep, dark, secret smell of ancient earth, something rank, something knowing and evil and worldly. Sharp, acid, sweet, heavy.

The eyes lowered, and noted a tiny glitter of light under them, the merest reflection of a reflection, bouncing off the wet wall, caught in the shine of a finger nail. The body crawled on.

The air thickened, became gravy rich with something awful. The light increased steadily, bouncing redly off the glistening throat of earth. Angela was now swimming in foulness and the head swung from side to side in an effort to evade the stench. The tunnel widened into a chamber, the chamber became a cave. Suddenly light was pouring in from a fissure in the ceiling, real light, daylight, glaring, blinding clean. A fern nodded in a crevice, bones of sheep and rabbits lay like hieroglyphs on the floor.

Angela crawled into the light and let it play on her face. She lay still for a long time, feeling life return to her body. Pain, fear, cold, relief – emotion and sensation mingled in a heady cocktail.

She rolled on her back, shuffled until she was immediately under the hole, and let clean rain drop on to her face. She opened her mouth and enjoyed the random dots of water on her tongue and her eyes.

She blinked, her eyes slid and noticed a shape on the side of the cavern.

She rolled on to her side and peered through the gloom. Her eyes adjusted.

She saw a body.

It was cradled in a mouldering net of rope, hanging against the wall. The arms were flung wide, the lips burst and shredded, teeth white in rotten gums, skull green, throat gaping, body a dark stew of flesh and gut and clothing and bone.

Angela stared, at first refusing to take it in. Then, as the details grew clearer and she saw the trick fate had played on her, shock and agony tore through her in wave after wave. She turned away. On the floor of the cavern was a marble slab, covered in mould.

The only word she could read on it was Angela.

After all she had been through, she had no resistance left. She simply could not take any more; the lights went out in her head. She sat in the mud, lifted her head and howled.

CHAPTER TWENTY-SIX

Angela concentrated and read the upside down letters.

Case notes for Angela White.
   Sex: female
   Age: 12.4
   Status: susp abuse (pat) penetration??? ritual*** + suspension.
   Symptoms—

But at that point the social worker saw what she was doing and unobtrusively moved her arm across the file. It wasn't fair, Angela thought, not letting her see. People should not write things about you and then not let you read them.

Secrets, secrets, still more secrets. The world was clamming up around her. You knew things but they did not make sense. Like Bill Fairley asking if she remembered about her father's signet ring, and she saying: Yes, he lost it a week or so ago. Like Bill Fairley asking about red mud, and her saying: Yes, there was some on Daddy's boots. It fell into my shoe, I had to get it out. Things like that were very clear. But the events of that afternoon, from the moment she left the house to the moment she woke up in hospital, were a complete blank. Angela could remember nothing at all. While Bill said it was all right, she could tell that he was worried.

She looked around the room. It was bright and cheerful. There were grass green armchairs like the ones she, her mother and the social worker were sitting in; posters on the wall of things like horses, pretty landscapes, a token racing car for the boys, mountains, and one in particular of a little cottage with roses growing round the front door that Angela thought was really nice.

A window with bright red curtains looked down over the car park. The ceiling was one of those funny ones with lots of holes drilled into it. In one corner there was a giant dolls' house, home to a couple of giant man and woman dolls. The man had an embarrassing and hairy willy; the woman had bosoms and a triangle of wool between her legs. On the first visit, the social worker had asked Angela if it would help her to play with them. If that's what she wants, Angela thought, and tried. But she was so crippled with embarrassment that in the end she just put the dolls down, her face smarting.

They got on all right now. Whatever Angela did was all right with the nice woman who wanted Angela to call her Nicola.

Angela wanted to read – well, that was all right, although she was quizzed pretty thoroughly on what she thought about the book.

Angela wanted to talk – fine too.

Angela wanted to stick her hands in her pockets and sit there with tears running down her face and snot bubbling in her nose – that was absolutely okay.

Angela wanted to shred a hanky because there was a hole in the middle of her head that really hurt her. Nicola just looked sympathetic.

It was all fine although it was embarrassing when her mother came too. Nicola called Mrs White Patricia. Patricia called Nicola Miss Hawkins. Angela knew that Patricia did not like Nicola. She was always asking Angela what she had been *made to say* by Miss Hawkins. Angela said over and over again that she was never made to say anything, in fact sometimes the silences made the session a complete squirm. If she talked, it was because she wanted to. No other reason, Mummy. And Mummy, please don't bite your lower lip because it makes me think that you don't really believe me.

'Angela.'

Angela stopped day-dreaming. She was back in the nice bright room with sunlight on her arm, warm and golden through the glass. She found it hard to concentrate on anything for very long these days. Her mind kept on wandering, back to – nothing. Into the painful hole, that colourless space that buzzed with emptiness. She had no memory of a day when something had happened to her that everybody knew about but would not tell her. It was important, apparently, that she find out for herself. Sometimes she remembered a cold, feathery little hand that had pulled her – somewhere.

'Whose hand?' Nicola asked.

Angela thought for a while. 'My little friend's hand,' she said.

'Angela!' Back into the nice bright room.

'Angela, would you like to tell us what you were thinking about? Could you share it with us.'

'I don't know,' Angela said. She couldn't really say that she was thinking that her mother didn't like Nicola. Now her mother was looking smug. Angela shifted her position on the armchair, uncrossed her legs. Miss Hawkins was sitting as she always sat, legs tucked under her in a position

of poised informality. Her mother was as stiff as a shop
window dummy.

A long silence. 'I was thinking about my little friend.'

'Your little friend who helped you?'

Angela shrugged. She did not like it when other people
talked about the ghost.

'Maybe she's a friend, maybe she isn't. She's really more
of a—'

'Yes?'

'A hand. Anyway, she's called Angela. Like me.'

'How do you know that?'

'I worked it out for myself. It's all in the diary.'

'There is no diary.'

'Then someone must have stolen it.'

Angela's mother made a noise that said: Do we really
have to put up with this nonsense?

'Is she, Angela, with you all the time?'

'No, not all the time.'

'You're leading her,' Mrs White said quickly.

Angela shook her head, anxious to help Nicola. Sometimes her mother tried to be too controlling. 'She visits me
sometimes.'

'How does she visit you? Does she visit your house?'

'No. Not the house. Well, she does come to the house,
but only because she's . . . she's . . .'

One of those silences that went on and on.

'She was inside me,' Angela said. It was funny how that
had not occurred to her before. If the voice she had heard
had been inside her head, then the little friend had to be
inside her.

'Inside your head?'

'No, my body. She gets inside my body. Like I'm . . . like
I'm her pyjamas.'

'Oh, really.'

Just to show her mother, Angela continued. She had only mentioned the girl twice. The first time had been to a policewoman when she was making a statement. She had not commented, just looked at her rather strangely from underneath her eyebrows. The second time had been to Nicola, who had just nodded when Angela told her about the voice in her ear, how she had heard it in her bedroom, how she had thought that she was being chased in gym, how there were always roses.

'What do you mean by that?'

'She's cold,' Angela said, thinking out loud now, discovering things for herself. 'She's cold. I think she gets inside me because she's cold and wants to go to bed. I don't know.' Now she felt like crying, but did not want to. Now she wanted to keep the memory away. 'She smells. She's horrible!'

There was a pause. 'But you said that she wanted you to help her, Angela. That's a good feeling isn't it? She wanted to be your friend.'

Angela shook her head. How could she explain the particular pitiless, rotting sense of need that filled her. The same thing happened in school: nobody ever wanted to be the friend of the person who needed friends. You kept away from them. It was one of those things.

'She wanted something from me, but I don't want to, don't want to—' The sobs kept on rising inside her like lines of waves. Every time she climbed one there was another. '—I don't want to help her. I want her to leave me alone.'

Another long pause. 'Are you sure, Angela?'

'YES!' she howled. 'I just WANT her to LEAVE me ALONE!'

'That's enough! I've seen enough! I can't bear to see her like this. What do you mean by dragging her through all this? Come on, Angela. We're going home.'

But Angela did not want to go home. Nicola handed her a box of tissues and stood up. Very politely but very firmly she led Mrs White out of the room. Through her sobs and sniffles, Angela heard her mother's high voice and Nicola's low voice to-ing and fro-ing.

She stood up. Nicola had left the folder on the table by the side of the chair. Next to the word 'symptoms' the letters MPD had been scrawled, followed by an asterisk. Then there was a lot of stuff about her physical examination which her eyes slid over. She did not want to be reminded of the metal instruments that slid inside her with a pain like toothache in the belly. Her hands and knees were still bandaged from the half day she had spent crawling in the tunnels.

She moved over to the door. Nicola was talking patiently now.

'The best way of describing it is this. Under stress the personality can fracture, fragment. The individual can then take refuge in any number of different personalities, all within him or herself – I forget what the most recorded is, but we're talking over ten. There's a film, perhaps you saw it, with Sally Fields – *Sybil* it's called – that explains things very well. Now we know that your daughter has a history of nightmares going back quite some way—'

'What?'

'Mrs White. Both you and your husband were interviewed on that occasion – you must remember. I believe it was a teacher from school who alerted Social Services.'

'That cow! Accusing us of— But it was years ago, and it was only Bill Fairley who came and talked to us. I mean at the time he was practically a colleague.' Her mother sounded frightened.

'Yes, and as far as I can tell it went no further than that, or at any rate no action was recommended. But it was filed.

Now, getting back to your daughter, Patricia. At present she seems to have invented a twin, a little girl. She has on more than one occasion called her Angela, just like herself. She's an only child, so it isn't that unusual, although by her age children are usually developing other ways of coping. What interests me is the extent to which this alternative person is articulated. In MPD, multiple personality disorder cases, the patient often retreats into one of the alternative personalities if they feel threatened; or they might use an alternative personality to help them cope with a stressful situation. What is unusual is the degree that this other Angela is associated with ambiguous things, just like in a real relationship. It's almost as if your daughter has given her a life of her own that has now really taken root.'

'What does that mean?'

'Well, it's too early to make a diagnosis.'

'Tell me what you think about my daughter, damn it!'

There was a pause. Angela strained to hear Nicola's voice, which was low and serious. Behind the words she seemed to be saying: You asked for it. 'Angela has created this other self to help her deal with certain unpleasant experiences. Firstly it is highly significant that she refers to this other Angela as visiting her for weeks before the night that traumatized her. Secondly she does not retreat into the personality. Instead she has given the alternative personality itself the bad experiences and then banished it from her thoughts. That is why she associates it with bad things the whole time: horrid smells, coldness. I'm not sure about the rose bush motif, but the mind is a peculiar thing you know. Now, what I have to say is that I think the shock of her attempted murder has brought a lot of things back to the surface. This alternative personality is attempting to reassert itself. In other words it is trying to force Angela to come to terms with the bad experiences in her past.'

There was a pause. When her mother spoke again she sounded worried. 'But I've told you, them, everyone, time and time again, they were just nightmares. Angela's got an imagination. She let it run away with her. She even wrote a school essay about it – I remember her showing us.' Her mother sounded desperate now.

'That is as may be, but until we can be certain, regardless of the criminal investigation, I have to recommend that Mr White be kept away from Angela.'

'You're saying you think he abused her and then tried to—'

'I'm saying it's a possibility. Apart from the cuts and bruises picked up in the tunnels, there were clear indications that she had been tied by the wrists and gagged. It's my responsibility to make sure Angela is as safe as possible.'

'Why not arrest me and have done with it? If he was abusing her, then aren't I to blame? Doesn't that show that I'm a terrible mother? Just arrest me and have done with it.'

'Patricia, I can't comment. I'm just a social worker.'

'It all comes down to that bloody little imaginary friend, doesn't it?'

Angela moved away from the door. Nicola was saying that the other Angela was nothing more than a figment of her imagination. But she wasn't. She wasn't! She was real, or if not real, then apart, different from her. She had not simply thought her up. If she could prove that, then perhaps they would let Daddy out of prison.

The door knob rattled. Angela scurried back to the armchair and began busying herself with paper handkerchiefs. Her mother looked as if she had been whipped.

'I'll show them,' Angela said to herself. 'I'll show them.'

*

They drove back in silence, through the busy centre of town, past the bus station, out on to the ring road with the crowded grey housing estates, tower blocks and wide, windswept roads. Glancing across at her, it looked as if Angela's mother was on the verge of tears the whole time. She kept on biting her lower lip until there was a red crescent in the flesh. At the Long Barrow turn-off she almost ran over a young family at a zebra crossing.

Then they were climbing the edge of the moor. Two miles from the Edgerton road they got stuck behind the old bus that was grinding up the steep incline, almost stopping between gear changes, black smoke hanging in a drifting veil behind it.

Angela thought back to the evening when she had been so frightened on the road. Somehow, in the course of the weeks in between, her past had rolled itself into a great raggedy blind-eyed bundle that went bouncing and leaping behind her whenever she moved, threatening to knock her over, to split and pour its rotten memories all over her.

Suppose all those nightmare monsters that she had had when she was a kid had been real? Nicola had asked her a lot about them, but why had her parents got into trouble over them? Why had Uncle Bill asked questions about them? Did the police have a nightmare squad like they had a speed squad and a drug squad? And why did they blame her father?

'Are you all right now, Mum?'

'Yes, pet. Thanks.'

'Then what's wrong with you today? I mean what did Nicola say to you?'

'You mean you weren't listening?' Her mother tried a smile and sniffed. She changed down for the rise just after the Snare Brook bridge. 'She just said some things that

. . . that worried me, that's all.'

'About what?'

'I'll tell you when we get inside.'

A white shape detached itself from the roadside and floated in front of the car. A face, a terrible grinning face, surrounded by a frizz of red curls. Angela screamed: 'That's her!'

Mrs White slammed on the brakes, but the carrier bag advertising a children's toy shop just blew away across the moor towards the church. Angela's mother hit the steering wheel. 'NO! NO! NO!' she shouted. 'This has got to stop. Who? Who did you think that was?'

'The other Angela!'

'There is no other Angela! This horrid, stupid little game is what had your father arrested. Do you understand that? He is rotting in Long Barrow prison among real child molesters because of you! It's got to stop. DO YOU UNDERSTAND?'

'I can't make it stop!' Angela shouted back. 'I can't make it stop.'

'You must.'

'I can't. I can't help it that Daddy was arrested.'

'It's because of what you told them.'

Angela stared at her mother, her face a white mask of shock. Then she opened the car door and slipped outside.

'You come back here! You come back here this instant. Angela White, you come back here!'

Angela heard the car door slam as her mother got out. She left the road and darted on to the moor.

'Angela, you come here! I can't follow you.'

Angela turned. Her mother was teetering on her heels by the roadside.

'I'm walking home,' she said. 'I'll be all right.'

'Please.'

'Mummy, we'll talk when we get home.'

And she set off to walk the last half-mile home across the moor.

The wide horizon and the great marble dome of the sky above her lifted the top of her head off. She was hollow, light as a bird, her thoughts as clear as the air. She would just have to show people the other Angela. Then they would believe her and Daddy would be let out of prison.

She had not been looking where she was going, and too late saw the family of ramblers in bright anoraks and bobble hats. They were leaning on the wall, looking at the village, Cragside House in particular, through binoculars. One turned and saw her, then nudged another. She heard them say 'Look. D'you think?'

'Don't know.'

'No you ask.'

Another said: 'Oh for goodness sakes, leave the poor child be.' Their faces were rude and staring, naked in their curiosity, arrogant in their disregard for her feelings.

Even though there had been no pictures of her in the press, her hair colour and age had been referred to. How many twelve-year-old red-heads were there wandering around near Edgerton?

'D'you think she's all right?'

'She looks funny, Dad.' That from a girl her own age.

'Can we help you, pet?' Smirk, smirk.

They were standing between her and the shortest route home. There was nothing for it. She turned sharp right and headed for the churchyard. She could shin over the wall, then cut round the back of the church.

'Let her go.'

'All I did was ask.'

'Did you see her face?'

'Let her go.'

The wall was higher than she thought and she made quite a hash of climbing it, but it was a good barrier between her and them. She was closer to the village now. Lights on in windows. She saw the yuppies' outside spotlight flick on.

The ground was uneven under her feet. Sam Mossop had been in there with his new machine, cutting grass that had been uncut all summer. It lay in thick green swatches on the graves.

'Ow!'

A noose of bramble had ridden over her track shoes and snared her ankle, pricking the shin through her sock. She half turned, trying to kick her leg free but the noose held and she fell sideways against an old, crumbling headstone, brown with bramble stems.

Not brambles. Roses.

The earth seemed to tremble, and a breath from nowhere made tiny frost-blighted heads tremble, sway. Nod.

'What's she doing, Dad?'

She could see the disembodied heads of the family like gargoyles above the wall, one bobbing up and down as it strove to get a better view.

Angela watched her hands as they gripped the headstone, then moved to part the crawling mantle of rose stems.

Angela Fitt
Dearly Beloved Daughter
Of
Margery and Thomas Fitt
Who Departed This Life
January 21st 1850
aged
12 years and 7 months

Lost but always loved
Suffer the Little Children to Come Unto Me
A blossom cut off before the bloom

'Angela,' she breathed. 'Angela.' The earth caught the sound of voice and echoed Angela. Vapours, both sweet and rotten, poured up from the matted grass. The grey sky had lowered. It was the dome of a giant's skull.

'Angela.' Buried here, under her nose. Suffer the little children to come unto me. A blossom, cut off before the bloom. What did that mean?

Her mind raced. This was what she needed. If Mummy really thought that she was making it up, now she would understand that there was another Angela, that there was somebody talking to her, begging her to help.

'How can I help? How can I help?' she said out loud.

'Ooh-er. Reckon she's gone mad.'

'Should we get help?'

'Clear off. That's what's best.'

Angela stood and turned towards the wall. The heads disappeared like tin ducks in a fair ground. Then she turned and ran for home.

Her mother was in the kitchen, sitting at the table, staring blankly out of the window. Angela rushed in, excitement bubbling up inside her.

'Mummy, Mummy I've found it!'

Her mother rose silently and tried to hug her. Her arms were stiff and she used far too much force. She smelled slightly unwashed. Angela tried to pull away.

'Mummy, I've found it! I found where the voice is coming from.'

The words came out all muffled because she was being held so tightly, her face crushed against her mother's rib

cage. Her mother's hands were rubbing her head rhythmi-
cally and strongly, but it was as if she was not there.

'I'm so sorry, Angela. I'm so sorry. I let you down.'

Angela pulled her head away and looked up. She could
just see her mother's white, tear-stained face above the jut
of her breasts.

'I'll listen to you now, sweetheart. You can tell me about
everything. I'll listen. It's just so hard for me, but I will
now, I have to. Your voices. I'll try and listen too.'

'But that's just it,' Angela said. 'The voice isn't just inside
my head. It's outside. I found out where she's buried.'

'Darling, it's the strain. Nicola explained to me what it
is.'

'It's not the strain. Don't you see? It's making the
strain.'

'Wait there, darling.' Her mother left the room and
walked quickly upstairs. Angela followed the creaks along
the ceiling, waited until the telephone in the sitting-room
gave a quiet 'ting', then lifted the handset while it was still
ringing. Melanie said this was the best time to do it – they
always heard if you lifted it while someone was speaking.

A man answered with a number. 'Oh, could I speak to
Miss Hawkins please?' Her mother.

'Yes?'

'Oh Miss Hawkins, Nicola. You said to call if there were
any—'

'Yes, problems.'

'I'm sorry, am I interrupting you? Were you in the
middle of something?'

'Just hold on.' Angela heard a muffled voice shout to
turn the grill right down or they would burn. 'No. It's fine.'

'It's just that she came in, looking wildly over-excited,
claiming she knew where the voice was coming from. I
think she wants to show me something.'

'Let her. It's very important to let her play out her fantasies. If you can get involved too, then so much the better.'

'Oh.' Her mother sounded disappointed. 'So I just go along with it.' A distant man's voice could be heard down the phone.

'I think that would be best.'

'Right. Well thank you for your time. Sorry to disturb you.' Angela's mother hung up.

Angela did not bother to pretend. She was waiting downstairs with her anorak on, holding her mother's coat out for her. She led her outside.

Darkness was deep over the town in the valley, creeping up the moors towards them. Behind the village to the west the sky was clotted crimson. Half light, twilight, trick-light. It was like a gentle mist; you did not realize how little you could see until you were in the middle of it.

The ramblers had gone. The church steeple leaned against a pale moon which spread a trail of wet silver on the grass beneath their feet. Angela followed the trail and her mother walked behind. When Angela got to the grave she knelt. The branches of the rose bush had fallen back over the flat stone. She did not notice how thickly they grew.

'Look Mummy.' The moonlight blazed more brightly on the stone.

'Look Mummy, you can read it.' The rose stems moved.

Her mother screamed, but the light had clogged her lungs and filled her nose. 'Oh my God Angela, what have -you done? What are you doing?'

'She's here Mummy, she's here!'

Mrs White staggered back, caught her foot and fell. The ground was rippling, crawling. A million thorns were rippling down her back, her legs, prickling her head.

'Angela get back!'

Angela stood still, her arms outstretched in welcome.
The roses gathered.

It was a girl of buds and leaves. Moonlight mottled her,
blotching the petals of her flesh with shades of grey and
white. Her head was small, tilted to one side; her face a
dreadful mass of rotting buds, eyes like ripped darkness,
mouth a small, part open bloom, lips the crinkled edge of
frost browned petals, teeth the brown, curved thorns of last
year's growth. Her neck was a single broken stem. She
reached out with her thin arms, shook her rocking head
and trails of dead leaves fell in a dry, russet rain. She moved
her thin, twig hands over her pale body, showing where
decomposition had melted flesh, blackened and rotted her,
then tricked her with a single rose head nipple. When she
moved, thorns rattled in her thin legs, tapering to points
perhaps two feet off the ground, twitching and jerking in
the memory of the last snapping moment of pain.

Angela stretched out a hand. An arm of briars floated
lazily towards her, petals falling in soft flakes as she moved.
Angela took the hand. The Rose Girl began to move, gently,
haphazardly across the graveyard, her head leading the
way, her body trailing loosely behind like a crackling
cloak.

Time slipped away as they moved from the graveyard.
Angela was not aware of it at all, but her mother felt a
great rushing, as wide and relentless as an avalanche. The
lights in the valley dimmed, the stars grew brighter. A fox
barked; the moor was busy suddenly with sheep. The smell
of burning wood and peat hung over the village like a
shroud.

The moor must have been cultivated then because they
were walking on a springy blanket of closely cropped grass;

to her left Patricia saw the great chimney of the smithy belching black smoke and sparks into the still night air.

And she heard the sound of weaving coming from a tiny cottage in a dip.

'No. NO!' Angela's voice cut across her thoughts. She looked up. At first she could not see what was happening, but then it became clear that the Rose Girl was growing. Stars showed through her terrible sides now. She was made of moonlight and darkness. Higher and higher she soared into the heavens, past The Plough, past Castor and Pollux. Far far above them, they saw Orion's belt loosen. It dangled now. It twitched. It looped itself into a rough noose and fell over the Rose Girl's neck.

'NO!'

But the shape floated higher, higher. Stopped. Held for a second.

Then fell.

The world rattled. The sound of the loom filled their ears as the neck broke in the heavens. Stars bled. Blackness rushed like a howling dog across the void. At first they thought that stars were falling but it was not stars but roses, tumbling from the heavens to land softly at their feet.

The loom sound stopped. Stars jerked back to their places, dimmed and the sky grew red above the town while a car horn sounded outside the village pub and a little heap of thorns and petals twitched at Angela's feet.

Part Three

CHAPTER TWENTY SEVEN

Aworkman in white overalls, a roll-up glued to his lower lip, was chipping away at one of the main pillars of the prison.

'If it's cracks in this you're in trouble,' he said to an uninterested guard. 'Thing is, these builders didn't know what they were doing half the time. Some of them put iron rods through the piers. Well that might be all right for Tom and Dick, but what about Harry? That's what I say. If there's damp in it, the iron rusts, it rots the brick, and Bob's your uncle. I mean look at this. You've got water coming in through that light up there, dripping right down on your rendering over there. It's got under the skin, I'll promise you that. In fact.' He pulled away a lump of plaster. 'Look at that.'

The plaster was a solid slab, the size of a hand. 'Hello, looks like some joker's been at this. Look at this. It's a bloody disgrace! Bloody hell, the whole pile's almost rotted through.'

'Sooner the place falls down the better, as far as I'm concerned,' the guard said.

'At this bloody rate it's going to be bloody soon and all,' the man said. 'I can't do work on this. I can't be involved.

If this pile's this bad, you've got to shore up those beams somehow, bring it right down and put up a new one.'

'You!' The guard pointed at Jim. 'Get the fuck out of here now.'

Jim walked on. Things were easier now that he had a red band. He could move around the prison without an escort and was trying to organize a mobile library – in other words a trolley he could load books on to and wheel around from cell to cell. Having a table left out on recreation nights had proved successful, but he had to limit the number of books taken to two each, and there was no way of anticipating the next time they might be let out for 'association', the new word for being allowed to talk to one another. It was a good trick. If you called it association, the prison officers could object to it officially. It sounded better to say that they wanted to limit association, than saying they wanted to stop the men from talking to one another.

Jim knocked on the library door, waited. To his surprise it was opened by Jack Lyall. He looked at Jim with something approaching pity in his eyes. Shook his head and waved him to a chair.

'What's the matter?' Jim asked.

Lyall sat down heavily. 'No use beating about the bush. Good news and bad news. Here. You'd better read this.' He took a copy of the local paper out of his pocket.

'It's a bit old. Well ten days to be precise. It's down the bottom right hand corner.'

The father of Angela White, the little girl found battered and suffering from memory loss in a cavern on the moors, was arrested last Sunday in a spectacular dawn swoop. Brian White is a security consultant and retired police officer of Edgerton on the Moor. While yet to be charged, his arrest is also being linked with the murder of Mary Hendersley, who disappeared five years ago, whose remains were also found in the cavern. It is rumoured that certain items found in the cave may link Brian White to the location at this time or an earlier date.

Jim pushed the paper away. The first thing he thought was that he needed a solicitor. The second was that he could not believe that Brian White was a murderer. The third was that Brian had been quite happy to believe that he was a murderer, so what was he worried about?

'You always maintained you had nothing to do with the prostitute, didn't you?' Lyall said.

'That and everything else,' Jim said.

'I have to confess I always thought you were as guilty as hell,' Lyall said.

'And now?'

'Well, this doesn't prove that you're innocent. It might just prove that you were in it with this Brian White character and he's only just got caught.'

'Right,' said Jim.

'Is there anything else you want me to do?' Lyall asked.

Jim thought for a moment. 'I'd be grateful if you could tell me who the arresting officer was.'

Lyall nodded, then said: 'Oh, read on a bit if you want another gruesome little titbit. The box in bold type at the bottom of the page.'

Jim looked down. The headline said: 'Ancient Grave May Yield Clue to Past.'

Events of the weekend leading to the arrest of former police sergeant Brian White, may also shed light on a mystery that has perplexed local crime historians for over a hundred and forty years. A search of the cave on

the moors where Brian White's daughter was found
revealed a memorial slab, dedicated to the memory of a
young girl, her murdered and brutalized body found on
that very spot, over one hundred years ago. Thomas
Lestrange, a local weaver, although arrested and subsequently hanged for the murder, always protested his
innocence. And the site, once a tourist attraction, was
lost.

Jim read the second piece twice, wondering if it contra-
vened the sub judice laws in any way and deciding that it
probably did not – quite. Then he put his head in his hands
and thought. Lestrange was now in the prison and out of
it, somehow cutting off his means of escape. He knew it
shouldn't seem personal, but he couldn't help feeling a bit
victimized. Which, for all he knew, was the point.

CHAPTER TWENTY EIGHT

'As I was walking on the stair I met a man who wasn't there. I met him there again today, I wish that man would go away.' That seemed to sum it up better than the old standby that fast track cadets, graduates mostly, used to stick above their desks just to show that they could read and write. 'When you have eliminated the impossible, whatever remains, however improbable, must be the truth.'

The problem was that you never got to the stage of eliminating the impossible. You couldn't. It was possible that an elephant had been smuggled into the cells at night; it was possible that the Queen Mother had a spare set of keys to the prison and ran amok whenever one of her horses lost a race. It was possible – anything was possible. After the longest and most exhaustive man-hunt in British criminal history, the Yorkshire Ripper was finally caught by a uniformed policeman on the beat. The Ripper had been pulled in twice previously for questioning. The constable who finally arrested him only did so on a hunch.

So anything was possible when the crimes were impossible. Locked cells. Too much blood for any of the staff or any of the men to commit a murder and go undetected. No secret tunnels. No hollow walls.

A sparrow made a stupid noise above his head. Jim had opened one of the high windows of the library by winding a long, brass crank but then had found that he could not shut it. The birds treated the library as a bit of outside, flitting in and out, nesting, squabbling, staring down with that idiotic jerking of the head.

One bird detached itself from the group on the window ledge and began to flit around the room, dipping and turning as if it was looking for something. It landed on a bookcase. Jim pursed his lips and whistled, trying to make a sparrow sound. The bird cocked its head. It was listening. He chirruped some more. The bird looked at him, hopped into space, fell, picked itself up. But this time, instead of dipping, it flew, straight as a bullet, for the embroidered rug.

'No!'

Jim's cry and the chair hitting the ground behind him were simultaneous. The bird was going straight for the wall, straight for the hanging, going to crash into it – through it?

The bird had gone. The room was suddenly silent.

Jim looked around. It was not there. It had been swallowed, absorbed, like a coin in a conjuror's handkerchief. He checked every shelf, every corner. Feeling self-conscious he lifted the rug away from the wall and checked behind it. Nothing. The birds had gone from the window ledge. Under the hanging was a feather, a single soft, brown feather, and when he put it to his cheek he imagined it was warm.

He stood in front of the blanket.

'All right,' he said. 'Tell me. Tell me what's going on. Tell me what really happened. Now. Then. I don't care. Just tell me! Come out and tell me!'

As he spoke he felt his anger ball up inside him. He punched the blanket, half expecting his fist to go through. It slammed against the cold wall behind, and hurt.

He waited.

And waited.

He began to feel stupid and laughed. Perhaps it was like watching a kettle boil or waiting for a meal to come in a fancy restaurant. When finally you couldn't wait another minute, all you had to do was light up a fag and hey presto! after two drags it was there.

It was there.

The S of Strange was a double-ended hook. It slipped invisibly through the air, cut through the soft skin underneath Jim's chin, and pinioned his tongue to the roof of his mouth. The pain was distant, anaesthetized and dull. Silence wrapped itself around his head like a duvet.

His head was jerked up. The blanket began to glow. Light dissolved the wall behind like acid, leaving the feathery lines of the village intact, but swinging out now into full perspective.

There was smoke billowing out from chimneys, wood smoke. A man was pulling a horse slowly up the lane past the graveyard which was empty now but for a few tombstones. He saw birds flying free over the rolling moor, heard the bleating of lambs, the steady clanging of a blacksmiths, little sounds, familiar sounds coming to him one by one, as if he were a child and a patient adult was trying to teach him something. No, not teach exactly, but show him enough so he could find it all out for himself from observation.

He turned his head this way and that, following the sounds. The creak of wagon wheels were from the hay wain just coming to stop outside the inn. The joyful whinny of a horse: that from a field below the blacksmith's.

The steady clacking of a loom drifted out of an open cottage door, a cottage that was almost smothered with dogroses. There was a man, standing by the pump in the middle of the village, seemingly lost but with a big, happy smile on his face. Jim thought the man looked a lot like Joe Cohen.

Then he heard the cry of a child, floating up from the village, right at the top above the little cottage – where the big house stood. Another cry, not from the house – no, not quite, but from the grounds. That funny shaped building seemingly half underground, what did they call them? Ice Houses.

The creak of a rope. A sudden silence. In the silence a sudden snap.

Oh my God.

Jim swallowed. Something dropped in the middle of his mind, a trap door, snapping open, bringing with it a blinding revelation.

Lestrange. Strange. He did not know if he was calling out loud or just thinking. *The ghost was taking people to his village. That was what he was offering them: a way out. Freedom.*

He tried to pull away from the hanging but as he did so microscopic threads of blackness flew from it, pierced his lips, drew his mouth open and dragged his face nearer. His face distorted. His lips were pulled further apart, then out, forming a loose tunnel. He wanted to close his mouth but the threads would not let him. They pulled him towards the rug until his lips met it.

Vacuum. Stillness. Something gathered in front of him. He could not see it clearly because his eyes were too close to the rug, but he sensed something was moving through the warp and weft of the fabric, something not only in the fabric, but of it, searching blindly for him, so it could—

His body suddenly burned. He was hooked. All over his

body tiny threads were working their way through his skin. His arms were jerked upwards, his legs hauled apart until he was spreadeagled against the wall. Still the threads worked through him, pulling him closer and closer until it seemed that he would be absorbed and woven into the fabric.

The wool twitched under him. A man shape grew, becoming stronger, harder, more definite.

Jim struggled to get away but he was sewn into the material now. Something was happening.

The rug gave a massive convulsion. Jim grunted and tried to scream. The shape in the rug was trying to join him, get into him, force its way through his body as if he were somehow a sieve, not a man at all, just a loose mesh of cells.

His skin resisted, then suddenly gave. Something dark and cold and vigorous coursed through him, freezing him with the cold of eternity, then boiling him with the power of its hatred. For a terrible bloated second his body held two forms, then time burst open like a rotten fruit and the thing was through him, streaming through him in a filthy, tattered wave. A scream of laughter, hatred, fear, passion that thrilled and appalled him, then . . .

The rug disintegrated into rotten tatters. Jim threw himself at the door but it was locked.

He rattled it. Put his mouth to the keyhole and yelled through it, banged on it with his fists.

A key. Was there a key in Tindall's desk?

He flung the top open. Nothing, just stale digestives, tea bags and a piece of folded paper. He took the paper out and spread it on the desk top.

It was the diagram of the wooden loom, with arrows to show how the frame, the beams, the treadle, and the harness all fitted together. The blanket would have been made on a loom.

He ran to the door again, and banged on it. There was no reply. It was a good hour before he was due to be let out for lunch.

The loom. He remembered how on the first day he had seen a pile of timbers in the corner of the cellar, right at the back where the blanket had been folded.

The weaver's loom. Lestrange had woven that village. Could he weave something else?

Jim collected the timbers in three journeys to and from the cellar. As he started fitting them together he felt almost as if his hands were being guided. He worked in a daze until a guard unlocked the library door at tea time. Jim stood up, almost finished. The loom looked like a complicated wooden box.

'Bloody great,' the guard said. 'What are you doing? Building a fucking time machine?'

That night Jim lay awake a long time in the darkness. At midnight, at one, at two, at three, he heard the guards doing the rounds. At four, and at five. At six o'clock he was jerked out of a light, swooping sleep by a sound in the corridor. Rustling.

He rushed to the door, pressing his ear to it, but then was forced back, hand over his mouth and nose as he caught a smell of something foul and awful and familiar, eddying into the cell.

His skin contracted. Sweat squeezed out. He put his lips to the keyhole and whispered, 'I understand, it's all right. I understand.'

Too late for that. He went to the window and began to suck in the cold outside air. There was the yard, the gallows yard, the earth looking faint and grey under the arc lights.

Birds were gathering on the perimeter wall, pouring out of the prison from the roofs, from the galleries, from the eaves and gutters where they nested. They dropped through the air, landing on the perimeter wall of the yard, all pointing in the same direction, staring in.

A scream wavered through the air. The birds rose in a chattering cloud, sparrows, starlings, robins, blackbirds. One detached itself from the wheeling mass and flapped raggedly towards the prison.

Jim clapped his hands, shouted, tried to keep the bird away. Oblivious, the bird flapped towards him, and then, at a point about twenty yards away, stopped dead. Jim watched it plummet, recover, fall again, seeming to scrape down an invisible wall in the air. Feathers were ripped away from his wing as it helicoptered slowly down. Patches of bare skin appeared on its wings, its back. It cawed once, was sucked through a shimmering wall in the darkness and then there was nothing, except a blur of black feathers, blowing in the wind.

CHAPTER TWENTY NINE

If it hadn't been a Sunday it might have been different.
Certain irregularities might have been picked up and
acted upon. Things would have started just the same, but
they might have been stopped sooner and the riot would
not have spread like an epileptic fit through the cells of the
old stone honeycomb. A fire-fighter said it was like not
smelling the smoke until your bed was on fire. Other people
talked about pressure cookers, brush fires, boilers, dam
bursts, dynamite situations, tinderboxes, and powder-kegs
(leading no doubt to explosions of evil). For a while it was
metaphor-a-go-go. The visible end result, in the immortal
words of the head of the Prison Officers' Association,
interviewed outside the main gates of the prison while the
riot was at its height, was 'criminal damage'.

But to be fair it was a difficult and confusing week and in
the end nobody really understood what had happened
except Jim Carroll, William Fairley, Brian White and young
Angela. And even they did not understand until the very
end.

In one prison there's a story that a group of drug barons
were playing poker one evening. It was getting close to

lights-out when one of them, who had been losing steadily
all evening, was dealt a particularly good hand. He called
his lieutenant over and whispered that if he could start a
diversion, just to keep the guards occupied for two or three
minutes, he'd be forever in his debt. Two days and a few
thousand roof slates later they finally finished the game
which had turned out to be a marathon. The man who had
started the riot was given eight ounces of Old Holborn, a
gram of cocaine and a bottle of Johnny Walker by his
grateful boss.

It doesn't always happen like that. A group of prisoners
in the 1980s called themselves the Backbench Committee
and set themselves up as a national protest group – easy
enough when it is estimated that as much as a third of the
prison population of the UK is in transit between penal
establishments at any one time. Word travels fast between
prisons – one explanation for the spate of riots in the long
hot summer of 1989 which had the government screaming conspiracy and anarchy at the prison service and the
prison service screaming 'we told you so' at the government. And the prisoners gave the world the finger which
was all most of them wanted to do anyway.

Then there was a case up in Scotland where a prison
nearly went up in flames when one of the men found a rat-
dropping in his cornflakes. There were rat-droppings in the
cornflakes, bird-shit in the marge, hairs in the mashed
potatoes every single day but on that particular day it sent
someone, and then the entire prison, berserk. And when
that happens there is nothing the authorities can do except
withdraw behind the wall and wait.

Looking back no one really ever knew how the Long
Barrow riot happened. It seemed to start at about four
different times. Whether the first three were abortive
attempts to start it or just turns of the screw, so to speak,

bringing the tension up to an unbearable pitch, we just don't know.

Seven o'clock in the morning and the relief shift was getting late. That was unusual. The officer on duty in the perspex observation box seemed to be dozing, his head smeared slackly against the perspex, which was rare too. The air was heavy, but cold. There were two officers on A Wing that night, Mitchel and Harrison. Harrison was still training officially; Mitchel was due to retire in four months' time. They got on all right, although sometimes Mitchel thought that Harrison had about as much sense as a hamster and was considerably less alert.

At seven-fifteen he said he was sick of waiting, told Harrison to wait at his post, and went off to the locker rooms to see what was keeping the selfish bastards.

Harrison fingered his panic button, jangled his keys importantly and went for a walk down the corridor.

At the second cell he came to, he heard a voice hiss: 'Hey boss, what's wrong?'

'Oh, nothing that should concern you. Just a little delay. Probably someone lost a key. Ho ho.' He had a kind voice, a sort of slippers-and-cardigan brummie burr, and a useless sense of humour.

He walked on down the landing. Banging started behind him. It sounded as if someone was hitting their bed frame with a hammer. He dashed back, looked in through the peep-hole. Nothing. Nobody. The cell looked empty. The bastards had to be hiding, probably standing on either side of the door. He put his mouth to the peep-hole and said: 'Okay, men. Very funny I don't think.'

Banging started at the other end of the landing. He ran down there and was about to look through the keyhole when it started in a cell somewhere between them.

He radioed down to the observation post.

'What's the problem? Christ is that the time?'

'Trouble on Level Three. A Wing.'

The man asked sleepily what sort of trouble.

'Banging and crashing.'

'Is that Harrison? Where's Mitchel?'

'Gone looking for the relief shift.'

'Maintain cell integrity. Wait for him. I've got you on video. Under no circumstances compromise cell integrity.'

Harrison dropped the handset. The noise was getting awful. He put his hands over his ears, remembered it did not look very professional and took them away.

The banging stopped. Relief for a second. Then a gurgling cry, suddenly cut off.

Which cell? The first one looked empty again. As did the second.

In the third one, he saw a man hanging by a pair of knotted trousers from the light fitting, turning this way and that, his feet twitching and jerking in the air.

He cried out and reached for his keys.

His radio fizzed. 'Maintain cell integrity. Maintain cell integrity.' But he did not hear. He opened the door, dashed inside and was suddenly enveloped in white as a pillowcase was dropped over his head. The man swinging from the light fitting twisted in mid-air and aimed a strong accurate kick at his throat. Harrison went down like a cow in a slaughterhouse.

It was a three-man cell. One of the men snatched the key ring in his belt loops. The other two men secured the pillowcase around Harrison's head and tied his wrists and ankles. They looped a sheet around his armpits, tied another round his neck. The plan was to hang him over the railings by the sheet under his arms and threaten to snatch it away if anyone tried to get close, breaking his neck. At that moment Mitchel appeared at the head of the stairs with the relief shift.

If they had been a minute later, it would have been different. Another cell would have been opened; the odds would have been more even. But it was an unequal battle. The guards were well fed, two of them were very fit, and they were angry. The prisoners were badly fed, unfit and caught at the psychological moment, just before their plan could be put into effect.

They were beaten back into their cells, then one of them, picked at random, had his front teeth knocked out on the end of his bed, *pour encourager les autres*. Nobody realized at the time that he had also been concussed by a blow to the head. Later that day he would fall unconscious and drown in the blood welling from the craters in his gums.

Brian White woke up in his cell on C Wing on the landing where the sectioned prisoners and men on remand were held. Under section 43 of criminal law, inmates of Her Majesty's prisons who are likely to be killed or seriously injured during their stay in prison can be isolated from the other men, watched over by guards whose role is not so much to see that they don't escape as to make sure they are not caught in the open by the other cons.

Brian shared a cell with a man called Smith who had banged his eight-month-old baby's head on the wall until she stopped crying and a minor celebrity called Maguire the Mouth who had shopped an East End gang in the mid-seventies but had since been unable to avoid an eight-year sentence for pushing drugs to minors.

Brian had not been inside for long enough to know that at seven o'clock in the morning, if you hadn't heard the screws beginning to open doors for slopping out, you were in trouble. The sectioned prisoners slopped out before anyone else and had to be back in their cells before the

regular prisoners lined up. This was to stop the regular
prisoners emptying the buckets on the beasts, as they were
known, rather than in official receptacles. Smith and the
Mouth woke him and told him to get dressed. They were
nervous but Brian did not know why. They sat and waited
in silence.

After he had seen the bird die, Jim had not slept. The sky
was white and throbbing a morse code of sickness. And he
was trying to get his tired and shocked mind to think.

   The prison, temporary home to seven hundred odd men,
was the permanent home to a ghost. Say it like that and it
almost seems reasonable. This ghost had been killing
people as well. People who were in despair, people who felt
that they were a cut above the rest of the prisoners, people
who wanted to go and live in that trick village embroidered
on the blanket – oh the whole thing was absurd. And yet
he had seen it and felt it. He knew what it could do. Dear
God. It might take over the whole prison. And yet what
was containing it? Or what had contained it until now?
And he had the oddest feeling that he was still missing the
point.

   Eight o'clock. The prison was getting noisy. Men were
banging on their cell doors, rattling the bars of their cages.
Everything was running an hour late and would be
running later still now because they would have to double
the screws on each landing to supervise slopping out,
which meant that everything would take twice as long.
Not only that, breakfast would be either stone cold or burnt
to a crisp, and that would make everyone even happier.

   Ten o'clock. Breakfast had been eaten in enforced
silence. Cold rather than crisped. Back in his cell Jim tried
to read, tried to think and couldn't do either.

   Shouting from a cell down the landing, followed by

bellows from the screw, followed by the sound of a door being opened. A fight. A man being dragged off to solitary.

So what? Jim thought. We're all in solitary more or less. But what about that man Lestrange? When you came to think of it, it was funny that there weren't more ghosts in prison. Perhaps they were kept in cells too.

Jesus Christ, was that a clue? Where did the ghost live? Where did it come from when it was summoned? Where did the damn thing live? Ghosts don't live anywhere. They're dead. So where did the damn thing die? Where did it die?

Lestrange had been hanged.

Jim walked quickly to the window. Some of the prisoners had been allowed out today at any rate. They were working in a small gang, digging what looked like manure into the ground of Old Yard. All the flags had been taken up now. They were leaning against the wall like toppled tombstones.

Old Yard. Tombstones. Gallows Yard. Oh my God.

Then Jim saw the ghost.

The men all had their backs to him. They were looking at something that one of them had dug up, standing in a circle. But Lestrange stood apart, a black shadow in the shadow of a buttress, watching, his head tilted to one side while the guard threw away his roll-up and sauntered over to the men.

The guard joined the group, which was peering down at the ground. The prisoners all stood back. Let him into the middle of a loose circle. Then they stood back, lifted their shovels, and let them fall, like the petals of a metal flower closing.

Jim's spit hit the window as he shouted. The guard was on his knees now, the shovels smashing on to his back, his head, his legs, in unison. Thud. Thud. Thud.

You might even think they were being controlled.

When Jim opened his eyes the ghost was dancing. The creature hovered above the ground, its legs twitching loosely, his arms raised, imitating the movement of the men, or a hanged man's last kick repeated over and over again. Blood was staining the ground red when the shovels stopped. A prisoner knelt and took the keys from the officer's belt and ran inside.

Jim's mind poured into and through the prison like liquid filling a maze. He saw the guards at an early lunch, relaxing because the men were all in their cells. He saw the empty perspex observation post and a man in uniform at an open cell door, putting a wad of bank notes in his pocket. He saw the prisoner with the keys running along the top landing on A Wing, opening doors. He saw another guard bludgeoned to the ground. His keys snatched. Prisoners running silently through the prison in grey waves, opening doors, overpowering guards.

Gradually he heard the sound build. First a murmur, then a roar, then a howling hurricane of sound. His own door was flung open by a man with a wild face, blood streaming from a cut above his eye.

'Come on! Out, out, out!'

The ghost was gone from his garden.

Feeling sick, Jim walked from his cell. The siren began to wail.

A bed ripped from the floor, sailed through the air and crashed through the rotten wire netting. Startled guards were running across the floor. A posse of them made a rough wedge and tried to force a way through a scrum of prisoners who were all heading for the sectioned landing on C Wing. Two guards were standing at the head of the landing, beating back prisoners who were trying to get to the cells with their truncheons. A guard was hustled out of the observation post and carried on the shoulders of prisoners to a cell where he was thrown to the floor and the door locked. The posse of guards had made it to the staircase of C Wing. Prisoners, beaten from behind were forced up, past the two men who seemed to disappear under a sea of grey. Then they realized what was happening. One turned and began to unlock the cells. He managed to open four doors, before the prisoners who had gone past them saw what was happening. The twelve or so sectioned prisoners were hustled out and down the steps, then bustled in a swirling scrum of blue and grey across the floor. Bed legs, slop buckets, radios – anything that came to hand – slammed into the floor around them. A group of guards at the door to the administration block ran out, met the scrum, ushered them in, then slammed the door behind them.

Jim noticed that about five prisoners slipped through with them with their hands on their heads, obviously determined not to get involved with the riot.

He looked around. As far as he could see there were no guards anywhere in the prison. There was a brief commotion as the chaplain was hustled across the hall and thrown at the door. It opened briefly and was slammed shut again.

Smoke. There were fires in some of the cells now. A burning mattress was dragged on to a balcony and tossed down. Then another, and another. They were piled together in the middle of the floor. Tables and chairs were hurled on to it. Men began to dance around the pile.

Someone had taken a music box and turned it up full volume. The beat, furred by distortion, slammed through the prison.

Jim looked at his watch. An hour had passed like a minute. Someone found a firehose and began dousing the fire in the centre of the hall. Then a loudspeaker cut through the cacophony.

'Enough! Enough. It's ours boys. It's ours!'

Jim looked across to a balcony on C Wing. There was a group of prisoners standing in a line. Randall with a megaphone in his hand stood in the middle flanked by George and a couple of other men, body builders by the look of them, with muscles like melons.

'That's enough. That's enough. Time for more of that later. Now listen everyone. Listen to me.'

Gradually the sounds of destruction ceased. Men looked up from the floor. Men left their cells. Men stopped shouting. Men stood and watched. The music was turned off. There was a moment of dead silence.

'We've done it, men. We've done it and we never even knew that we could. We've done what no one else had ever managed to do. We've cleared the prison. You've cleared the prison. The prison is ours!'

There was a half-hearted cheer from the floor.

'Don't be afraid to cheer. I said don't be afraid to cheer! There's no one to stop you now.'

This time the response was louder but by no means unanimous. Randall held up his hands. 'Over the past few months we've put up with a lot. We've put up with too much. We've put up with beatings, with bad food. Only today Tommy Chambers was dragged off to the cells for complaining, complaining about the food he was given to eat for breakfast.'

This time the men roared. 'Just this morning Harry Johnson was beaten up and left. He's dead now, men. Dead. He drowned in his own blood. Left in his cell to die like a rat. Do we have to put up with that? Do we have to put up with that?'

This time it seemed like the entire prison roared 'NO!'

'Do we have to put up with the treatment? Being treated like animals. I tell you this. If you're treated like an animal, you act like one.'

This time the place erupted. Men cheered, barked, squawked, yelped, but looking down Jim saw that it was still not everyone. Some of them were looking around, moving uneasily from the central hall that was filling with prisoners from the balconies.

He hasn't got them all yet, Jim thought. *Not all of them. There's a chance this could be turned.* Randall leant on the balcony.

'This is our chance to do something,' he said. 'This is our chance to really make a difference.' The tone of his voice changed. It was easy now, more conversational. 'But tell me, what is it that we all want?'

Silence.

'What is it that we all really want?' His voice was lighter again. He cupped a hand to his ear and bent his head.

'I want to get the fuck out of here, boss,' a voice said. It might as well have been staged. Randall looked delighted and clapped his hands. Laughter erupted. When it had died down he held his hands out to the crowd below.

'Right, men. Get out of here. And what does that mean? It means one thing: freedom. Freedom.' He paused again. 'Do you think we'll get it?'

'Course we bloody will.' That voice again. More laughter.

'How?' Randall asked. His voice dropped. It was sneering now, low and sarcastic. 'How will we get it? Look around you. Look at this place. What do you think'll happen when you walk out of here? Do you think they'll give you a cup of tea, and a pat on the back for giving yourselves up? Oh no. Oh no. Blood's been spilt, men. And they want blood. Look out in the old yard. You'll see a screw out there, and he's dead. He's lying on the ground with his head flattened.

Not all of you knew that, did you? And you don't know who did it either. They don't outside and they don't care. It'll be blood for blood. I tell you this. Anyone, any one of you can walk up to that door there and knock on it. They'll let you out and none of us will stop you. But what'll happen to you, nobody knows. What you've got to do is make a choice. And the choice is this. Go out there and take the consequences. Or stay with me. Because I can offer you freedom.'

'And who the fuck do you think you are?' A voice shouted.

In answer Randall lifted his arms. There was silence for a second. Jim looked up at the windows high above them and noticed what looked like darkness creeping across the glass. It pressed inwards. Something groaned. A shiver went through the building and small chunks of masonry fell from one of the pillars. The darkness out there was not just an absence of light. It was physical, heavy. The glass groaned. Wisps of black, like wet, sticky smoke began to drip downwards.

Mass hypnosis, Jim thought. It has to be mass hypnosis of some kind. He stepped forward to the railings.

'Don't listen!' he shouted. 'Don't listen.'

The air lightened slightly and seemed to grow thinner. Randall looked across at him. Jim tore his eyes away and gripped the railing of the balcony.

'Don't listen to him. It's not true what he says. He just wants control. He'll sell you down the river as soon as you blink. Give yourselves up and we'll all get a fair hearing. There was someone killed. I saw it. The ones who did it are the ones who'll be punished. You'll get justice.'

Like your justice? I'll give them justice. My justice.
And freedom.

He could not say where the voice came from. It was enough to rock him. The darkness grew. Randall was pointing at him. The men around him were moving away, heading for the staircases.

'I tell you—' he began, but the air was suddenly thick in his lungs. His hands began to grip the railing. He looked down and saw that they were twisting, the muscles on his forearm standing out like ropes, his whole arm was being pulled over and round and the railing was writhing in his palms. It was no longer metal but something soft and growing, fleshy and strong. Thorns began to spout along its length. He felt them under his palm, pushing upwards into the skin, up and through. He screamed as a great hooked spike broke though the back of his hand, shaggy with his flesh like seaweed on a shark's fin. Then another and another, until he had hands of thorns, like a rose himself, and he was standing there, screaming with pain and fear, fighting to stay upright, terrified of what would happen to him if he fell. But the pain was too great. A red shutter fell over his eyes. He staggered back from the railing and fell into blackness.

CHAPTER THIRTY

His head pounded and ropes were burning his ankles. He opened his eyes and closed them fast. The world was upside down and his head and hands were full of blood and throbbing dully. Over the roaring in his ears he heard another deeper roaring, punctuated by dull crashes. The prison was falling apart.

His head swam. The world was swaying. To steady himself he risked opening his eyes again, and this time he saw rich and luminous shards of colour, red earth, azure sky, still, ivory faces. A man on a cross. Upside down.

The scene swayed and twisted. Jim tried to turn back but only succeeded in twisting himself in the opposite direction. Nausea swam downwards. Tears flooded into his eyes. He blinked, upwards, and wet ran down the bridge of his nose and over his forehead. He felt panic, tried to steady himself by looking down and thought he was going mad. He was floating above a floor that dipped away from him, like the hull of a boat. He looked up and saw a chequered floor, twenty, thirty feet above, below his head. Below his head.

He was not floating. He was hanging. Hanging by his feet, suspended from a beam high above the floor. He twisted his neck. Those colours had come from the big, stained-glass window above the altar, blooming with the afternoon sun, where Christ in his glory was welcoming the saved to paradise.

The pain hit him as he became aware of his situation. His feet felt as if they were being torn from his ankles. His hands had been dangling down above, no below, his head and were dark with pooled blood. He brought them up to his waist and tried to hold on to his waistband with them but they were heavy and numb. He flexed them gingerly and feeling came back with a dull burning, then a rush of pins and needles. His split cheek was throbbing terribly. His whole head felt like a rotten orange.

He tried to flex his back, but could only twitch up a pathetic six inches from the perpendicular. How did they do it in the films? It was as if the blood in his head were a lead weight. He simply could not move, and now to make matters worse his movements were making him spin slowly round. As he completed the last arc of the revolution a dark, swollen face, drifted past his. He recoiled and closed his eyes, then had to wait for the next slow pass to see ...

A dead man hanging, his hands tied behind his back, dressed in prison uniform like himself, but the heart had stopped and blood had drifted down the feathery maze of capillaries to pool in the lowest part of his body. His face was blue, heavy with the clotting blood, the eyes bulging behind thickened eyelids. The lips had swollen, the tongue hung down past his nose like a thick tie. His ears were aubergine blue, the skin shiny and taut like a ripe fruit.

Jim swallowed bile upwards, flexed his hands, twitched his back, tried to get even the slightest amount of bend in his knees, anything to try to get circulation going.

So what do I do? Hang here and die? He fought to control his panic. And just what the hell was going on out there? It sounded as if every bed in the place were being thrown

off the landings and crashing down on to the floor. It was
not the sound of a riot so much as methodical destruction.

As he rotated, he began to look more closely around him.
Something long and grey that snaked away diagonally
flashed across the corner of his eye and was gone. He
wiggled, to get more speed, twisted again, ignoring the
burning in his ankles, and the thought that if the knot
slipped he would go crashing down on to the floor below
like a high diver. Christ though, it was hard to control the
movement. Every reaction produces an equal and opposite
reaction, or something, and whatever he did deliberately
seemed to cancel out the last movement. He twisted again,
this time flinging his arms out to try and give his body some
torque.

There. There! That was what he had seen. The rope.
They must have flung it over the beam, tied his feet to it,
then hoisted him high into the roof like a side of meat. How
to get over to it? How to swing, rather than twist?

He jerked his body again. God it was hard – his back was
on the rack of his own weight – but he had moved through
space. Back and forth. Back and forth. He jerked again.
This time he only succeeded in cancelling out the movement and he slowed again. Careful, careful. It was like
trying to start a yoyo off from scratch. He felt the rope
around his ankle slip, and desperately bent his foot out at
a right angle, forcing the knot back to his Achilles tendon.
Cramp splayed his toes. Don't think about it. Just swing,
baby, swing.

He swung. He found that the best way, once he had a bit
of momentum going, was to flex his back and neck very
slightly at the dead moment which came at the end of each
swing. The rope creaked. He blessed whoever had strung
him for giving him enough. The tiled floor arched below
him in a long blur and he suddenly realized that he had

been so intent on blocking out the pain and getting moving that he had forgotten where the rope was. He looked around. Down. To the wall. There.

His heart nearly stopped. The rope had been attached to an old gas light fitting. He could see it move as he swung. A gap opening and closing in the plaster. God damn it, the whole wall was bulging around it. It was about to tear itself loose. He reached out as he swung, his fingertips still feet away from the rope.

Something cannoned into him. The slight movement transmitted through the beam had set the corpse moving in its own arc. Muscles creaked up and down Jim's back. His hand was a good two feet away from the rope. At the dead point he bent his knees and tried to twist the whole movement of the swing around. There! But he mis-timed the grab. His hand closed on empty air. Back again. A chunk of plaster fell from the wall. Up. Closer.

Missed it again! As he swung back he felt the rope around his ankles go dead. He flew like a sack of grain, stretched out with a cry to embrace the empty air, and instead found his arms wrapping themselves around the corpse's legs. He slipped down, past the knees. His chin hit the forked pocket of the crotch and stuck.

He struggled and kicked. Forced a foot into the armpit and using it like a sling straightened up. There, he could lift a knee and force it into the crotch, use the open mouth as a toe hold. Up, up. Hands on the rope now. Ignore the pain. Forget what you're doing. Stand. Forget where you're standing. With both his feet crammed into the fork of the legs he could reach the beam, wrap arms around them, lever himself up, up, up.

With one mighty bound ...

Thanks mate.

He lay there, fighting for his breath, feeling the hard

wood under his ribs and the pain in his head subside. A hundred years of bitter dust had gathered on top of that beam. He stifled a sneeze and lay still, flexing his fingers, feeling the stretched muscles of his back begin to contract, and waiting for the singing in his head to stop.

At last he reached behind him and began to fumble with the knot around his ankles. But he was careless and the rope, heavier than he thought, slipped through his fingers and fell to the ground.

He swore.

That was that. He was tempted to follow it down. Then he noticed how there was a ledge all the way round the wall of the chapel, just above the level of the beam. The wall was pierced by small dormer windows, cutting through the slope of the roof, and set into one of them was a small, latched door.

Jim straddled the beam and began to inch his way along it.

CHAPTER THIRTY ONE

The weather forecast had been fine to start off with, clouding over later. The telephone went just as Jack Lyall was staring out of his kitchen window at his garden, the day's first mug of tea in his hand. He was thinking how odd it was that there was no equivalent word for twilight to describe the peculiar watery clarity of first light on a cloudless winter's morning, and was looking forward to tidying up the lawn edges, and cutting back the roses before the frosts. Little tasks, none of them important in themselves, but making a difference when taken together. But he'd have to get out there fast. Storm clouds were smearing the western horizon, looking like a memory of night. If the rain held off until midday he'd be amazed.

The phone rang. Then, as if to hammer it in, the bleeper that he had deliberately left by his bed in his uniform tunic pocket went off upstairs.

'Mitchel here sir.' The voice at the other end sounded flat.

Jack glanced up at the kitchen clock. 'Still at work there?'

'The new shift were late getting in. Something about fog, they said.'

A silence spread between them.

'Well?'

'There's something funny going on here, sir. Harrison was seriously assaulted. They were late for breakfast you see and got a bit restless.'

'Is he all right?'

'Shaken up. I sent him right home for a rest. No injuries. It looked ... It looked like they were trying to hang him, sir.'

An old worm writhed in Lyall's throat and twitched its tail in his stomach.

'HANG him?'

'Over the balcony, with a sheet. I should never have left him, but I had to go and see where the relief had got to.'

'So he went in on his own. That's not going to look good in his file.'

'He was tricked. Well tricked. It would've got me at his age and all. It's like it was planned, though. I mean they half got his keys away. I got back just in time and sorted it out. But why try and hang him?'

Jack looked at his garden. The rain would hold off. Shit. He half wanted the heavens to open to help him make up his mind.

'Do you want me down there?'

'I'm going home for a kip, sir. I just thought you should know, that's all.'

'Well, I've got things to do here. I'll be there later anyway.'

'Governor back soon, sir?'

'Yup.' They all knew that the governor was away too much but Lyall never liked to complain to anyone.

'Well, I'll be getting off home now.'

'Thanks for calling and sleep well.'

*

It was a strange morning. The smear of cloud that Lyall saw seemed to keep hanging on in the same place, up over the moor. He gardened but without much pleasure. He knew he should be over at the prison. Mobbs, senior officer on that shift, was decent enough but a bit slow to make decisions. He looked over creosoted fences and neat, wooden garden sheds to where the prison stood, five miles away. Was it his imagination or was there low cloud there too? It was hard to say. Hard to tell. He brushed the earth off his hands and went inside.

This time he heard the bleeper first. He dialled the number to the prison. It was engaged, dialled again a few minutes later. Still busy. He began to get worried. He could make it over there in under ten minutes if he pushed it.

As he was backing the car out of the garage the phone rang. It was Mobbs desperately asking for instructions.

There was a traffic jam on the flyover and by the time Jack got to the prison it was lost.

'I don't believe it. I don't fucking believe it.' This was worse than mutiny. This was like being a captain of a liner and finding out that it had been sailed on to the rocks while you were having a piss. 'How?'

'We got most of the beasts – I mean the sectioned prisoners out, sir. I would like to commend officers—'

Mobbs read from a list. Always anxious to give credit where credit was due.

'You've had time to write that list while the bloody place is going up in flames? Are all the men recalled from leave?'

'Those I could reach, sir.'

'Have you notified the Home Office?'

'I left a message.'

'You left a message?' Lyall's voice was savage.

'For the Home Secretary.'

'Ye Gods. Where can we go?'

'Anywhere in the admin wing. They've got the kitchens and the stores. All the cells are taken and the chapel. As far as I know they're not outside anywhere. Apart from Old Yard. That's where they killed Ross.'

'I'll have to speak to his wife. Widow. Make a note of that. I want all the men assembled in the locker room in full emergency gear in ten minutes. We are going in through that door and—' There was a cheer from inside the prison. 'What's going on? Get all the men ready. Now!'

The heavy door swung open. Shouting, Jack led the column of men through, three abreast, the first three with high, curved perspex riot shields held in front of them, the next three with shields held above their heads. The other men had to make do with dustbin lids. They might as well have been holding cocktail umbrellas.

Bed frames had been hung from the landings above the entrance, and pulled back. Jack looked up to see three frames come scything through the air towards him. He managed to scream 'Down!' One frame caught a guard with its corner and knocked the riot shield into his face. The leg caught his shoulder and knocked him clean off his feet.

The momentum lost, the charge was doomed. A mat-tress soaked in oil and set alight was thrown down, smothering two officers. The men scattered – some ran straight back to the door, others pulled the mattress to one side and tried to stamp it out.

Jack Lyall looked up. The balconies were lined with prisoners. Ahead of him stood a man with his arms raised.

He dropped them suddenly. A figure, burnt and bent, arms flung out as if begging for mercy, was manhandled off a landing and thrown down. There was a snap as the rope around his neck tautened. Then a crack, and the head went spinning off while the stiff body crashed to the floor beneath and shattered.

Jack recognized the Christ figure from the chapel.

'Leave us be, Mr Lyall. Leave us be.'

Jack looked once more in disbelief at the men standing around the balconies, silent as statues and lit by the last rays of the afternoon sun, then followed the last of his men through the door.

CHAPTER THIRTY TWO

Angela put her hand up.

Miss Sims noticed her immediately and interrupted Mark Hebden's description of his father's funeral parlour, all part of the new Life Awareness course. So far they had listened to a zookeeper from the local theme park tell them about looking after llamas in captivity, they had read a short story about a tramp, improvized a play about Bush People in the Kalahari, and started work on a project to do with rainforests, yawn, yawn.

'Please Miss, I'm just feeling a bit strange. I think I'd like to go and lie down.'

Heads still turned whenever she did anything out of the ordinary.

Miss Sims gave a sugary smile. 'Of course, Angela. Would you like someone to walk with you?'

Angela bit her bottom lip and shook her head bravely. She reached into her desk to take her homework books out, but stopped herself just in time.

She did not want anyone to suspect what she was doing. Her mother would be at the gates in two hours to pick her up, but that should give her enough time to sneak back into school through the gap in the fence by the bicycle sheds, hide out there until the school started to empty and then nip into the classroom to pick her books up.

She walked shakily out. Nick Chalmers (Chalmers by name, charming by nature) smiled at her sensitively and even though she thought he was an insincere creep she felt herself blushing the same colour as her hair.

Once outside the classroom she headed towards the science labs, walked confidently out of the side door which was left open for sports, and made for the bike sheds. She slipped through the fence.

Cars slid past her in hard coloured blurs. No one else seemed to be walking on the ring road and it was bitterly cold. She hugged her blazer to her, wishing she had put a vest on that morning. At the bus stop she hopped on one foot, then another, trying not to look too closely at the advertisement for headache pills that consisted of lime green letters on a fluorescent pink background.

She had a headache. It came from the cold that was pinching the skin tight around her head.

Come on bus. Come on. It was risky standing in a bus shelter so close to the school. Any member of staff might be passing in their car.

Angela White? Are you all right? Going home? Let me give you a lift. Are you sure you've got permission? It's easy for me to check, you know.

A car did slow down as it passed, heading in the direction of the school. It was grey, slippery and anonymous. She shrank back into the shelter, her feet crunching on broken glass. A head turned – a middle-aged man. He had looked at her, she was sure of it, in a way that people did when they were sizing you up. A flasher? It could be. Last year the school had been told that if anyone saw a black Ford Escort parked outside the school, they were not, repeat not to look inside it for any reason, but to go straight back inside and report it to a member of staff. Of course the next day there was a scrum of students outside the gates all looking out for the car. Sharon Edwards claimed that she *had* looked inside and seen a man stroking his dick with a paint brush.

Angela peered back along the road. On her side was a modern housing estate, hiding behind high wooden fencing. On the other was a bare winter wood, its undergrowth clogged with soggy chip papers and supermarket bags full of rubbish.

Come on bus. Come on.

The road was empty. She waited.

'Weaving?' Mr Appleby had said when she told him that she wanted to change her history project. 'Weaving? And what makes you interested in that all of a sudden?'

She shrugged. 'I just want to change.'

Mr Appleby thought. 'Well, Angela,' he said after a pause. 'I think it would be a mistake for you to change at this stage. Far better to keep on with your original idea.' Whatever that is, his face said. 'Of course if you need any help with it – I mean, that is, I know that you've had to miss school because . . . Well, so if you want me to help, just – er – you know . . . I'd be more than happy.'

But he didn't sound it. The teachers had all been told of course. Some treated her just the same; some were sugar sweet; some, like Mr Appleby, tried to be nice but became awkward and distant, as if she had some disease and they wanted to get a long way away from her.

She followed him out of the classroom. 'But if I wanted to find out about weaving, sir, where would I go?'

'The County Museum,' he said breezily. 'Next to the town hall. Ask your father to take you there some—' The expression of frozen dread on his face as he realized what he had said almost made her feel happy.

It was one of the new minibuses and it seemed to take an age to get anywhere near the town centre. It meandered around housing estates which had been quarantined from the world by gritty parks and smashed up playgrounds, along dual carriageways, by the side of filthy black canals and brand new industrial estates, through places that Angela had never heard of. Long Barrow, for example, what sort of place was that? Over the rooftops of the terraced houses she saw a bank of spotlights and a big sloping roof which she assumed was a football stadium. The next stop was a giant hangar-like building painted blue and yellow called 'Kitchens 4 U', then they were on the dual carriageway and heading for the bus terminal in the Market Square.

The town hall was a mass of spires and towers, windows and steps. A gothic masterpiece. Next to it was the simpler domed museum with its Roman pillars and white marble front. Angela climbed the steps between two concrete sphinxes and walked through the heavy, panelled doors of beaten brass.

The weaving exhibition was in a huge, high room, empty of people, flickering with the dull white light of distant strip lights. Hot, dry air, smelling faintly of oil, pumped up through brass grilles in the floor. The only sound was Angela's footsteps clacking over a mosaic floor which celebrated the town's past achievements: the installation of the sewage system, the hygienic civic slaughter house, the growth of heavy industry, all expressed by stiff Greek maidens doing something symbolic: drinking a glass of water, growing up healthy and strong, looking at a forest of smoking chimneys.

No chimneys now and her father was thinking of going into do-it-yourself water filters. And she felt sick.

She wandered between glass cases tracing the development of the shuttle and the bobbin, dyeing techniques, sources of flax, the impact of textiles on society . . .

The town had grown rich on weaving. There had been a rich coal seam nearby to power the new steam engines. There was a steady supply of workers flooding in from the villages as the sheep drove them off the land. The damp air on the plain kept the threads moist and supple – the biggest problem in the past had been threads losing their elasticity. In the slums the people coughed blood and died but the threads did not break.

The first mill had been built in Long Barrow. Before the age of steam there had been a small factory there, its mill wheel driven by the Snaresbrook which then spread out and meandered through the flat plain, flooding it in spring, keeping it wet and green in summer.

There were before and after pictures of the town. Before the industrial revolution it had been a sleepy little market town with a cattle trough in the square, a church and low houses making up the High Street – not so very different from Edgerton really.

Then suddenly, in the space of forty or fifty years, it had exploded. Brick canyons spread out across the land like the tendrils of some giant fungus. Chimneys belching black smoke pointed at the dirty sky. Where once there had been watermeadows, there was now street after street of grey houses. Where once there had been woods, great warehouses and factories stared at the ruined land with blank eyes.

There were photographs of people in narrow streets, staring with blurred, dark faces at the camera. There were pictures of pubs, vast empty spaces, bare of decoration –

straightforward drink factories. Gin traps. There were pictures of chapels which sprung up everywhere to try and counteract the lure of the gin. Pictures of shops. An itinerant preacher with a sandwich board around his neck. Repent or Burn. Pictures of chimneys, many with names painted on them in large white letters. A huge oil painting called 'Holding the Line' which showed a row of badly painted soldiers defending a factory gate against what looked like a mob of gorillas in rags, led by a white-haired, red-eyed lunatic. The weaver? The mad weaver who had killed Angela Fitt?

'Contemporary representation of riots caused by allegedly poor conditions in Loveyards Mills, 1850. Riot put down by local militia, subsequently blamed on alcohol and incitements by an itinerant preacher.'

She walked from one picture to the next, stopping in front of a picture of the prison. What had prisons got to do with weaving?

Long Barrow prison was completed in 1849 to take care of the needs of the rapidly growing town and the burgeoning urban underclass, it being considered that the existing facility was not sufficiently large. Subscriptions were sought from local businesses to speed the process. Built on strict principles of science and hygiene, Long Barrow prison still serves the community in much the same way that was originally intended.

And there was a picture of the prison, as it was then with the chimneys in the background. Angela thought back to the bus journey. Funny to think how things changed.

She wandered on. The whole room was indeed devoted to weaving, but it was not quite what she had been expecting. She had thought there might be a mock-up of a little one-roomed cottage on the moor, a man with a patient face hunched over the loom, a fire in the grate, a cat on the hearth. Instead there were just more photographs of rows and rows of machines powered by great looped belts hanging down from the ceiling, pinched miserable faces looking at the camera. Some of them were kids. Some were no older than she was.

The next stage of the exhibition was called 'Men of the Broadcloth: Portraits of an Age'. It consisted of portraits of men with vast tummies, high collars and white waistcoats staring at the world from huge oil canvasses. They made Angela yawn. She walked slowly on, stopping every now and again to look at a dog at his master's feet, or a photograph taken later, then ...

Angela froze.

The photograph.

A family group was standing on a lawn. They were dressed up, the men in suits leaning on croquet mallets, apart from one who was sitting in a bath chair with a blanket over his knee. The women wore long white dresses and held frilled umbrellas above their heads. A dog lolled at their feet, its tongue hanging out.

And behind them, absolutely unmistakable in the sharp sunshine, was Cragside House.

It looked newer then, but of course it would. There were blinds over the ground floor windows, and the gardens were neatly tended with rose bushes in front and something like honeysuckle growing above the high French windows giving on to the grass.

'Thomas Loveyard of Loveyard Mills, and family outside Cragside House, Edgerton on the Moor.'

Loveyard of Loveyard Mills had lived in Edgerton on the Moor. There had been a weaver in Edgerton on the Moor. A girl had been murdered in Edgerton on the Moor. She had come to look for one weaver, and had found another. She looked at the picture again. The men had hard, old-fashioned faces and tiny bright eyes. She looked at the seated man. He was older than all the rest, had mutton-chop whiskers and eyes that stared out at her.

At her.

She walked back to the portraits. There he was. Thomas Loveyard. But how had she missed that expression the first time? There was such ... anger in the eyes, as if he were furious that she was alive and he was dead.

She sat on a padded bench with her back to the pictures, clenched her fists into her cheeks and tried to think.

Survival was a matter of keeping the past at bay, William Fairley thought. It was that simple. It had always been that simple. It had to remain that simple.

Simple. The trail from the back seat of a Volkswagon beetle full of a whore's swollen corpse had led Jim Carroll straight to prison and how long was a policeman meant to survive in prison? Not only had he survived but that smug bastard had somehow got his act together sufficiently to get a message to Brian White. Brian White had actually been about to resurrect the whole affair, and that would never do. Now Brian White was inside. Somehow he and Jim Carroll would have to burn together.

Keeping the past at bay. If he could just clear this matter up he would be home and dry, all evidence mopped up.

That just left the little girl, who as far as he could see was a complete fruit and nut case – barking in fact; brain in a basket. Or was she? You couldn't tell with kids, they were tricky. She's whispering with her sweet kiddy breath and little white teeth that she knows about a murder. I mean a man has to act, has to be decisive, has to be clever. Kill the girl and let her father take the rap. Neat. Two birds with

one stone. And make it look disgusting. Make sure the
bastard goes down for ever.

But fuck it all, he couldn't have told, nobody could have
told that she was going to pull that stunt and get out of the
ice house. Now she was spouting some stuff and nonsense
about being helped out by a friend. All she could remember
was that she had been helped by a friend. Someone had
tried to kill her and she had been helped by a friend. She
had been tied up by a monster and helped by a friend.

What fucking friend?

Nicola Hawkins thought she was an aspect of the girl's
disturbed psyche, disturbed because she had just been
abused by her father. Unfortunately he knew that he had
cooked up the whole thing. He knew the girl had not been
abused. So who was this mysterious helper?

The hemispheres of his brain were two great millstones,
grinding out the future. He'd think the little bitch dead
then pulp her pathetic bones and make them red.

Time to call her mother. Time to play Inspector Helpful.
Again. He opened his wallet and found the business card
she had pressed into his hand after her husband had been
arrested. Pathetic woman.

A uniformed officer put his head round the door and
made a T with his index fingers. Fairley nodded and hissed
'two sugars' at him. Gave him a wink. Easy to make some
people happy.

'I'd like to speak with Mrs White, please. Patricia White.'

'Not in at the moment,' a nasal, sing-song secretary
voice.

'Could you tell me when she's going to be in?'

'Not for the rest of today, I'm afraid. Can I pass you on
to another member of our staff who will be pleased to help
you in any way?'

'Isn't she on mobile? I thought she had a car phone.'

Hurried whispers. 'Is this a client, may I ask?'

Fairley sensed something wrong. 'No, I'm a friend, a close personal friend. Is there anything the matter?'

'Oh a friend. It's terrible. Her little girl—'

'Angela,' he interrupted.

'That's right,' the receptionist sounded delighted, 'the little girl, Angela, well, she's gone missing from school. Walked out of class, saying she was ill, then was seen getting on a bus, would you believe? Right outside the school grounds.'

'Do you know the name of the school?' he asked.

'Hold on. I'll just ask around.' A couple of seconds later. 'Nightingale, Nightingale Close.'

'Right, thank you.'

He put the telephone down, found the number in the directory and called the school, this time talking official, giving his name as Inspector Barlow. Ho ho.

After a short break he got through to the headmistress who told him that the mother had been informed but as far as she knew the police had not.

Fairley did not tell her how he found out. She would assume that Mrs White had contacted him. The more confusing the actual chain of events, the better for him.

No, they did not know where the girl was. They assumed that she was in one of the chip shops near the school. Things like this were always happening. People panicked so. A member of staff was going to check. Oh, another member of staff had just told her that he was feeling guilty. She might have gone to the museum in the town centre. Apparently he had been insensitive and would never forgive himself.

Fairley smiled at the voice, dripping with sarcasm, thanked it, and put the phone down as his cup of tea arrived. He waited until he was alone, poured it into a spider plant, put the cup on his desk (Yes, I did go out. I had my tea, finished it and left a few minutes after that. Why are you interested?) and walked out by the fire escape (short cut to the car park). The museum. He had an instinct.

'Angela.' She was a funny little thing, with her hair spreading out from a centre parting. Weird looking really, with those big green eyes and skin so white that you could see a blue vein running up her forehead. There was a red patch on her cheek where she had been cupping her face in her hands.

Skin white, blood red, funny to think that she might have been dead. Hair red, veins blue, funny to think it might have been you.

Fairley hears his breath roar like a blast furnace. Before she looks up, time has split like a cell, doubling, redoubling, spreading, expanding. Time holds still for everything except for him. He feels a hair grow a fraction of an inch. His finger nails creak outwards from their soft pink roots. Blood whispers through his veins. His nipples harden. They are cold pebbles against his white shirt.

She looks up. Good. What does the expression say? Well, there's recognition there, which is good, but she doesn't like me any more. Okay. I don't care. I'm a cop. A family friend. Her mother relies on me. Her mother's very worried. Her mother might fuck me but that will make the pink shrimp hate me. Her mother sent me, no, asked me to come here just on the off-chance. Lucky she thought of it, eh? She's waiting by the phone. Shall we go and call her from my car? You can talk to her if you want IN MY CAR.

WE CAN DRIVE SOMEWHERE.

Thoughts creak on like a rusty train on a moon-bleached track in blue midnight dreams. Rust and oil. Oil and slick. There's always vomit in your guts. Pink and white. Vomit her up. Fart out your dirty lust. You've got to think.

Calm down. It isn't nice to think like that. Then again, it isn't nice the way the little bitch is looking at me. Right little madam. Like to—

'Hello, Angela.' Come on face, smile. 'Do you mind if I sit down?'

That was wrong. My lips feel like sick tyres, my teeth are rotten wooden pegs. Should have given her a nice big smile, all shining lick-pink gums and ivory, and said: 'Oh Angela, thank God I found you. The school told your mother that you might be here. Apparently you've made one of your teachers feel rather guilty.'

There, I said it. There is sunlight on my brain. The sponge is warm. Aha. That was working. She gave a little smile. Now pretend you're out of your depth. Look a little bit uncomfortable.

'Am I in trouble?' she asks.

You betcha.

'I don't know, Angela.' Look around. Try and pretend to be normal. 'Find out anything interesting in here? Looks rather dull and boring to me.'

'I was thinking.'

I can believe that. There's a little furrow between your red-haired eyebrows, sweetheart. Dark. Soft. Downy. Down boy.

'What were you thinking?'

'About history. I was wondering whether it might catch up with you.'

Careful, careful. Don't sweat. Keep the diesel out of your voice. Try and keep your head together – put bands around it, the skull is breaking, old pottery and porridge! She's smiling at you, so she doesn't suspect or she wouldn't be smiling. Concentrate. There's a freckle on her upper lip. CONCENTRATE.

Smile. No. Look really interested. 'Would you like to tell

someone about it? No, I've got a better idea – why don't we go and call your mother and you can tell me on the way?'

She stands up, cutely. Smoothes her skirt. 'I hope Mummy won't be angry,' she says.

'I'll take care of her, don't you worry.'

Try and keep your hands off her. Don't push her. Just let her take her time. Just remember this. She knows it was you that tried to hang her. She's forgotten but she knows. What do I do? Kill her again? But how? It was perfect last time. Perfect.

Angela thought Bill Fairley was getting ill. His face turned a sort of grey-green colour and the sweat suddenly squeezed through the skin between his lip and nose like little blisters. It was a bit awesome, like watching a building think about falling down.

She looked up at him. He was thinking very hard. She could see that. Suddenly he handed her a set of car keys and said: 'I tell you what. I've just got to go and do something. Why don't you let yourself into my car? It's parked round the front. You can call your mother on the phone.'

He seemed very insistent about telephones and her getting into his car.

She shrugged. 'How do I know it's yours?'

He smiled toothily. 'Just hold this out and press this button. If you see the locks jump up on the inside of the door, you'll know it's my car.'

He walked quickly off as if he was anxious not to be seen with her.

She looked at the key ring. It had a button in the middle of it. It must be one of those fancy modern ones. Shame he ran off like that. Perhaps he needed to go to the loo. It would have been nice to try her theory out on someone about who killed Angela. Or who didn't kill her. That was the important thing.

Outside it was getting dark. The black car glowed. It looked like a crouching animal, about to pounce. It had shining windows the colour of smoke that held the spires and turrets of the town hall in a curved frame, distorting them, darkening them, like a nightmare castle in a fairy story. Alarm bells clanged in her brain – a sense of menace surrounded her. She looked at the key ring. Tried to think. It was odd the way he was behaving, come to think of it. Her mother was always telling her not to get into strange men's cars, not to accept lifts from strangers. But he wasn't there, so she couldn't be in danger. And he wasn't a stranger.

She pressed the button on the key ring.

The locks sprang up.

Bolts shot sideways in her brain. A door opened in the dark.

Cracked.

Gaped.

A stinking rush of memory poured over her in a terrible wave, paralysing her. The bonds were on her legs, her wrists. She felt her back arch. Her mouth was stretched to burning, her tongue held down with a plug, the hood over her head, the rope, the rope—

She was dimly aware of the car door opening, and a hand on her neck pushing her down and in, so fast that she could not react. Her head cracked on the sill. She fell in, loosely.

'Just sit there, Angela, and do not say a word or I will kill you. If you move or scream I'll put you in the boot. Now GET ON THE FLOOR.'

Angela crouched in the well under the passenger seat, not quite understanding why she was doing what he said, but so frightened that she had to. She watched Bill Fairley's polished shoes move up and down on the pedals. For some reason she thought of red mud.

CHAPTER THIRTY THREE

Jim pushed the door open. A dark and dusty world stretched away in front of him. There was a low attic beneath the roof slates, easy enough to crawl through if you were a skinny midget, but a tight fit for anyone else. The slates were unlined. The joists were black with generations of coal soot. It might be a place to hide.

What would they think when they returned to the chapel and found only one of those swollen fruit swinging from the roof beams? Assume that he'd managed to clamber back up, tie the rope to the beams and slide down it? No, that wouldn't do. If he had done that, the rope would still be tied to a beam. Must be getting tired. Loop the rope over the beam? Too long a drop at the end. Shin down the corpse's rope? The fixing would have given. Still, unless you tried it you would not know. They might just assume he had got down and escaped from the chapel.

The slates were rotten. He found that just by tugging at them they came away from the fixing nails. He made a hole easily in the roof and put his head through cautiously.

He was almost blinded by a shaft of the setting sun that broke through the clouds and made the windows of the prison blaze. But even as he looked a dark fog seemed to pour across the bloody wound in the sky and a cold, thick mist descended. It poured over the buildings like liquid, tumbling down the roof and walls, pooling within the perimeter walls, shifting, eddying.

Ten feet below him a lip of rotten guttering was full of black mud, but back towards the body of the prison he saw how he could break through the roof and get on to the main body of the prison itself. He would have to squeeze through the roof space to get there.

His nostrils itched abominably. At one point the air exploded into shivering screeches above his head as he disturbed a small colony of bats. He smelt the ammonia of their droppings, and pressed on, feeling each step of the way with his toes, convinced that the beams under his feet were rotten and would give way at any moment.

Then he felt space all around him. When he stretched out his hands they touched nothing but cobwebs and darkness. He must be out of the chapel.

In front of him was a curved wall of tongue and groove. There was a small brick corridor around it, from which the main wings of the prison opened.

From what he could hear, there seemed to be very little movement along the landings. Everything was terribly subdued. It was funny, now he thought of it, that they had not broken out on to the roof. Funny that there was no sound of riot anywhere. He could hear crashing, but it sounded organized, as if the men were systematically destroying the fabric of the prison. But for what reason, or for whom?

For whom. That was the question. Randall was trying to organize something for himself – it was inconceivable that he would do it for anyone else. He would have to get back into the prison somehow and try and find out what was going on.

At night with all the lights off, it might be possible to move around. Nobody would be expecting him still to be inside the prison.

He woke up with voices in his ear, low voices, thin voices, voices as scratchy and grey as old spiders. Men whispering below.

Scared ... I know ... going to do? ... how long ... killed ... oh God ... why?

Then a stronger voice cut in, high-pitched and impatient. 'Oh for Christ's sake! It's no use just sitting here whingeing. What are we prepared to do?'

'Oh yeah, listen to the big man. What was big brave Brian fucking White doing when they came to take us away? Shitting his pants and begging for mercy. "I'm only here on remand. I didn't do anything. I'm innocent."'

Jim stiffened. Brian White? Here?

'Okay. I was scared. I admit it. We all were. But the point is that they've got us here like rabbits in a trap. They've already taken Burton God knows where—'

'They strung him up from the chapel roof – I saw,' a voice interrupted.

'That just confirms what I'm saying. What are we going to do? Sit here and be taken away, one by one?'

'Burton was different.'

Brian's voice shouted: 'We're all different. To them we're just beasts. Beasts. All of us! They are not concerned with fine distinctions! We've got to get out!'

'We wouldn't stand a chance out there. Randall put us in here for our own protection.'

'Bullshit! If he wanted us protected he would have let us fucking well go, you shit brained moron! We are about as far from being rescued as – listen. We are on the top floor of C Wing. They have ripped out the landings between us and the stairs. The only way out is to jump from girder to girder. I tell you, they are saving us for something!'

'Oh, what?' The other voice was flat and sarcastic.

'Just because you can't imagine it, doesn't mean it's not going to happen. Christ. What's that?'

Up in the loft, Jim was suddenly caught in a bright lattice of fierce white. The slates began to shudder with the whupwhupwhup of helicopter rotors – a siren, sirens began to scream. The whole prison was resonating.

Below him he heard the cell of the sectioned prisoners begin to cheer. Jim ran, crouching under the beams, back to the wall of tongue and groove. He peered down.

A scene from hell. Twists of fabric, soaked in oil, sent red flames spiralling up to the shadow-mottled ceiling. Men with soot-blackened bodies, streaked with sweat, flickered yellow and gold in the torchlight.

Most of the landings were gone. Cell doors opened crazily on to singing space. The prison walls were a great smooth rock face; the cells like caves. Flames burned in some like angry Cyclops' eyes; in the others the smoke had stained the wall above. Old iron girders jutted sharply from walls where the balconies had been. Staircases gasped at landings that had gone. Spiral stairs twisted into nothing, swayed as the prison rocked. The men had moved along the landings, methodically smashing the floor behind them as they went. The most agile jumped from beam to beam like monkey gods and had nests high up in the walls. The others slept ten to a cell on D Wing which had been left comparatively undamaged, lived in the kitchens, talked in the dining-rooms. Listened to the radio.

Right now, as Jim looked down, they were working. In the centre of the hall, rising from a scree of metal plates, wooden beams, grilles, bed struts, a metal pile was growing, a vertical

upright was being bound and bolted and stressed by a
handful of men stripped to the waist.

But all around the ends of the wings, where a counter
attack might fall, barricades were going up, mazes of
sharpened scaffolding, traps. Great cauldrons had been
carried up from the kitchens and filled with cooking oil
from massive drums. They stood ready over small bonfires,
waiting to be heated, waiting to be tipped over the heads of
anyone trying to break in.

The second assault by the guards took place at three o'clock
that morning. Lyall now had a full complement of prison
officers under his command and was planning a three
pronged attack: one through the main C Wing door between
the admin wing and the prison, and two others via small outside doors, rat-holes as they were called, in A and D Wings.
These were barred and bolted on the outside and opened
directly into the canyon-like space between the outer and
perimeter walls. If the prisoners did manage to repulse the
attack and regain the unlocked doors, they would be going
nowhere fast. As such it did not matter if these attacks failed.
The main thrust once again was to be concentrated on C Wing.

Harrison, standing some way down the phalanx that
was due to assault C Wing, felt so light and nervous that
he thought he might float away. It was just the weirdest
feeling to be standing outside the reception area with its
neat little booths and lockers for the cons' civvy clothes,
and feel that the prison was no longer yours, that you were
an alien in it. The emergency lights gave only a dull yellow
glow. From the outside they had seen the light of flames
flaring and flickering against the high windows. The old
man had decided against torches and flashlights. He
thought they would just get in the way. But the helicopter
was due to switch on its big spot three minutes after they

went in and hit the prison with its siren. On the trial run
it had sounded quite frightening.

He felt cold but supposed that was just nerves too. The
thing to do was try and concentrate on what had been
going on. They had killed one of his mates. They were
animals. Animals. And animals had to be beaten until they
understood who was boss.

He tapped his truncheon against the perspex shield, and
shifted his shoulders against the riot padding. Helmet on
tightly. Visor down. A bit like *Robocop* really.

'Half a minute!'

Their column was led by Mobbs. He began to stamp his
feet and bang his truncheon against the shield.

'Beasts Beasts Beasts Beasts Beasts Beasts Beasts Beasts.'

They were all shouting now and stamping. Now moving
forwards.

'Beasts Beasts Beasts Beasts Beasts Beasts Beasts Beasts.'

Moving faster. Faster. The doors swung open.

Harrison felt the men in front slow down, then try to
stop. He bumped into a back, staggered, then was pushed
forwards by the man behind him, pushed the man in front
of him, was in the doorway, in the prison, looking up.

He saw a man swing towards him on a rope, waving a long
pole. He flung the shield up and heard the scrape as the point
seared the plastic. He looked again. More prisoners on the
balconies, hurling rocks at them. All the men had their
shields over their heads now, (Beasts Beasts) but they were
hemmed in by a wall of twisted metal and sharpened wood.
He felt a sharp pain on his ankle. There. A spear had darted
through the barrier and had pricked him. They were on the
other side. They were behind. All he could do was move
forwards to where a huge fire burned in the central hall. A
vast gallows was standing there and hanging from it was an
awful parody of a man made from old mattresses, his neck

stretched to horrid length, his feet tapering to points.

Panic. On. On! They were being forced steadily through a narrow maze of metal. Spears kept on darting through the wall and pricking him. The man in front of him was shouting 'Come and fight, you bastards!' but there was nothing to hold on to, no one to hit. The cold rage inside Harrison turned to something like panic. He began hitting out wildly around him at nothing, forced on by the pressure of men behind him, held back by the men in front.

He turned and shouted 'Get back!' but guessed that it was too late. The men were being forced slowly into the middle of the hall. Somewhere behind him he thought he heard a door slam.

And the missiles never stopped. The bastards were jeering now, sneering. A huge pole, scaffolding by the size of it but sliced off at one end and sharpened like a giant quill, glanced off his shield, knocked it away and buried its point in Hawkins' shoulder. He staggered, the weight of the spear dragging him down. Harrison caught him under the arm, tried to turn but was caught up in a stampede of officers, who were being forced forward by a wave of bricks wrapped in burning rags.

Two men were down and were being dragged forwards by their colleagues. Mobbs was bleeding from a cut above one eye, screaming, crying, waving his truncheon at the prisoners who stood on the balconies and jeered or rushed along, stabbing downwards with their spears. A couple of men ran towards a staircase, yelling. They were beaten back so easily it made Harrison want to weep.

They were forced relentlessly into the main hall. Light splashed around them from the helicopter. The siren wailed. It all seemed like a sarcastic joke. Looking round, Harrison realized that there had been no diversion attacks from the other wings. Somehow they had been prevented

from even getting through the doors. The prisoners must
have been working solidly to secure the place.

As Hawkins sank to his knees, bleeding heavily from the
wound in his shoulder, Harrison thought with some
surprise that the prison was probably more secure now
than it had ever been. It took a bloody riot to achieve that.
'They want us in here,' Hawkins said dully.

Harrison shook his head, unable to take it in.

'They want us in here,' Hawkins said. 'They could have
stopped us if they wanted to, but they wanted us in here.
They're going to kill all of us.'

Up in the loft, Jim saw the lull in the fighting. The guards
were effectively trapped. If they moved away from the
centre, they would be met with a hail of missiles. If they
stayed where they were, they were out of range of all but
small lumps of concrete that forced them to keep their
shields up. If they moved back to the main door they would
be met with a rain of missiles – and the fires were now
alight under the cauldrons of oil. A, D and C Wings were
just dead-end traps. But if they stayed where they were . . .

He was aware that the shouting had stopped, and the
prison was growing quiet again. There was a movement on
the balcony immediately below him. He pressed his cheek
up against the woodwork.

George walked to the railing, waited for complete silence,
then said: 'Your position's hopeless. It's time you gave
yourselves up.'

Mobbs shouted: 'What do you want from us?'

Silence.

'What do you want, you animals?'

There was an angry murmur from the balconies, cut
short by a quick gesture by George.

He paused, then said one word. 'Justice.'

CHAPTER THIRTY FOUR

By cricking her neck she could see a strip of window. The town flicked past. Tops of warehouses, that ugly skyscraper near the Corn Exchange, street lamps. An aeroplane followed them briefly, drifting through the blotched clouds like a ghost.

A girl, a man, a plane, a rope.
A skip, a tip, a road, a dope.

If she cried, would he take pity on her? His face was blank and he was whistling through slightly parted teeth in a musical sort of a hiss. She knew the tune. 'Angie Baby'.

She opened her mouth.

'STOP FUCKING THINKING!'

He did not even tilt his head to look at her. The words bounced back off the inside of the windscreen, making her cower back further under the dashboard. They were out of town now, near the flyover. A helicopter chatterwhumped overhead, and she saw him crane his neck, staring up from under lifted eyebrows.

They floated over the tarmac. He switched on the radio

301

and a froth of easy-listening music flooded the car. He pressed a button on the radio and it began to scan the frequencies automatically, soundbites sheared off by dark bursts of static.

Ba Ba baba baba BAAA ... Fight the power ... Coming now into the home straight ... too sexy for my ... Standing here outside the prison ... Pompompom POM ...

He swore and tuned into the news report.

'... dull glow, an orange glow, flickering through the small windows. If I hold the microphone out – I don't know if you can hear it – but there's the sound of glass breaking as the heat smashes the windows in the administration block. I can see a hand thrust through the windows there, scattering papers to the four winds. There – he's given me the thumbs up as if he can hear me. Perhaps they have radios on. I'll ask him to give me a sign. Oh dear, not that kind of sign. But as I stand here I can see there's no one actually on the roof. That's peculiar as most often in protests like this they break through immediately and hang out banners. What's that? It's just been put to me that perhaps this isn't a protest. It might be something different. I've just been handed an update. Fire engines have got water on to the blaze now. They are directing the massed weight of their hosepipe nozzles through the smashed windows and that could be many thousands of gallons of water per minute flooding through the building ...

'What's this? Oh my God. That's sickening. That really is absolutely sickening. There are reports of executions in the prison. Sick behaviour. Really bad. A fireman involved in a skirmish reports having seen a man float through the air, spitting at him – that can't be right, surely. Another says he saw prisoners dangling from balconies. From landings. I've got the head warder here, Jack Lyall. Mr Lyall, can you comment on this? On these reports?'

'I can't because as yet we have no clear idea what is going on.'

'Have you been unable to break into the prison?'

'Obviously I have to take into consideration the safety of my own men—'

'But there have been attempts—'

'There have.'

'That staff have got inside.'

'Yes.'

'And what did they report?'

'Er, they—'

'Have they reported back?'

'Not exactly. As yet they have been unable to secure safe passage out of the prison. Now if you will excuse me.'

'Mr Lyall. Mr Lyall! No he's gone. Well sensational news from Long Barrow. Remember you heard it first here on Broadway Radio—'

Fairley cut off the jingle half-way through, pursed his lips and looked to the left. Angela followed his gaze. The sky was orange over there. As she watched she felt a tiny quickening of interest inside her. Long Barrow.

> *A field, a sheep, a house, a tree.*
> *A girl, a man, a moor – and me.*

The voice came from far away: not inside her this time, but high on the moor where her house was. She suddenly remembered her mother, her bedroom, all the things she did like swimming and homework and drama. She was gripped by awful sadness and desperation.

'What are you going to do with me?' she asked.

Without taking his eyes off the road, William Fairley said: 'I'm going to take you back and do the job properly.

They'll never think of looking there again, not for a while anyway.'

It was dusk when they turned off the main road to Edgerton on the Moor. She knew it so well and it was the last time she was ever going to see it. There was so much sadness inside her that it blocked her throat, and no tears would come. She felt like a balloon. She feared the fear, and was filling with grief.

In the Snare Brook Hollow they turned left along the track to the disused quarry, the car bumping and rolling in the pot-holes. He stopped the car, hidden from the road by the edge of the cutting, and waited. It grew dark. Cramp began to bite Angela in the thigh. Her knees felt as if they were on fire. The moon fell through the windows.

Where are you, oh where are you? She thought the words out loud and she heard nothing, but a shaft of moonlight seemed to clot for a second on the seat above her and for a fleeting second she caught a glimpse of a figure sitting there, very still, the head cocked to one side. Faintly, like a distant tune, she smelled roses.

William Fairley stretched and checked the handbrake.

'Right Angela. From here we walk.'

He pointed to a narrow path that led from the edge of the quarry up towards the village. She got out of the car and began to walk. At one point she stopped. Fairley stopped too and breathed deeply. Behind her, very faintly, she heard the paper rustle of the thing that was following them.

CHAPTER THIRTY FIVE

High pressure water drummed on the slate skin of the roof. It was angled from below and found ways under the lips of the overhanging slates. In places it ripped the loose slates free and Jim could only imagine that they were trying to soak the prison through to make it uninhabitable for the men inside. More charitably he supposed that they might be trying to make the roof timbers so wet that if the flames ever did reach them, they would not catch.

But why hadn't the men got up there? It was what rioters did. It was their way of showing the bastards out there that they were alive, free – well almost. Top of the world ma, that kind of thing. Apart from all that there must be something terribly satisfying in watching all the slates go spiralling down and smash on the stones beneath.

The smell of cooking was filtered up to him. Jim's mouth filled with saliva. What was it they were eating? Baked beans and bacon. He had to eat. He had to, but how the hell was he going to get down unnoticed, especially if all the landing floors really had been taken up?

B Wing. It might be possible in B Wing. He walked across the rafters to the central drum, and put his head round the corner. All clear. No wait. What's that? There!

The sloping roof joists merged greyly in the distance. Half-way down the tunnel a sliver of light had just slit the floor as if something was opening in it. A trap door.

Jim hesitated, torn between staying and running. He wanted to see what was happening, but suppose that they were coming after him? No. They would have been up here already. It did not make sense. Nothing made sense.

He saw a man's head and shoulders appear. The man put something long and white on the floor, then began to lever himself up through the hole. He crouched for a second. Jim heard him panting. He slid the trap door back.

Silence. Jim pictured him crouched over the trap, listening. Why else would he be so still? Perhaps the prison was retaken. Perhaps he was trying to hide from the guards. That meant Jim should wait until he had moved away, then swing himself down and give himself up.

A scraping sound. The flat crack of a slate breaking. That didn't make sense. Why draw attention to yourself if you're trying to escape? There'd be no let up on the roof, not with the helicopters and fire hoses.

A patch of grey appeared. The man's head was briefly silhouetted in the gap, moving from side to side to try and get his shoulders through, but the hole was not wide enough. He tore more slates away, then stooped and picked up something from the floor. It unfolded as he lifted it and Jim saw that it was a sheet. He pushed it through the hole and shook it. Suddenly he was bathed in white light, impaled on a spotlight beam, unable to move. He continued trying to shake the sheet but was having difficulty. Perhaps it was sticking to the wet tiles. He had to lean out to try and free it.

Jim heard the trap door open before he saw it. In the bleached white light he saw Gorgeous George's head rise effortlessly into the roof space, as if propelled by hydraulic rams. He too crouched for a second, assessing the possibilities. Then, still at a crouch, he moved swiftly over to the man's legs, wrapped his arms around them, and lifted. His shoulders punched a bigger hole in the roof. They skiddered down. Jim heard fingers scrabble. There was a snap as the guttering broke. Then nothing.

The police had lent Jack Lyall a mobile command and control centre. He was trying to get a line through to New Orleans, where the governor was attending a conference on security, but the electronic switching in the van was knackered and the engineer kept on trying to explain to him how it was really interesting that the bit that was faulty was the only spare he did not have but he would probably be able to fix it if he re-routed a couple of circuits and installed a—

Lyall was close to snapping.

The problem with a command and control centre was that people expected you to command and control. But he did not have the authority to command and as for control . . .

Frustration numbed him. It was like the fog that swirled around the prison hollow like a cloud of poison gas. He had been interviewed by a local radio station and when they had asked him what he thought about the destruction of his prison he had been unable to say anything intelligent. Was he pleased, on one level, that the prison was going?

His prison. Why weren't the bastards on the roof where they could pick them off with the hoses?

The head of the Prison Officers' Association wanted assurances on overtime and safety. A man from the Home Office was four hours late. The Home Secretary was meant to be telephoning. There was a sinister individual with

sandy eyelashes and a small moustache hanging around.
One theory said he was SAS and had a team of snipers in
a bus. Another that he was a vigilante. And another that
he was planning to blow the perimeter wall and spring half
the prison.

Why weren't the bastards on the roof?

It was the first thing they were meant to do. The shrinks
called it 'a display reaction concommitant with an emo-
tional state in which the individual asserts his authority
subsequent to the destruction of a real or imagined power
structure.' What did that mean? Simply that they were
supposed to be up there showing their hairy arses to the
world, screaming insults, bitching about conditions, waiting to be hosed down. Instead the place was just a great
dead hulk, a black lump with fires flickering in the cell
windows. And nobody knew what was happening inside.
Fuck Mobbs. Should he send another team in to rescue
him? One man dead already. Could he risk another, and
another?

The caravan rocked as Mobbs climbed in. 'There's
something happening sir. One of the policemen has got
hold of a night scope. He says he can see slates falling off
the B Wing roof.'

Mobbs was trying to make himself useful, but he
reminded Lyall horribly of Pike from *Dad's Army*. Could he
risk that boy's life for a stinking old prison and a few cons?
Throw a cordon round. Let them starve.

They pushed through the crowds. Vultures. Gawpers.
Press. Radio. TV. Relatives being interviewed in pools of
light. Cables snaking along the ground. He smelt frying
onions. Someone had set up a hot dog stand. The oily pant
of a huge old generator reminded him of fairgrounds. The
whole thing was a fucking circus.

'There sir! Up there sir!' Mobbs pointed to the roof. Lyall

could not see a thing, though perhaps there was a dark patch on it, growing – yes. A slate, wetted by the firehoses, flashed orange as it fell.

'Can we get a spotlight on this?' he bellowed.

Two men trotted off. He was handed the night scope by Mobbs. The colours were different inside it. The hands that ripped at the slates were dead white. A bundle was thrust out and shaken, but it stuck to the wet roof in folds. The hole was widened. The man's head and shoulders appeared, but this time the wind took the sheet. Lyall saw a flash of letters.

IT'S STR

What's that? What's it say? Hold that fucking light steady. Get the light on to him. All right. All right.

There was a heavy clunk. The light wavered then swept towards the man who dropped the sheet in order to shield his eyes.

The sheet glowed white and rippled in the wind.

IT'S STRANGE SAVE US

Then, as if he were a diver on a spring board, the man rose smoothly into the sir. Taken by surprise he flung his arms out wide. Lyall saw his mouth open, a small O in the white disk of his face. He somersaulted once, slid down the slates, then fell silently out of sight behind the perimeter wall.

Nobody spoke. The prison was a killing ground. 'That's it.' Lyall spoke after a long silence. 'We're going in if it brings the whole fucking place down around us.'

What was strange, anyway?

Five minutes. Ten minutes. Fifteen minutes. Half an hour. Jim waited then moved as quietly as he could over to the trap door. It was simple and crude – a panel that had to be pushed or lifted, depending on which side you were. It was hard to get a decent hand hold. Try not to make too much noise. If Gorgeous George was there, prowling . . .

You couldn't think like that.

He lifted the trap door a few inches and peered down. There was a chipped table below him, but as far as he could see, no one in the corridor. The prison was quiet.

A corridor stinking of bonfires, like piss and old meat. Smoke-blackened ceiling. Sodden, charred paper. He was past one of the office doors when he heard the snore.

A man was curled up on a table, a length of wood with nails driven into it lying by his hand. They were guarding the place to stop people getting out. That meant that some were with Randall and some against him. But what did Randall want them for?

In the next office he saw a dead man, a kitchen knife sticking out of his back. From his sprawl he must have been caught running. Stairs on the left, the treads slippery with wet ash. Half-way down, on a half landing, a table was laid on its side and chairs piled on top of it to make a barrier, the legs pointing downwards.

As quietly as he could, Jim started to work his way through.

In the middle of the hall a structure had been built from scaffolding, bed frames, scrap metal. It rose to a rough platform about fifteen feet from the ground with a row of vertical scaffolding poles along one side. The flickering torches had now gone out and the only light came from the few emergency lamps along the landings that had not been smashed.

Jim could not believe the devastation. Hardly a landing was intact. Many of the staircases had been destroyed. The floor was sticky with a gritty paste of water, brick and plaster. Ripped mattresses soaked up the liquid. In some of the cells, high in the scarred walls, the prisoners looked down on him incuriously, put on hold, waiting.

And then he saw the light.

On the first floor, between A and D Wings a short corridor had been sunk into the walls. The light was coming from the cell at the end of it. It was a strange light, neither the pale blue of the emergency lamps, nor the warm flicker of a fire. It was a steady light, grey, white, and weary.

The cell was unlike any other he had seen in the prison. For one thing there was only one bed in it; a proper bed, rather than a bunk. The mattress was bare, thicker than usual and striped. It looked old-fashioned. Against one wall was a heavy porcelain washbasin without taps. Next to it was a lavatory.

Old. Victorian. Special. Familiar.

Randall was sitting on the bed. He looked up as Jim walked in.

'What are you trying to do, Randall?' Jim asked.

'What am I trying to do? What do you think, Mr Carroll? I am trying to create order out of chaos.'

His voice was like silk running over a hang nail. His face was waxy white, his eyes almost black, so black you could not see where the pupils ended and irises began. It was like looking into two dark caves. Jim took a deep breath.

'What's all this with keeping the sectioned prisoners separate? You're not doing it for their own good, are you?'

Randall stood up and stretched. His back clicked. He sat down again, suddenly.

'It may have escaped your notice Mr Carroll, but there is a very strong force at work in this prison. Something rather old, rather nasty and rather dead. I suspect it was behind the killings, and I suspect that someone who shall remain nameless has been messing about and has released something that should have been left well alone.'

Jim thought of the ghost passing through him, passing through and moving out into the stone channels of the prison.

'So what do we do?' he asked.

'We pool our knowledge and we try and work out a way of containing the thing.'

'You won't contain it by feeding it sectioned prisoners.'

'I might. Did it never occur to you that all those mysterious deaths might in some way have kept it in check?'

'I don't know.'

'Come, Mr Carroll, think. Society takes victims and puts them inside prisons. For peace, for order, for stability. As a policeman you understand that. This ghost – or whatever you like to call it – is just trying to take things one step further.'

'I don't know,' Jim said. 'All I know is that he was called William Lestrange, and he was a weaver. He murdered a little girl up on the moors somewhere and was hanged here.'

'It doesn't sound like a very great deal to go on,' Randall said. 'What do you suggest we do?'

'I don't know. But I know that we can't just feed it people.'

'I don't know if you're in any position to tell me what I can or cannot do. As far as I can tell, I am the only person trying to contain whatever is in here.'

'You just want to find out how it operates. You want to use it.'

Randall shrugged. 'Why not?' he said. 'Money stopped mattering to me some time ago. Power, control ... that is what interests me at the moment. Perhaps we should just look on this as a challenge. Whatever happens,' Randall said, 'we can't keep on like this. I think we should call it.'

'You've no idea what you're talking about.'

'And you're so thick you can't shit straight without a plumb line, Mr Jim Carroll. Interfering. Poking. Prying. I'm certain you had something to do with this thing getting loose. Well, I'm not going to just sit here and worry. I'm going to see what it is.'

'You're mad,' Jim said. 'You're just a megalomaniac. You think he's a rival.' The walls of the cell were softening now, glowing with a calmer, steadier light.

'William Lestrange,' Randall said. 'I call you.'

All the light went from the world. A moment of utter, piercing blackness. Then the light was back, pulsing with dark veins, throbbing with the beat of some half-remembered life. It was with them so quick, Jim thought, it must have been waiting.

Above the bed, behind Randall's head, Jim saw the walls soften and form giant lips. They were white. They glowed with a dead light. The room filled with the perfume of decay.

The lips pulled themselves apart, mouthed a word. An unheard whisper scurried over the dimples of his brain.

'No!' Jim shouted. 'That's not your real name.'

The lips parted again. Saliva spread between them in thorny strands. A tongue, maggot-white, flickered in the mouth.

No breath, but the whisper of rich, graveyard grass and the clattering rustle of rose stems.

This time Randall seemed to catch the breathless echo. Jim saw Randall following the movement of the white lips. He tried to shout but his mouth was full of something, soft things, flat things that clung to his palate and his tongue like wet communion wafers. He spat out rose petals that tasted of dead skin.

Randall was coming to it now.

'Strange,' he said. 'Strange.'

The pressure drop was so sudden that Jim's mind exploded. A screaming, scouring wind sucked consciousness from his eyes and ears and nose and mouth. The vacuum was sucking the walls together like giant cheeks. They closed around him, smothered him, and then, as he felt his flesh compress, his bones began to give like sappy twigs, the body of the prison squeezed through the warm, sharp honeycomb of his cells, mashing itself against the sieve of his being.

His brain was a dark mulch. It slopped over the edge of his eyes and he tumbled into blind oblivion.

It was the soft clatter of the helicopter that aroused him and the white beam of light that ran across his face. He pulled himself to his feet. The thought of what he would find appalled him.

'I'm not here. I am not doing this.' That made it seem better. How had he been drawn into this?

'It's not you. It's someone else.'

Jim made the someone else walk out of the cell.

The prisoners had been gathered in the main hall. They were standing in ranks, their heads bent back, staring up. The metal structure was a throne. A vast figure was seated on it, spilling over the edges, dripping through the gaps in the metal.

A bloated mass of light and shade; flesh and rot; softness and bone. Shivers ran up and down his sides, scurrying like dark squalls over his surface, knitting him up where will failed to hold the dreadful pile together, shivering off to another quarter of his bulk as another dark hole began to gape.

Only his head seemed solid. It was a blank sack of seamless skin. Puppy soft. Mole blind. Leprosy white. Floating like a flesh balloon.

It turned from side to side, distorting slightly and slowly. Slopping.

Jim felt revulsion rather than fear, and mixed with the revulsion was pity. The thing was so pathetic. As he looked a terrible commotion broke in the great ghost's chest. Rotten ribs splintered. A frothing heart, unused to movement, twitched through a tear in the skin's surface, pulsed, spilled out heavily like soft dough. A huge blunt hand rose, and tried to dab it back. The head slumped.

Randall stood on a table top by the flat, rotting feet.

'He has come! He has come to deliver us! The dark lord is risen to deliver us! He is risen!'

The men lifted their heads and said dully: 'He is risen.'

'He was hanged but now he lives. Join him. Live with him. Live in him.'

'That's not life—' Jim could not shout any more. A terrible tiredness was seeping into his body. Every time he opened his mouth, more flooded in. He was drowning in fatigue.

But he could still think. That's not life. That's death. Or was it? Was it? Might not that be peace? And wasn't peace what they wanted? Wasn't peace freedom?

A current in the soupy air pushed his legs. One step. Two steps. Three steps.

He was down in the main hall now, staring up at the ghost. Where was the danger? Where was the threat? Had he misunderstood?

'Come with him. Come with him on a great journey.'

Oh to travel! The cells were windows. He saw blue sky, wheeling sea birds, an emerald sea streaked with foam and heaving waves which crashed against glittering cliffs. He

saw red deserts, purpled with deepening shadows; vast
forests; towering mountains; wide rivers; a rolling turf
moor with a high marbled sky above it and a village
nestling in its folds. Yes. Yes! To leave this weary body with
its dusty haze of dead cells behind. To be free!

'Who will come forward and be saved?'

Meme. Me. mememe.

Jim was walking forwards but so was everyone else. The
man in front of him turned and said: 'Steady on, brother.
We'll all get a turn.'

His face swam in front of Jim's. He knew it. File cards of
memory flickered. Once upon a time there had been a man
called Jim Carroll, and he had known a man called Brian
White. Brian White was the man in front of him. And
neither of them belonged in here.

He felt the air lighten. He grabbed Brian's face, feeling
the skin slip over bone. Brian struggled, started waving his
arms ineffectually around.

'Let go,' Brian said. 'Let go. Listen. Listen. Leave me free
to listen.'

Jim felt his energy drain away. He tried to force himself
to grab Brian again, but he was too weak. He dropped his
hand, lifted his head and listened.

The sound came down like a cloud, the slow sound of
peace. It was a whispering, a loosening, an unpicking, an
unravelling, a relaxation of everything. He heard the slow
mumbling of the earth, the whisper of rocks dissolving, the
airless keening of the stars as they spun themselves to dust.
The sound of dissolution. Falling dust. Decay. *Peace*.

Fuck it, that was death.

Loosen. Relax. Unravel. Fall.

Think opposites.

Dissolve. Rot. Melt. Flow.

Opposites. Come on.

Loosen, TIGHT. *Relax*, TENSE. *Unravel*, RAVEL? What sort of word is that?

Fall.

Come on. Ravel means knitting, knotting, weaving.

Shit.

Jim looked into Brian White's face. Suddenly his mind was clear. 'Sorry for this, but I'm going to need your help,' he said. And hit him.

Strange moved his hands. He drew eleven strands of light from the air and began to twist them into a rope. The men below looked up and sighed. The rope completed, he began to tie a knot.

Jim found that it was easier to convince himself if he talked to Brian. He talked hurriedly as he bustled him down the corridors.

'He was a fucking weaver, not the Boston strangler. And he was innocent, not guilty. I'm not saying he couldn't have killed the little girl, I'm just saying that he didn't. Are you with me, mate?'

Brian's face was losing its awful smoothness. He looked lumpy now, and sick, as if he were trying to remember something, or forget it.

'He thought he was saving prisoners. As far as he was concerned, everyone had been wrongly imprisoned like he had. He tried to show me so many times. He let me hear it too. I heard the sound of the loom and the sound of the rope. While the girl was hanged he was actually weaving. In his little cottage. Somehow he was contained inside the prison. If the prison falls—'

They were in the library now. The loom stood there. Undamaged.

'Come on mate, we're carrying this out with us. Now lift!'

It was heavy and the frame unstable, but together they managed to manhandle the loom out of the library and into the corridor.

'He came to me because I was innocent,' Jim grunted. They were in the hall now. The air glowed with the light of a gigantic noose, its loop containing utter darkness.

'So who the fuck put me away?' Jim said, more to himself than anyone else.

Brian spoke for the first time. 'The same man who tried to hang my little girl in the ice house. Fairley.'

Outside in the yard Lyall heard a scream pierce the air. He thought it had come from far away, from high up on the moors. He staggered, as if the earth had stopped turning.

Inside the ice house Angela lay on a slab of rock. She had been tied hand and foot. Bill Fairley reached above his head for the noose that was hanging from the hook in the roof.

Jim and Brian White put the loom down. The great central hall of Long Barrow prison was the loop of a giant noose. Inside it there was nothing.

The world stopped turning. Air shivered. Ripped. A howling tunnel tore through earth and sky. Inside the prison hall a whirling vortex opened. Wind tore through the prison with scouring force, as if it wanted to suck everything into the glowing circle.

In the ice house Fairley's hand touched the rope and was sucked inside the loop. He screamed. A thousand red-hot teeth tore into his flesh. The blood in his hand boiled. He tried to pull it out but it was held fast. Inside the noose was swirling darkness, as black and opaque as ink. His hand stopped feeling anything. When he looked up it had disappeared, drowned by a dark, welling swirl of bitterness.

Cold wind started howling through the ice house. Two vortices, twisting space and time like hanks of wool, joined together and formed a screaming tunnel between Long Barrow and Edgerton. Ropes were torn from Angela's body. They frothed like spun sugar and were whirled in grey clouds into the void. Fairley was dancing like a mad man, his clothes ripped, shredded, flapping, the skin of his arm lifting from the limb in a long, pink glove. He screamed in pain and anger, in pain again.

Leave this place, a little voice said. *Leave this place and leave him here and come with me. Safe with me.*

Angela was folded in rose petals. Two soft hands gripped hers. She rose from the table and floated into the vortex. She was as light and free as a wisp of silk.

As she floated through the void she turned. She saw Fairley, his face grinning with effort, try to follow her through the noose, his face looming like the man in the moon's. Now his head was through, now his neck.

The noose jerked shut. She heard a grunt and a snap and wet dying sounds. She closed her eyes. She did not want to see him die.

And then she was flying, flying through the air, light as a petal, through darkness, into light and then back into a flickering darkness and a great cave of brick. Arms closed around her.

She looked up, and saw her father.

CHAPTER THIRTY SIX

T here were other people in there but she hardly noticed
them. It was a dream and she was safe. She saw the
prison, smelled burning, but could not be frightened. She
felt the comforting weight and support of her father's
hands on her shoulders. Then she saw the figure in front
of her.

He had been a giant but he was shrinking into a thin
man with burning eyes, walking with cautious, floating
steps towards the loom. A ghost, woven from threads of
bitterness and anger, but now just the ghost of a weaver.

He stood behind the loom, stretched out his hand and
ran a finger gently over the frame. He reached for the
shuttle and hefted it. He threw it across the frame once and
there was all the care of a craftsman in his movements.

The shuttle moved on a weft of light, the warp of
darkness. Faster and faster it moved, as the ghost balanced
the threads, holding them in gentle tension.

And a wonderful pattern grew.

It was indistinct at first but Angela saw that it was
history. First she saw the rolling moor, then the houses,
snuggling into hollows. She saw the church with its
steeple, she saw the weaver's cottage.

The picture shimmered with all the desperate energy of longing: a village, her village, his village. The darkness was utter darkness, soft and extreme, but the light held all the colours of the spectrum, bathed everything in the light of pearls, or the colours of a dew drop caught in the newly opened bud of a rose, fresh and sweet and clear.

There was the street, lined with houses. Trees moved their branches slowly in the wind. The church bell tolled. A breeze frosted the surface of the pond, clouds moved across the sky.

The weaver wove clouds and flowers, grass and wind. He made a world that was perfect, peaceful and empty.

Angela felt something move inside her. She opened her mouth and exhaled gently. A tinted cloud rose from her lips, spread, contracted, and coalesced.

In front of her stood Angela Fitt, the rose girl. She was smaller than Angela White. Her body was thin and her hair fell lankly over slightly hunched shoulders. She turned. Her face was hollows and ridges and her eyes were sunken and sad. When she saw Angela White she stopped, then a smile lit up her face. For a second the ghosts in her eyes were extinguished. It was a smile of recognition, of horrors shared and overcome, a smile that two girls of the same age from the same village might give each other if they share a great secret. And if they know each other inside out.

Angela smiled back but she felt like crying. The girl turned and walked into the weaving.

It was hard for Angela White to see what exactly happened, but she thought the girl turned and waved to her, and Angela would have walked into the world of light then and there but her father's hands stopped her, holding her shoulders.

The old man laid the shuttle down. He stood before Angela.

She said: 'Loveyard killed the girl. You are innocent. Leave us now.'

The old man nodded. He looked at the men in the prison and seemed to be weighing something in his mind. To invite them to join him? To force them to join him and people his world?

Jim shook his head. He said: 'It's not a fair choice to give people. It may look like heaven from here but—' he paused. What did he mean? '— but at least they're still alive.'

Again Strange nodded and stepped into his world.

Jim called after him: 'You could leave a gate open just in case.'

Strange was walking across the turf. He was joined by other figures: men who were horribly damaged, horribly hurt, but when the light caught them, their injuries seemed to weave themselves together.

Jim recognized some of them. This was Strange's way of saying sorry. A strange way of saying sorry. It seemed a poor substitute for life but better than . . . the other thing.

The world began to fade. There was a muffled cry of anguish. A man, his face twisted in terror, raced towards them. He leapt into the air like a hurdler, but as he touched the fabric of Strange's world, the surface shimmered, greyed, fogged and swallowed him into oblivion.

Nobody knew what happened to Randall.

CHAPTER THIRTY SEVEN

The Press had a field-day of sorts. As no one knew what was going on, they were able to make it all up. Nobody could remember anything, apart from Jim, Angela and Lyall, who had left his men standing behind their shields and walked through the hole in the wall to witness the final end of William Lestrange.

Long Barrow prison was condemned. The fabric of the building was rotten anyway, and the massive hole in the wall, caused by a 'gas explosion', had weakened the structure to the extent that bits just kept on falling off.

Good riddance to bad rubbish.

The Victorian Society wanted to preserve B Wing, the least damaged section of the building, and dish it up with waxwork dummies as a piece of Our National Heritage. But rootling around in some old papers Mr Tindall had discovered that the prison was built on the site, albeit disputed, of a neolithic long barrow – hence the name. In the end it was decided to level the site, excavate the area then grass it over. It could be used as playing fields for the new prison, Long Barrow II.

Amid all the furore, not many people noticed a small item in the local press, dated a week after the riot was put down.

BODY FOUND IN VILLAGE

The body of Chief Superintendent Fairley was discovered in the grounds of Cragside House, Edgerton on the Moor, last weekend by a prospective buyer of the property. A rope was found at the scene and police are apparently not taking the matter any further.

However, sources at police headquarters are speculating that Fairley's death might be connected with a murder enquiry going back five years, the outcome of which led to the arrest and imprisonment of Inspector James Carroll. While his appeal is currently being examined, his solicitor is confident that his conviction will be overturned.

Angela got a C+ on her history project. Mr Appleby thought it was creative but short on facts.

CHAPTER THIRTY EIGHT

Appeals take a long time, especially when the evidence depends on the findings of internal police investigations. It was a long year later that Jim walked out of the gates of the open prison to which he had been transferred, with a feeling of deep anticlimax.

There was a booklet in his pocket called 'The Weaver of the Moors' by Clarence Tindall, published by The Midlands Heritage Press. It told the story of Lestrange, but properly this time.

With it, Mr Tindall had enclosed a letter, written in a strong italic hand.

My dear Mr Carroll,
How pleased I was to hear of your transfer to more salubrious surroundings, and the fact that your evident innocence is greasing the rusty cogwheels of justice.
You may think it strange (!) that I rather faded away, but I was afflicted with a debilitating and excruciatingly painful crick in my neck which incapacitated me for fully two months. Fortunately my sister, with whom I live, ensured that I had plenty with which to occupy my mind. Telling her one evening about that tapestry that interested us both so

much (what did happen to it, I wonder, and what a frightful tragedy it would be if it were destroyed) she immediately insisted that I start to work on the subject, as an article for our society's quarterly publication, or even as a monograph to be published separately.

As soon as I began to research the matter in some depth, certain anomalies in the case became clear, and it was these I focused on. Could Lestrange have been so evil? In my experience of visiting prisons, banality rules the day. The idea of this demonic creature with long white hair striding the moors, his eyes alight with murderous lust, became ridiculous. It sounded to me like a 'put up job'.

We shall of course never know who murdered little Angela Fitt. It was planned that way, of course, so that when the body was found, the trail to the real killer would be cold, even as the false trail to poor Lestrange was built up. However, to my mind it is too much of a coincidence that Lestrange lived in the same village as the mighty Loveyard family, who had little reason to love him, and every reason to do him down. But perhaps I am jumping the gun.

Lestrange was a weaver. He was also a non-denominational preacher – a 'freelance' if you will, and so low-church he was practically underground. Perhaps he was a troublemaker, perhaps he was prompted by self-interest. The days of his kind of life and work were numbered: the small, solitary weaver sitting in his moorland village could not compete in terms of cost or quality. Mechanisation was the name of the game, and Loveyards' mills with their infernal machinery were famous for their speed and power throughout the land. It was Lestrange who led the riots of 1850. A mill-worker, an eight-year-old boy who had been told to clear a shuttle while the loom was still running, fell into the machinery and his arm was near enough ripped off by the belt. The rest of the hands were obliged to keep

*working 'while the boy lay twitching and blood was being
swabbed from the floor' as a contemporary report has it.*

*As far as I can gather, Lestrange had always hated the
factories and towns. He wanted men to return to a simpler
relationship with God and nature. How Loveyard must have
hated him! Imagine how he must have looked out of his
window at Cragside House every morning – remember the
tapestry – and seen the weaver's cottage in the dell. It is well
within the bounds of possibility that he conceived the idea of
framing Lestrange for the murder of the wretched Fitt girl.
She was a friend of the weaver's incidentally, and one of the
few converts in the village. She used to visit him and tend his
roses. Before she was taken on at the Loveyards she sold
roses in the town where she was known as the Rose Girl. The
evil of Loveyard, if indeed it was him, defies imagination. The
Victorians for all their cant about family values, cared little
for children.*

*So it was all there, laid out in the tapestry, if only we had
known where to look. Of course we shall never know for
certain what happened, but if I am not convinced of
Loveyard's guilt, I am certain of Lestrange's innocence.
Three of the witnesses at the trial who testified against
Lestrange were tenant farmers of the Loveyards. How ironic
all this must seem to you! And how extraordinary. Remember the only evidence was the girl's bloodstained shift. Easily
'planted' indeed!*

*Well, once again I must congratulate you, and believe me,
am yours sincerely, Clarence Tindall.*

The minicab pulled up outside the prison and the duty
officer gave Jim a vague salute. Jim threw two bags, one
much heavier than the other, into the back seat. He had a
train to catch and a simple ceremony to perform.

Fairley was dead, and that was a good thing. He had

ruined too many lives around him. Fairley had been mad, but whether he started out that way or the spirit of the place, the spirit of the ice house had somehow entered his veins, and rotted him still further, he did not know. On reflection, he had always been an evil bastard, and if it hadn't been for the little girl, he still would be.

The Whites had visited him in prison, three people who looked at each other a lot for reassurance, a family which was drawing closer, pulling the wagons in a ring around them while the world outside still seemed bad and uncertain. That would change. Things would get better. If anyone were living proof of that, he was.

The minicab driver dropped him off at the station. 'Can't tell the difference between cons and screws these days,' he said. 'Off on your holidays?'

'Got to see a girl about a ghost,' Jim said. He did not offer a tip. He changed trains in London, trying to notice things. Skirts and hairstyles were shorter again, cars smoother. Men seemed to wear heavier glasses. Whisky cost a bomb but then he had a lot of back pay to work through.

He slept for most of the journey, only waking up when the train slowed down. You used to be able to see the prison as you drew into the station, standing like a castle and silhouetted against the soft drab of the moors. It had gone and that shocked him. Instead there was something that looked like a nuclear reactor in its place – the governor's new model prison. High-tech. Ghost-free.

Perhaps.

Personally he thought the problem all came down to the burial. He had read books about it, able to suspend his disbelief all too easily.

Hanged men, after the doctor pronounced them dead, were cut down and either given away for medical students to practice on or dropped into an unmarked grave inside the prison walls. There was no burial service. Lime was spread over the corpse and the ground filled in. Someone had planted a rose bush on the very spot. As he had been hanged for murdering the Rose Girl, it must have seemed like a bitter joke to Strange.

The train pulled into the station. Brian had offered to pick him up, but he said that he would take a bus. Little things like that still seemed like fun.

The bus crawled and smoked out of the town, and began to grind through the gears as it climbed the edge of the moors. He got off at the Edgerton turn-off and walked. This was where Angela said she had first felt the presence of her twin, as she now called her.

The Snare Brook valley was deep and shaded from the low winter sun. A track led off to a disused quarry on the left. That was where Fairley had parked. Over the next rise and he would see the church spire, the one he had first seen on that rug. This terrain was like a swamp of memory. Every footstep squeezed more from the ground. That was where—

Oh stop it. That was then. This is now.

He paused at the top of the rise and looked at the village. It was pretty. He caught a flash of colour – a red-haired girl was running across the rolling ground towards him. He waved. She disappeared into a dip, and though he waited for her to reappear, she must have gone off somewhere else.

It was a still, crisp day. Smoke from chimneys rose straight up into the air, thin grey columns that hardly wavered. His stomach rumbled. He'd missed a sandwich on the train because it cost four times more than he thought it would, although the filling did look nice.

By the time he reached the Whites' front door he was starving.

Patricia White opened the front door and led him into the sitting-room. Kitchen smells wafted in: roast beef, vegetables, pastry. He closed his eyes and smiled.

'It's good to see you, Jim. Brian's been looking forward to it, though it may not look that way. It'll be good for Angela too. She's out—'

'I know, I saw her.'

'Did you pop round the back already?'

'No, I – I must have been mistaken.'

He felt a single cold finger run up his spine.

He looked out of the back window. He saw Angela, the real Angela, now. She was dressed in gumboots and an anorak. Her father was holding up a dog rose, its roots in a black plastic bag, explaining something.

'Lunch'll be about twenty minutes. Do you want to . . .' Her mother tapped on the window, 'meet her out the front? Best if we leave you two on your own.'

They had spoken on the phone about it, and decided on this course of action. Jim carried the heavy bag with him out to the front. Angela met him carrying the rose.

'Hello Angela.'

'Hello Jim.'

Together they walked down the road to the graveyard. The vast dog rose that had smothered the old cottage died that night of a year ago, its roots blasted. It had spread from the child's grave, over the graveyard wall, across the grass to the old weaver's cottage where it had set about trying to bury it.

Angela pulled a few dead stems from the headstone and dug with a trowel until she had made a hole about a foot square. Jim opened his bag and took out a shoe box. It was full of light earth. It hadn't taken much to persuade Jack Lyall to let him have it. After that night he was ready for anything.

'That's all?' Angela said.

'It's enough,' Jim said.

He emptied the last remains of William Lestrange into the hole which the girl had dug. She knelt and planted the dogrose. It was small, and as yet only had two pinky red flowers on it but with its roots in that soil, it would soon grow.

They both patted the earth down. 'There,' she said. 'Will she rest now?'

She trailed a loose stem over the headstone. 'Or will she still—'

'Perhaps we should think of her as free, wherever she chooses to be,' Jim said.

'What, sort of in the grave or out of it? In prison or out of it?'

'That kind of thing.'

She pulled her hand away. Tiny thorns caught on the sleeve of her anorak. 'Did you know that it all came down to red mud?' Angela said flatly. She talked quickly and obsessively. Jim did not try to stop her. 'In the diary, Loveyard's wife said the husband had turned up at a picnic covered with red mud. You can get to the cave where he killed her through the ice house. He dragged her through the tunnels – I dare say there must have been mud falls and what have you since then – and then climbed out of the cave. He must have been horribly shocked to find his wife having a picnic twenty yards away. He hid the diary because it was evidence. You know, if he hadn't hidden it, I'd never have found it. That's funny, isn't it? Fairley knew all about the mud as well, because he'd used that cave too. Do you suppose—'

'I don't suppose anything,' Jim said. Her voice had been running on faster and faster. He wanted to stop her now.

'No, but, do you suppose bad people think in the same

way as other people? I mean Bill tried to blame you and then my father for the murders he'd committed, just like Loveyard, and used the same place more or less. And the same girl, in a way.'

Jim wanted her to stop. 'Yes,' he said. 'No. I don't know. I mean I really don't know.' And what was more, he thought, he did not want to know. The thought that Fairley had used the same place as Loveyard somehow suggested that evil act could call to evil act, that across the centuries crimes might echo crimes, that the world was cradled in a web of evil ... It was too awful to contemplate.

He held his hand out; he just wanted to feel a human touch. He looked at the village. Smoke from chimneys was still rising in dead straight lines. The air was fresh and crisp. Things did change, faster than you wanted sometimes, other times not as much as you thought. He thought of a long-playing record, how a scratch across the grooves could make a record skip a line. Jump time.

But they did not have long-playing records any more, they had compact discs.

'Come on,' he said. 'Never talk philosophy before lunch. I've been looking forward to this for years.'

'Look,' Angela said, peering over her shoulder at the graves as they walked away.

'Don't,' said Jim.

The air was as still as ice. An iron gate clanged. A dog yapped. Then the world was still.

And on a tombstone in a country graveyard two rose blooms, their frilled heads heavy on thin stalks, nodded on a breeze that was not there.